# Seven Perfect Things

# Also by Catherine Ryan Hyde

*My Name Is Anton*

*Brave Girl, Quiet Girl*

*Stay*

*Have You Seen Luis Velez?*

*Just After Midnight*

*Heaven Adjacent*

*The Wake Up*

*Allie and Bea*

*Say Goodbye for Now*

*Leaving Blythe River*

*Ask Him Why*

*Worthy*

*The Language of Hoofbeats*

*Pay It Forward: Young Readers Edition*

*Take Me with You*

*Paw It Forward*

*365 Days of Gratitude: Photos from a Beautiful World*

*Where We Belong*

*Subway Dancer and Other Stories*

*Walk Me Home*

*Always Chloe and Other Stories*

*The Long, Steep Path: Everyday Inspiration from the Author of* Pay It Forward

*How to Be a Writer in the E-Age: A Self-Help Guide*

*When You Were Older*

*Don't Let Me Go*

*Jumpstart the World*

*Second Hand Heart*

*When I Found You*

*Diary of a Witness*
*The Day I Killed James*
*Chasing Windmills*
*The Year of My Miraculous Reappearance*
*Love in the Present Tense*
*Becoming Chloe*
*Walter's Purple Heart*
*Electric God/The Hardest Part of Love*
*Pay It Forward*
*Earthquake Weather and Other Stories*
*Funerals for Horses*

# Seven Perfect Things

*A Novel*

# Catherine Ryan Hyde

LAKE UNION
PUBLISHING

Published by Lake Union Publishing, Seattle

www.apub.com

Amazon, the Amazon logo, and Lake Union Publishing are trademarks of Amazon.com, Inc., or its affiliates.

ISBN-13: 9781542021548 (paperback)
ISBN-10: 1542021545 (paperback)

ISBN-13: 9781542027731 (hardcover)
ISBN-10: 154202773X (hardcover)

Cover design by Shasti O'Leary Soudant

Printed in the United States of America

# Seven Perfect Things

# Chapter One

## The Fish Would Think So

**Elliot**

When Elliot opened the door, the woman on his welcome mat struck him as bizarrely young. For a moment he doubted whether she was the volunteer he'd been waiting for. Maybe she was his new newspaper delivery person, or something else besides a hospice worker.

Then he was struck by the disturbing thought that he'd gotten old. Or at least old enough that grown adult human beings looked bizarrely young to him.

Meanwhile he was just standing there, one hand on the knob. Looking at her.

"Mr. Colvin?"

"Elliot's fine," he said. "Are you the volunteer?"

"Yes," she said. "Julia."

"Come in, come in." He stepped out of the doorway to allow her in, and closed the door behind her. "Thank you for coming. My wife is upstairs."

They walked to the stairs together and began to climb.

Elliot was seized with an uncomfortable sense of exposure. As though the sadness of his life was on too microscopic a display. But he wasn't sure why so suddenly, and why now. Nurses came to, and went from, his home on a daily basis. Maybe he expected them to have a more clinical view of illness and loss. Young Julia seemed more wide-eyed, as if taking in his pain in real time.

"Is she . . . ," Julia began as they climbed the stairs, ". . . conscious?"

"From time to time," he said. And did not elaborate.

He led her to the door of the master bedroom.

"Honey?" he called at the doorway. "Pat?"

Her eyes were open. She seemed to be staring at a spot in the corner of the room, near the ceiling. She offered no indication that she had heard him.

He had taken great pains to get her ready to be visited. He'd given her a careful sponge bath, and dressed her in her best blue nightgown. He had brushed her hair, though he had never once gotten it looking the way she had used to. Maybe because it was drier and more lifeless now, or maybe Elliot simply did not know how to make a woman's hair look presentable. He saw her now through the volunteer's eyes, which was unfortunate. He almost wanted to tell Julia, or show her in a photo, what Pat really looked like, minus the progression of the disease. Of course he didn't. Because the only person it mattered to was him.

"She's on a lot of pain medication," he told Julia. Quietly. "So it's hard to know what's as a result of that sedation and what's the actual . . . condition."

They approached the bed together.

"Darling, this is Julia. She's a volunteer. She's going to stay with you while I go out and do some errands." Pause. Nothing. No reply or reaction. "Is that okay?"

They waited in silence for a moment.

"Just go," Julia said. "We'll be fine here."

Elliot kissed his wife on the forehead. Julia walked him to the bedroom door.

"When's the last time you were able to get out of the house?"

"Oh. Let's see. It's been a while. I've been having groceries delivered. Pat's mother was here for two weeks, so that was helpful. But that was more than a month ago."

"Just go," Julia said. "Take a well-earned break. We'll be fine."

———

He stepped into the consignment store with the first of his trophies. A moose head, from a trip to Maine more than a decade earlier. It was the largest of everything he had brought to sell, and all he could carry in one trip from the car.

The bell on the door jingled, and the shop owner, Ralph, looked up from his newspaper.

"Elliot," Ralph said.

"Ralph."

"Don't tell me."

"Don't tell you what?"

"Oh. Nothing. How's Pat?"

"About the same."

It was a lie. She was worse. But it was a lie that comforted him. *Maybe "fiction" would be a better word than "lie,"* he thought. It was, simply, a story he liked better than the truth.

"You're selling your moose?"

"I'm selling all of them."

He'd thought of simply throwing them into the trash. But somehow it seemed disrespectful to the animals who had, after all, given their lives.

"Really." It was a statement on Ralph's part. Not a question. Elliot could feel the shop owner wanting to ask why, but holding the question in check. "Now, if I didn't know you, I'd assume you'd just inherited some taxidermy from an older relative. People either love that stuff or they hate it. Not much room for sentiment in between. But forty years in this store and I've never seen a guy let go of those animals he took with his own hands. You planning to go out and bag a lot more?"

"No," Elliot said.

"Okay. Your call."

"I'll go bring the rest in."

"I'll help you."

For several minutes both men walked, and carried. Ralph made no more comments about Elliot's decision and asked no more questions.

That was a relief.

———

Elliot was sitting at an outside table on the patio of the coffeehouse when he heard his name called. He was reading the newspaper and drinking an espresso—a ridiculously lavish luxury by his current standards.

He looked up to see Roger, from work, standing over his chair.

"Oh, hey, Roger."

It felt good to see someone from work. After nearly a year of leave, the old company and its employees felt like an uncomfortably ancient part of his past.

"How's Pat doing?"

Elliot opened his mouth to answer, but could not seem to find words. He wasn't going to create fiction for Roger, but the truth was hard to spit out.

"Never mind," Roger said. "That wasn't exactly what I meant to ask anyway. I think what I meant was . . . how are you doing with how Pat's doing?"

Still feeling mute, Elliot spread his hands wide, palms up, as if to encompass the entire universe. As if to suggest that the arena of his feelings could not be compressed into the smallness of words.

"Mind if I sit?"

Elliot gestured toward a chair to indicate that his friend was welcome.

Roger had a hot drink—probably coffee—in a to-go cup, suggesting to Elliot that he had been planning to go. But for a minute they sat.

"You had somebody to stay home with her while you went out?"

"Hospice volunteer."

"Must be nice to get out."

"The sun feels great. I'd almost forgotten."

"You used to be a real outdoorsman. You still go up to your cabin?"

"How could I do that?"

"Well, you know. If you had somebody to stay with her for a few days."

"I couldn't leave her for a few days."

While Roger was not answering, Elliot ran a finger around the rim of his espresso cup. He did not add, "Because those could be the last few days." But maybe it didn't need to be added. It seemed to sit there on the metal table between them, obvious to anyone who owned senses and was paying attention.

"Besides," Elliot added, "I'm not going to hunt anymore."

"But you loved that so much."

"I'll have to find something new to love."

They remained silent for a beat or two. Elliot was hoping Roger wouldn't ask. But, in time, Roger did.

"Anything you can say to help me understand why?"

"Might sound strange," Elliot said.

"Try me."

"Okay. Well." He sipped his espresso, which was stone cold. The sun slipped behind a cloud. It felt as though everything good about his little outing had suddenly abandoned him. "It's the whole thing about death and dying, I guess. It looks different from a distance. Like we have this fairly cavalier attitude about the whole thing. We look at the animals and we think, *Well, everything lives and dies. It's perfectly natural.* But then death comes to take one of our own, and it feels like a whole different ball game. It's a big deal. To lose someone like that."

"You're not suggesting that the animals mourn like we do . . ."

"I have no idea what they do," Elliot said. "I only know what the whole thing means to me. Now. And how it colors things. Changes everything."

"But you were so proud of the fact that you ate every ounce, and how the animals had better lives than the ones in the factory farms. You know. Right up to the moment you shot them."

"I did feel that way," Elliot said. "Yes."

"But you still eat meat, though. Right?"

"No."

"Oh."

The conversation took a moment to recover. Elliot could feel it. He also knew that Roger would likely push no further in that direction— that he had already been told more than he wanted to know. Elliot sat still, hearing and feeling the wind blowing by his ears. It felt strange.

"Well . . . ," Roger began. "When you can, you should still go up there." Elliot knew what "when you can" meant. "I mean, I know it's kind of a long drive and all . . ."

"What would I do up there?"

"I don't know. But you loved it so much up there in the foothills. You know. The nature and everything."

"I feel like nature goes better with a purpose. You can just sit and stare at nature, but for how long? And, anyway, I think the experience lights up when you're in search of something in the natural world. When you have something you want from it."

"The river is really close by up there. Right? You could do some fishing."

Elliot didn't answer. His mind flickered to the massive plaque-mounted ocean sailfish he had just abandoned at the consignment shop. He hoped if he waited long enough, Roger would arrive at the destination on his own.

"Oh, right," Roger said, clearly having arrived. "That has death involved with it, too, doesn't it?"

"I suppose the fish would think so."

"You could take up hiking."

"I could."

"How long has it been, anyway? Since you went up there?"

"Let me think. Not since Pat's diagnosis. So more than three years."

"Too long."

They sat in silence for an uncomfortable length of time. Several minutes. Then Roger picked up his to-go cup.

"I should be moving along. But it was great seeing you, Elliot. Try to get in a little vacation. You know. When you can. Whatever you do with it. I don't think that's the important thing. Just to get your head clear." He pushed to his feet. "And then come back to work. We miss you there. We need you. You're the best damned engineer Meade's got. And in the meantime, give Pat my love."

"I will," Elliot said.

He did not add that Pat would likely not know that love had just been given, or from whom.

———

He let himself into the house, climbed the stairs, and stuck his head into the master bedroom.

Julia was reading to his wife. Elliot had no idea what book she was reading, or whether Pat heard and understood, but it struck him as thoughtful and kind. So much so, in fact, that it brought unannounced and unwelcome tears to his eyes. But he fought hard to keep them in check.

"Oh, Mr. Colvin. You're back."

"Elliot's fine."

"Was it a good morning out in the world?"

"It was and it wasn't."

"How so?"

"Well . . . first it was and then it wasn't."

But he noted that her face had fallen. He felt guilty, as though he had just devalued the service she'd provided. So he changed course.

"But of course I needed so much to get out, and it was a lovely day out there, so thank you for that."

For a moment the young woman made no move to leave.

Elliot watched his wife for a time, searching for some trace of her. Something he had known, something that had been fully on display before the damned disease got her. He could have done so longer, but Julia spoke, knocking him out of his thoughts.

"It's nice that you love her so much."

"How do you know how much I love her?"

"Oh, it's right there on your face when you look at her."

Elliot thought his face had been more a picture of devastation than love. But he could have been wrong. Or he could have been overlooking the fact that only great love brings one to the brink of that brand of devastation.

"I'll go now," Julia said. "I can come next week if you want."

"Thank you."

He found it comforting that she should be so sure that next week would be the same as this one. He wished he could be similarly sure.

———

After she left he sat on the bed with Pat for a long time, compressing himself back into the role he had briefly vacated. In many ways it was uncomfortable. In other ways it almost felt like a relief.

He took her hand and squeezed it, and, to his surprise, she squeezed back. Just the tiniest bit. Or, at least, he thought she did. And he would continue to believe she had, because he needed to believe it.

He needed something, even if something so small, to hold himself aloft.

# Chapter Two

*Alive in There*

**Abby**

The assistant principal yanked Abby out of swim class to take her down to the principal's office. That was too bad. Swim class was the one place she never felt cowed. Never felt *less than*. Never walked with her head down and her eyes trained toward the floor. But when Mrs. Neilson stepped into the girls' dressing room and barked her name, it changed the feeling of everything.

"Abigail Hubble."

"What?" Abby said, hoping she did not have to come along.

"Come along."

She walked down the dressing room aisle, between the cubbies where girls were changing, and listened to their quiet taunts. They were just sounds, really. Muttered sounds that the assistant principal likely didn't hear.

"Ooh." The same sound from each girl.

It was a language. A native language. They all knew how to speak it. They all knew what it meant.

*Girl, you are in trouble now.*

But Abby had no idea what she had done.

She followed Mrs. Neilson out of the pool area, walking a couple of steps behind. Properly subservient. Her heart hammered, and she wanted not to speak because she knew her voice would sound breathy and desperate and betray that she was afraid.

But she had to know. The suspense was killing her.

"Are my parents here?" Her voice sounded breathy and desperate, and betrayed her fear. Just as she'd known it would.

"No, Jamie Veitch's parents are here."

Abby stopped dead in the hallway. It took Mrs. Neilson a moment to notice.

"Come along," she said, when she finally did see.

"What does that have to do with me?"

"If you come along, you'll find out."

Abby sighed, and walked again. At least it was not her father. If her father had been here at school . . . that could have been . . . anything. That could have been bad.

They marched into the principal's office.

The principal stood with her arms folded across her ample chest. She hadn't seen Abby yet, but already she looked stern—locked and loaded to intimidate someone. It fluttered through Abby's mind that maybe she always was. Maybe she looked that way in the shower, or climbing into bed at night.

Jamie's parents sat in hard wooden chairs in front of the principal's desk, but they rose to their feet when they saw her.

"Sit down, Abigail," the principal said.

Abby did not want to sit down. All the grown-ups were standing. They already towered over her in a frightening way. Why make it worse?

"Couldn't I—"

"Sit," the principal said, as if talking to some kind of hound or terrier. Not a human girl.

Abby sat.

"Before Jamie's parents speak to you, I just want to say that this is a serious situation. The sheriff will be called in if something doesn't change soon. So be very careful with your answers, Abigail. Don't make the mistake of thinking you can take this lightly."

Abby stared at the floor and did not speak. She didn't dare.

Jamie's parents hovered over her, burning her with the dark anger of their energy. She could see them, peripherally. She purposely did not take a direct look.

"Abby," Jamie's mom said. "Do you know where Jamie is?"

"Isn't she in school?"

"Have you *seen* her at school today?" the principal interjected.

"No. But it's only third period."

Jamie's mom reached down and took Abby's chin in her hand. It felt alarming. She used that grasp to force Abby to look up into her face. Abby was still careful to avoid the woman's eyes.

"We understand all about loyalty between best friends, Abby. And we understand that Jamie has problems with our parenting decisions. What thirteen-year-old girl doesn't? But when we don't know where she is . . . this is a serious issue. So if you know, it's important that you tell us."

Abby thought it was interesting that Jamie's parents thought they were best friends. Probably a lot of people did. Maybe because nobody else seemed to hang around with Abby more. Nobody seemed to be a better friend. Then again, it was not a hard contest to win.

"I don't know where she is," Abby said, wishing she could have her chin back.

She had a guess, though. She waited to see if anyone would ask if she had a guess.

No one did.

———

Abby got off the school bus at the end of her day and began the long march toward home. Through the trees. Alongside the river. Then steeply uphill. It was a hard slog on any day, but today she had to go higher and farther than usual. She had to put her theory to the test.

She reminded herself that more exercise for her legs would only improve her swimming.

She purposely missed the dirt road turnoff for home and kept climbing. Here the paved road turned into a four-wheel-drive track, rutted and twisty. The trees encroached more and more on the road, nearly blocking her view of the navy-blue sky.

She panted as she climbed.

When the hunting cabin came into view, she stopped dead in the road, frozen, and waited quietly. She was trying to get a sense of whether anything was moving inside.

There had been a padlock on the door of the place. Always had been, as long as Abby could remember. But the lock had been cut a few months ago. Sheared off with something like a bolt cutter, and left to hang uselessly on its hasp.

Since then she and Jamie had been inside a grand total of once, just for the sheer audacity of going into somebody else's place. It had been Jamie's idea. In fact, it had been Jamie's dare. And Jamie had wanted to do it again, but it struck Abby as just another way to get in trouble.

Jamie was always getting her in trouble.

Seeing no movement, she began to walk again.

She stepped into the yard.

She felt shivery and jumpy as she walked up to the cabin's door, though she wasn't sure why. Either there would be nobody inside, or her best friend would be hiding here. Whoever owned the cabin had been gone for years, as far as Abby knew.

She touched the wood of the door with her fingertips, then pushed it lightly. It swung open, revealing the interior Abby remembered, but with more dirt. A leather couch, a brick fireplace. Brass floor lamps, and a few trophy animal heads on the walls.

Jamie was lying on her back on the couch, but she leapt to her feet as the door opened. She stood in a defensive pose, as if about to use karate to defend herself. But if she had ever learned karate, Abby would know it.

"Oh, it's only you," Jamie said.

Abby stepped inside, and they sat on the leather couch together. Perched there, looking and feeling uncomfortable. At least, Abby knew how uneasy *she* was. She knew only how her friend looked.

Abby looked around, wondering what might have been here before the burglary that was not here now. "What do you think they took?" she asked, even though she might have asked the same question when they were here before. "It seems to still have plenty of stuff."

"Well, they probably didn't want furniture."

"So I wonder what they wanted."

"Probably just food from the cupboard and a place to crash for the night."

They sat in silence for a minute more. Abby tried to gaze out the window, but it was streaked with dirt and water spots from years of storms. Everything in the room seemed to carry a layer of grime.

"You have to go home," Abby said.

"I expect that from my parents, but not from you. Why should I?"

"You can't stay here."

"Why can't I?"

"You don't own it. It belongs to somebody."

"Nobody comes here anymore. When have you seen somebody here? Last time there was a truck here was like three years ago."

"I know it. But that doesn't mean nobody ever will. They still own it. Besides, your parents are about to call the sheriff. Maybe they already did."

"How do you know that?"

"Because they came to school and pulled me out of swim class and tried to get me to tell them where you were. You got me in trouble."

"I didn't get you in trouble. You didn't know where I was. So that's not trouble."

"It felt like trouble." They sat in silence for a minute more. Then Abby said, "What about school?"

"It's out for the summer in a few days anyway."

"You're going to stay up here for *days*? What are you going to eat? How long can you do this, anyway?"

"No, I won't stay for days. Not really. I'll go home in a while. I just want them to think about how they treat me."

"You need to go home now, Jamie. I'm sorry. I don't mean to be bossy. But now I know where you are. And if anybody asks me, I'm not going to lie. Then I'd really be in trouble."

At first, nothing. No reaction.

Then Jamie sighed. "Okay, fine. I'm getting kind of hungry anyway."

They rose and walked to the door together. Stepped out into the yard. The cabin was set in a clearing in the trees, and the sun baked down on them as they stood. The air felt clear and thin, the way it always did when she climbed up into the foothills.

They both seemed hesitant to walk down the hill toward town.

Abby was feeling disgusted with her friend, but that was nothing new. Why go through all that just to give it up again because you're hungry? It seemed silly. Like a ploy by someone with nothing better to do.

"How do we keep the door closed?" Abby asked her friend.

"I guess we don't. It was open when I got here."

"All that nice furniture'll get ruined next time it rains and blows a gale."

"I don't know what to tell you, Abby. I didn't rob the place. It's just like I found it."

They walked side by side toward the road. But before they got there, Abby stopped dead.

"We can't go back down together," she said. "People'll see us together and they'll think I knew where you were all along. I'll get murdered."

"You go ahead, then."

"No, you go home. Quick, before they call the sheriff. I'll stay here and figure out how to keep this door closed."

"Nobody cares, Abby. The place is abandoned."

But Abby cared. She didn't know how to explain why she cared. She only knew that she did. "Just go," she said.

She watched for a minute as her friend trotted downhill. Then Jamie followed a curve in the road and was gone.

Abby walked to the shed behind the cabin and looked inside. In case there was something there she could use. There had been a padlock on the shed door, too, but it had been cut as well.

There was a huge stack of firewood beside the shed, carefully tarped to keep it dry. But inside, nothing. Just empty shelves and a concrete floor. Abby wondered if there had been anything stored in there before the burglary.

She crouched beside the wood pile and examined the way the tarp was tied. It had thin rope holding it down at the corners. But she didn't dare cut it, because then the firewood would no longer be fully covered. She wondered if it mattered, if no one was coming back. Then she wondered if it mattered if the cabin door was closed. Maybe the place really was abandoned.

She decided that just because an owner doesn't come visit a property for three years doesn't mean he never will. Or at least that he doesn't still care what happens to it, whether he uses it or not.

She dug into her jeans pocket and pulled out her house key. It was on a keychain with a small penknife. She opened the knife and cut off a few inches of trailing rope—the part on the outside of the knot, left hanging down. It wasn't much, but it might be enough to tie the two parts of the hasp together. Hold them the way the cut lock no longer could.

She carried the short piece of rope around to the front of the cabin, where she closed the door and threaded the rope through the two hasps. It was just enough rope to tie once. Not enough to tie a proper knot. But she stepped back and watched and waited, and the door didn't drift open again.

She sat cross-legged in the dirt, in the sun, feeling the warmth on her face. Just long enough to give her friend a good strong head start.

Then she headed downhill toward home.

———

She had descended from the foothills and was walking along the river when she saw it.

There was a bridge up ahead, where the cross street into town spanned the water. It was big enough for two cars to pass each other, but not big. It had a railing maybe as high as your elbow if you were driving along with your arm out the window.

There was a car stopped on the bridge. Which felt . . . unusual.

It was an old car, maybe from the sixties or seventies, but tricked out, like someone had bought it or kept it on purpose and restored it. It was a convertible with the top down, painted candy apple red. It was long—weirdly long—with those fins on the back.

Abby couldn't see the driver's face, but it was a man. Middle aged, from the look of him. Nobody she knew. She was looking at him both from behind and from the side, but mostly what she could see of him was black hair.

He raised a bundle. A sack, from the look of it. Like an old-fashioned burlap feed sack. Or maybe they still used them. How would Abby know? Her family didn't raise livestock.

To her surprise he swung it hard and let it go, and it sailed over the railing and landed on the surface of the river. Just for a split second it seemed to hesitate there, as the weight of it and the pull of the river began to take over. Or maybe it plunged right in, but time stopped for one beat in Abby's mind. However it happened, it felt strange.

In that split second, Abby saw the sack move. But not move the way the current moved it. Something jerky, from inside. It sliced into her belly like a cold knife.

Something was alive in there.

The car sped away.

Abby shrugged off her backpack of textbooks and ran like she had never run in her life. She was a swimmer, not a runner, though her gym teacher often forced them to run laps. Besides, you do what you have to do. You do what the situation requires.

The car had been on the upriver side, but the current was strong. Slow, but strong. So when Abby ran onto the bridge, she climbed the railing on the downriver side. The water was greenish but clear, and the sack had not completely sunk. The sun beat down, slicing through the water and showing it clearly. It was thrashing. Alive with distress.

She dove headfirst into the river.

As she sailed through the air, she felt the panic of what she might hit. People broke their necks diving into water that was not deep enough, and Abby knew it. She arched her back in an attempt to break the surface of the water at an angle.

It worked.

It also put her closer to the sack.

The cold was shocking, but she only registered the sensation in a distant way. She still had her shoes on, which made her feet feel heavy, but she ignored that as best she could. She opened her eyes—another stinging sensation of cold—and swam six powerful strokes. Downriver, with the current, and also down toward the rocky bottom. Because the bag was sinking fast.

She grabbed hold of it by its knotted top, then swam for the surface. Her head broke out into the air, and she struggled to raise the bag out of the water as well. It was heavy. It felt as though it would be heavy even if not soaking wet, but now, in addition to whatever else was in there, it was a bag of water. It took every ounce of strength she had to hold it over the surface.

She let the current take her for a moment, and watched the water drain through the burlap of the sack. Fortunately, that made it lighter.

And the panicky thrashing was still going on in there, which was good. Whatever was alive in there was still alive.

Now she had to get out of the current of the river. With no hands.

She knew better than to try to swim against the current, or even straight across it. Instead she set out at an angle, kicking her strong legs, trying to use the pull of the river to drive her closer to shore. Her arms ached, but she kept the bag above the surface.

She spotted a huge boulder at the shoreline and used it to her advantage. She sharpened her angle, and the river took her up against that boulder, on the safe side of it. She could no longer be forced downriver. She breathed for a moment and tossed the sack gently onto the muddy bank. Then she climbed out.

She couldn't undo the knot at the top of the burlap sack. It was too tight and too wet. So she took out her penknife again.

Just before she sliced into the fabric, her mind filled with frightening images. What if the sack was full of something you wouldn't want to save? A bag of rattlesnakes, maybe. But snakes would thrash in a very different motion. Something vicious, maybe. A weasel or a badger. She reached out with the knife, then recoiled. But she had come this far. She had saved whatever was alive in there.

She had to know what she had saved.

She sliced a long gash in the top of the bag and then stumbled backward two or three steps on the muddy bank.

A puppy came tumbling out.

He was not a newly born puppy, though he was small. He looked maybe just at the borderline of being weaned onto solid food. He had a black-and-white spotty coat—spotty in threads like a Queensland heeler—and black ears. He stood spraddle-legged in the mud of the riverbank and coughed. And coughed. And coughed.

Greenish water came up from his lungs and splashed into the mud.

Another head emerged. This one was tan and white, with the same spotty threads. One ear folded back. A tan patch over each eye. Coughing.

The next living being to emerge was black and tan, like a shepherd mix, with a streak of white across his chest. He shook himself so hard he unbalanced and fell into the slippery mud on his hip.

Then a fourth being emerged. All black except for a kite-shaped white chest marking.

Then a fifth. All black.

Then a sixth. Tan like the second one, but not so spotty. More just tan all over.

Then a seventh. All black but with a white tip to his tail, as though the very end hairs had been dipped into an open paint can.

Abby knew they couldn't all be boys, but she couldn't bring herself to think of them using the word "it." She figured it was that kind of thinking that had gotten them into trouble in the first place.

They stood in the mud, legs splayed for balance, unless they had already fallen on their hips or plump bellies. Abby watched them as they coughed and vomited water.

In time, seeming satisfied with having survived, a few of them began to approach her, tails swinging. Then they all did. They swarmed her, wagging and jumping and slipping and falling. She couldn't tell if they were grateful that she had saved them or just adored everybody they saw.

She plunked down into the mud and allowed them to swarm her, leaving perfect little black paw prints on her jeans and shirt.

Her arms and legs felt almost rubbery in their exhaustion, but she raised her arms to pet them. It was hard, because they never held still.

"Now what the heck am I supposed to do with all of you?" she asked them.

Not surprisingly, they had nothing to offer that would help her solve the dilemma.

# Chapter Three

## Stash

**Mary**

She thought her husband had left for his physical therapy appointment. But when Mary walked into the bedroom, feather duster in hand, she ran into him. Almost literally. He had her top dresser drawer open, and was counting the money she'd been keeping stashed in a sock at the very back—hidden. Or so she had always believed.

She stopped and stood statue-still, feeling her belly turn to ice. The sensation spread quickly. Soon her fingers and face also felt strangely cold, and tingled.

He looked directly into her face, missing her eyes by an inch or two. He didn't seem about to fly into a rage, but his energy was tight and dark.

Stan was not a large man. In fact, he was an inch shorter than Mary, who had not worn heels in all the years since their first date. But he was wiry and powerful. He had taken to combing his graying hair over a bald spot in back, but it didn't cover the truth. He had veins that throbbed in his temples when anything made him feel that his world was spinning beyond his control. Mary could see one of them throbbing now.

"Why don't I know about this?" he asked. He seemed to be working hard to keep his voice even. "There's almost three hundred dollars here. Why would you have three hundred dollars that I know nothing about? Where did all this come from?"

Her mind raced in what felt like several directions at once. But she had no time to waste, so she allowed a plan to drop into place. It felt like a penny rolling around and then dropping into a slot. A perfect fit.

"Well, that spoils the surprise." She could hear her voice tremble slightly. She hoped he couldn't.

"What surprise is that?" he asked, one eyebrow raised in suspicion.

"Month after next," she said, vaguely referring to his upcoming birthday. In honesty, she would have had to check her calendar for the exact date.

She watched his face as he rearranged his thoughts to accommodate this new information. She hoped he would not ask what she planned to buy him with all that money.

"For three hundred dollars? What do I want that costs three hundred dollars?"

"You've already spoiled half the surprise. I'm not going to go and ruin the rest of it."

In the silence that followed, she wondered when she had become so practiced and automatic at dodging and weaving. And lying.

"You're still not telling me where all this came from."

"I saved it out of my budget," she said, which was a truthful thing.

"So I've been eating on the cheap so you can stash some secrets?"

"I've been economical and efficient so I could get you something special."

For a moment he only stood, his beefy short fingers crumpling her hard-won stash. Then he sighed, folded the bills in half, and stuffed them back into the lacy pink sock, which he threw roughly into the back of the drawer. He closed the drawer with a bang that made her jump. And he was watching her reactions, too. Purposely watching.

"Why act so nervous if everything is all aboveboard?"

"Truthfully? Because you scare me sometimes when you're mad."

"If you've got nothing to hide, you've got nothing to be afraid of."

"That's not necessarily true. Sometimes I tell you the truth and you don't believe me."

It was a brave thing for a person to say to Stan, and she knew it. But in this case, honesty felt like her safest bet.

She watched his reactions to her words swirl around on his face. Then he walked to the bedroom door, and she felt it like a fever breaking. She breathed deeply for the first time since she'd walked into the room.

"You home all day today?" he called over his shoulder.

"I have the quilting bee."

"I never see quilts."

"I told you. It's one big quilt. For charity."

"Doesn't mean I can't see it. Take me a picture."

So that was yet another lie Mary would need to sort her way out of. It got so tangled. So complicated. Yet she never seemed to find a safer way. And not for lack of searching, either.

———

She met her friend Viv on the bank of the river, in their usual spot. In the nice dry grass, just up from the muddy part. Viv had an old blanket spread out for their late-lunch picnic, and she had brought wine. That seemed like a rare glimpse of heaven to Mary, who settled on the blanket and took a bag of sandwiches out of her purse.

Viv poured Mary a serving of wine in a colorful striped paper cup. Viv's kids were younger than Mary's daughter. Much younger. Almost everything in Viv's life was portrayed in bold primary colors.

"That's a treat," Mary said. "I never get to drink wine."

"Why the hell not?"

"Stan doesn't like it in the house. His parents were alcoholics, and he never touches any alcohol."

"But you're not him."

"But he kind of shapes the way he wants the house to be run."

"No kidding."

It was a rut they dropped into during every meeting. Viv would always ask questions intended to get to the heart of why Mary didn't have more rights in her marriage, and in her own home. Mary had not quite figured out if she was friends with Viv in spite of that pattern, or because of it.

"Cripes," Viv said when it was clear Mary would not answer. "Is there anything about that house that reflects how *you* want things to be?"

"I raise Abby the way I want. He pretty much stays out of that."

They sat in silence for a time, sipping the wine, which was a bold red. Mary watched the pull of the river current. Watched sticks and leaves swirl around on its surface, steadily pulled downriver.

Then Viv broke out the big guns. "So do you tell him you come meet me for lunches? Or am I a secret?"

"I tell him I'm in a quilting bee."

Viv laughed, hard enough to spit a little wine onto the blanket. "A quilting bee! How prosaic. What happens when you have to show him a finished quilt?"

"I told him it's to go to charity. But now he wants to see a picture."

"So now what are you going to do?"

"Somewhere in the world there's a quilt I can take a picture of."

Viv only shook her head. Then she plowed through Mary's brown paper bag until she found the tuna salad sandwich. She liked Mary's tuna salad. Mary, who was sick of tuna, chose egg salad.

They ate for a time in silence.

"He found my stash today," Mary said, her mouth still half-full.

"What stash is that?"

"The money I've been saving."

"Well, that can't be good. What did you tell him it was for?"

"I couldn't very well tell him the truth, now could I? 'Oh, Stan, that's nothing. Just a down payment on a dream that I could get away from you. Start a better life somehow.'"

"You still haven't answered the question of what you told him."

"It's embarrassing."

"But we're friends. And you have to have at least one person in your life you can be honest with."

"I told him I was saving it up to buy him something for his birthday."

Viv shook her head. Mary waited for her friend to offer thoughts on that pathetic excuse. Her face burned a little while waiting.

But Viv took the conversation in a new direction. "Did he take it away from you?"

"Not really."

"What does 'not really' mean? He either did or he didn't."

"He put it back. But now I have to spend it on his birthday present. So one way or another it's gone."

"You worked nearly a year to raise that."

"Oh, it doesn't matter, Viv."

"How can it not matter?"

"Because it wasn't enough anyway. I have a daughter to support. Where could we have gone on three hundred dollars?"

Viv seemed to chew on that sentiment for a while, along with Mary's tuna salad sandwich. "I still think it matters," she said after a time.

Truthfully, Mary thought it mattered, too. Even if she couldn't put into thoughts or words exactly why.

"So that's it?" Viv asked suddenly, startling her. "Two steps forward, three back? You just have to stay with him forever because he throws these obstacles in your way?"

"Not forever, I don't think. Oh, I don't know, Viv. I keep thinking it'll be better when he gets off disability and goes back to work."

Viv opened her mouth to answer, and it made Mary wince. Inwardly only, she hoped. In the past such pronouncements had not been well received. Viv tended to serve as a mirror, forcing her to see the truth reflected back.

Mary never got to find out what her friend would have said in reply.

A movement caught her eye. Mary whipped her head around to see Stan standing on the muddy part of the bank, quite a bit downriver. Holding a tree branch, twisting it in one beefy hand. Staring at her.

"Now that's got to reflect some big-league trying on his part," Viv said. "Because we always park where we can't be seen from the road."

"He must've spotted my car and walked in on foot." She struggled to her feet, but Stan was already half gone, slipping and sliding in the mud. Shaking his head. "I'd better get home."

"Wait. Are you going to be okay? Is it safe to go back there? Do you need some kind of help?"

"He doesn't beat me or anything. You know if he hit me, I would leave."

Viv's ex-husband had been a hitter. Except he'd only hit Viv once. Turned out you only got to hit Viv once. After that she would not be around for your second try.

"Well, whatever he does, are you sure you're okay?"

"I've made it this far," Mary said.

She walked back to her car without further comment, hoping that her assessment—that dealing with everything Stan had dished out so far meant she could deal with anything—would bear out.

—

He wasn't there when she got home. In fact, he did not get home for more than two hours. Mary sat at the kitchen table, drinking coffee, biting at a piece of uneven skin on the cuticle of her thumb.

She poured cup after cup, even though some voice in the back of her head noted that she was only helping herself worry in a sort of fast motion, like video run on 2x speed.

She semi-accidentally made her cuticle bleed, and had to go upstairs to get an adhesive bandage from the bathroom.

When she got back down to the kitchen, Stan was there.

He seemed to sense her presence, but he wasn't looking at her. Maybe he was refusing to look. She waited, heart pounding. She could hear the pulse of its accelerated beat in her ears.

"I've known for days there's no quilting bee in this town," he said. His voice sounded calm, but it was an artificial calm.

Mary jumped back in time in her head—to earlier that morning, when he had asked her to take a picture of the quilt. He had been playing with her, the way a cat torments a bird or mouse pre-kill. He had already known there was no quilt.

It also explained why he'd been searching her drawers.

Stan picked up her coffee mug and hurled it against the wall above the sink. It had been a gift from her late mother, and he knew that. It shattered into what looked like hundreds of pieces. They clattered into the sink with a tinkling sound. Coffee with cream splashed everywhere, including onto the white lace curtains.

"I thought you were seeing another man," he said.

"So now that you know I'm not, why are you still mad?"

"Must be something with this woman. If you kept it secret."

"Are you trying to suggest we're more than just friends?"

"You tell *me*, Mary."

"That's a perfectly ridiculous suspicion. We're both married women with children. We're friends. Don't I get to have a friend?"

Viv was actually a divorced woman with children, but it did not seem like the time to bring that up.

"Why sneak around, then?"

To Mary's surprise, it was now her turn to be angry. Mostly she didn't get angry. At least until she got into a room alone, away from him. Because you couldn't out-angry Stan. He was the champion. He would always win. It didn't even pay to try. It was only a waste of her carefully guarded life energy.

But this time it came up, and she couldn't stop it.

"Because you always get between me and my friends!" she shouted.

"When did I ever get between you and your friends?"

"Every time."

"Name one."

"Karen. Jacque. Joanne."

"That's not fair. That's entirely different. I wanted to protect you. They weren't good friends for you. They weren't good people."

"They were perfectly nice people, and you're not supposed to pick for me. You're not supposed to judge. I'm a grown woman."

"You don't always act like one."

"And that's another thing you don't get to judge! I'm forty-five years old, and I'm supposed to get to decide on my own friends!"

She stood in silence a moment, trying to read his reactions. Listening to a sort of silent ricochet of her shouted words bounce around the kitchen. Or maybe it was only bouncing around inside her head.

He seemed less angry than she'd imagined he would be.

"Well, if you want me to be someone who doesn't look after you," he said, "then you're out of luck. Because I'll always look after you. If you have a friend, I want to make sure she's good enough for you."

"But she'll never be good enough for *you*," Mary said. All the fight had drained out of her. She could hear it in her voice. The words came out sounding breathy and quiet. Defeated.

"Oh, nonsense," Stan said, seeming more comfortable now that he had defeated her. Again. "Half the time I don't even know what you're babbling about. You always talk such nonsense. Sometimes I wonder if you even believe it yourself."

But by then Mary was only half paying attention. Her eyes had gone to the little clock on the kitchen stove. It was splashed with light coffee. Impossibly, it said it was nearly five. Almost a quarter till.

"Wait," she said. "Wait a minute. It's almost five? Then where's Abby?"

"I have no idea. If you can't keep track of your own daughter . . ."

"*Our* daughter."

"Not right now she's not. Since you're the one who lost her. Until you find her, she gets to be *your* daughter. *Your* responsibility."

Mary trotted upstairs and looked in Abby's bedroom, in case she had slipped in unnoticed during the fight. But her daughter was not there. There was no backpack on the bed. No wet swimsuit or school clothes in the hamper.

She searched the rest of the house, but it looked as though Abby had not yet come home from school.

It seemed especially spooky coming on the same day as Jamie Veitch disappeared. But she called Jamie's mom, and learned that Jamie was back home.

Now it was only Mary's daughter whose whereabouts were unknown.

She called four of the other mothers, but nobody had seen the girl.

# Chapter Four

## Squirm

### Abby

Abby managed to get three of the puppies in her backpack, but of course to do so she had to jettison her textbooks and leave them by the side of the road. The other four she gathered into the sack, which could no longer be closed, and then into her arms. She began walking toward town with the ridiculous load, but it wasn't easy, to put it mildly. Because they were heavy, collectively. And they wouldn't stop squirming.

She couldn't waste time, either. She had to hurry—to walk fast, even as the weight of her load wore her down. She would be missed at home by now, and besides, the county dog pound would probably close at five. And if she missed that deadline, then what? She couldn't even imagine.

She puffed along, across the bridge toward town, then down the short business stretch of Main Street.

As she passed the hardware store, Mr. Barker stepped into the street to stare at her load.

"Hey, Abby," he said.

"Hey, Mr. Barker."

"Where'd you get all those puppies?"

"Somebody threw 'em in the river."

"Dang. What is wrong with people?"

"I know, right?"

"Two of the ones on your back are about to wiggle out."

"Oh no."

"They'll get hurt if they hit the concrete from so high up."

Abby dropped immediately into a sitting position on the sidewalk, stunned by the sudden weight of responsibility. She had taken over the care of these seven little beings, these helpless lives. And she had almost made a dreadful mistake. Was she even up to the task?

As Mr. Barker had predicted, two black puppies wiggled out. They immediately ran around Abby to greet their brothers or sisters in the sack. For a moment they all enjoyed an excited reunion, as though they had spent years apart.

"What you need," Mr. Barker said, "is a box with nice high sides."

"Got one?"

"I break my boxes down and put them in the dumpster out back. But I could tape one back together for you."

"That would be really nice. Thank you. But I have to hurry. The county pound probably closes at five."

Mr. Barker disappeared back into his shop.

"Oh dear," a new voice said. An older woman's voice. "I don't think you'll make it."

Abby looked up and around to see the widow Mrs. Whitman towering over her. Which seemed odd, since Mrs. Whitman was barely five feet tall and noticeably stooped. One really had to be down on the pavement to look up at her.

"Oh, hey, Mrs. Whitman."

Then Abby had to turn her attention back to the puppies. Six of them were out on the pavement now, and she had to keep herding them together so they wouldn't bounce out into the street. One was still at the bottom of her backpack. She could feel him squirming.

"The dog pound is nearly two miles, Abby. You'll never make it by five. It's ten till. You should let me drive you."

"Oh," Abby said. "That would be very nice. Thank you. I can't take 'em home. Not even for the night. My father would have a fit. So if I missed that five o'clock closing, I have no idea what I'd do."

"Someone threw them in the river, you said?"

"Yes, ma'am."

"Unimaginable. People can be so cruel. Why didn't they just go on to the pound themselves and drop them off? They'd be rid of them either way."

"No idea, ma'am. I really can't imagine."

But as Abby sat on the sidewalk, carefully herding puppies, she found herself overwhelmed by what had actually just happened. She'd been so consumed with saving them from drowning and then getting them somewhere safe that she'd barely had time to stop and consider how a person had tied them up in a sack and tried to drown them. Maybe she purposely had not stopped to consider it. Maybe she'd kept busy and preoccupied to give herself a few more minutes living in a world where such a thing could never happen. Where no human being could ever be so cruel.

———

There was a bell tied to the door handle of the shelter office, and it jingled as Abby stepped inside. She had to use the box to push the door open. She had no free hands.

The woman inside looked up from behind her desk. She was a pleasant-looking woman in her fifties with long, straight hair. She wore the Army-green uniform of a county animal control officer. Or maybe they called themselves animal services these days. In any case, she was in uniform.

She took one look into Abby's box and frowned. Then she tried to turn the frown into a smile, but it was a sad-looking thing.

"These yours?" she asked. "Your dog had puppies?"

"No, ma'am. I don't really know these guys. Somebody tied 'em up in a sack and threw the sack in the river."

Abby watched the woman's face change. Harden. She muttered something under her breath. Abby figured it was probably just as well she couldn't make out the words.

"I hope you're not mad at *me*, ma'am. I was only trying to help."

"No, I'm not mad at you. I'm mad at people who drown puppies. And you literally dove in there and fished them out." It didn't sound like a question.

"Yes, ma'am. How did you know?"

The woman laughed one short bark of a laugh. "Looked at yourself in a mirror lately?"

Abby hadn't. But she looked down. Her clothes were still wet, and covered with muddy paw prints. Her stringy wet hair dangled into her line of vision. She must have been quite a mess viewed straight on, and as a whole.

"Oh," she said. "Right."

"It was brave. But I wouldn't have advised you to do it. That river has a strong current. You could've drowned."

"Oh, but I'm a very good swimmer, ma'am. I'm on the team at school. We go to swim meets and everything. We might even get to the county finals next year."

"What's done is done. I'm just glad you're okay. How long ago did this happen? Obviously not too long if you haven't even air-dried yet."

"Just a few minutes ago."

"Good. Then you haven't had time to get attached yet. Which'll help this next piece of news go down a little easier. We're full. In fact, we're overfull. In an overflow situation. Now, if these were strays that might have an owner—somebody who could be looking for them—we'd have to put some other dogs down, so I could hold them ten days. That's law. But we know for a fact these guys were abandoned, and the owner won't want them back. So I'm not obliged to hold them."

"You mean . . ."

"I'm sorry. I know it seems harsh. But we only have just so much space. Stray dogs and abandoned dogs are a real problem in this county. People come up here from the city to dump them. I guess they figure it's so rural out here and the dogs can just live wild. Get by on their own. But that's a pipe dream. Anyway, we just don't have all the resources we need."

Abby looked past the woman's face to a clock on the wall behind her. In one minute it would be five o'clock. It made her feel as though she'd better talk fast.

"So you're just going to . . . *kill them?*" The last two words came out as a tense whisper. Extra quiet, as if she could keep the puppies from hearing. And as if she needed to.

She looked down into the box. The puppies had stopped squirming. No one was biting anyone else with needle-sharp puppy teeth. They were all sitting, except for the tan-all-over one, who had fallen over onto his hip and didn't have room to right himself. They were all looking up at Abby, except one that was looking up at the animal control lady.

Maybe they were just tired, Abby told herself. But that didn't seem to be their situation. It seemed as though they had caught the mood of the conversation and were now transfixed by the seriousness of things. Was that even possible? Abby had no idea. But that was the way it seemed.

She stared for a moment at their perfectly round, shiny eyes. Their velvety ears, folded over and flopping. Their pudgy sides puffing in and out with their breaths.

"That is so unfair!" Abby wailed, her voice a high, embarrassing whine. "Why does everybody want to *kill them*?" Much to her humiliation, she began to cry openly. There was no holding it in. "Look at 'em! Look! Look at those faces! They're just puppies. They're perfectly innocent. What could they possibly have done that everybody would want them to die? Look how perfect they are. They're these perfect little living things. Why doesn't that mean anything to anybody? I just don't get this at all."

Abby ran out of steam and stopped shouting. She was suddenly too tired and emotional even to stand on her feet at the dog pound. But what choice did she have?

She looked up at the clock again. It was one minute after five. But the woman hadn't thrown her out. Yet.

The animal control lady handed Abby a tissue from the box on her desk.

"Thank you," Abby said, and wiped her eyes. Then her nose.

The puppies watched in mute fascination.

"How old are you?" the lady asked.

"Thirteen."

"You're a good girl."

"Thank you, ma'am. That doesn't help *them*, though."

"I might be able to hold them three days. I'd have to bring in a portable cage and leave it in the aisle somewhere. But I wouldn't be too optimistic if I were you. We've got a lot of puppies. It's the season for them. Not too many people coming in wanting one. We even have ten from one litter that look like pure Aussies, with blue eyes. And only one of them's been adopted."

"Maybe you could hold 'em for three days and then if nobody takes 'em, I could come get 'em back again. Maybe find homes for 'em around town or something."

"But then you'd have to pay their adoption fee."

"Oh. How much is that?"

"Seventy-seven dollars."

"Seventy-seven dollars!" Abby repeated in her shock.

"It includes their shots and a deposit on their spaying or neutering."

"I sure don't have seventy-seven dollars I can spend."

"Right. And that's . . . you know. Per dog."

Abby felt her eyes go wide. She did some quick and approximate math in her head. Just the part where seven times seven equals forty-nine. "That's over five hundred dollars!"

"I know. I'm sorry."

"But I'm the one who found 'em. I brought 'em in."

"I know. But once you surrender them, they belong to the county. I wish I could say better for you. I really do. You're a nice girl, and I know you're in a bind. Unfortunately this is not Linda's Private Dog Shelter. I'm a county employee. I have to follow their rules."

"Who's Linda?"

"Me."

"Oh."

They stood silent a moment, even though it was three minutes after five.

"I guess my advice to you would be . . . if you think you can find homes for the puppies around town, try that first. Now I really don't mean to be short with you . . ."

"I know," Abby said. "You need to close up and go home."

"Good luck."

Abby sighed deeply. She picked up the box again. It felt significantly heavier, as though the puppies had grown or gained weight while she was talking to the lady. More likely Abby had lost her drive and adrenaline, and was now feeling her exhaustion more acutely.

She carried the puppies out onto the street, her shaky arms wrapped around their box. She heard the click of the lock as Linda closed up shop behind her.

She looked into their perfect faces, and they looked back.

For the second time in just twenty or so minutes she asked them, "Now what the heck am I supposed to do with all of you?"

But they were still only puppies, and they still had no ideas that would help her. There was nobody to help her. She was completely and utterly alone, dependent on her own resources. Seven lives depended on those resources. And she wasn't even sure yet what resources they might be.

———

She carried them to the little storefront market on Main Street, each step feeling like an impossible trial, and tried to figure out how to safely leave them out front. She knew they would not be welcome in the store.

A lady she didn't know was sitting on a bus bench near the door.

"Hey," Abby said. "You think you could keep an eye on these guys while I run real quick into the store? In case one of 'em figures out how to climb out of there?"

"Well, I don't know," the woman said. "What would I do if one was getting away?"

"Just holler for me."

"And if my bus comes?"

"Just holler for me."

"I guess that would be okay."

Abby ran into the store. Literally ran.

She grabbed a quart of milk out of the refrigerator case. Then she grabbed a plastic bag from the roll in the produce section. Because she didn't have a dog dish for them to drink from. And she wouldn't have enough money to buy one once she bought the milk. And it was the only idea she had.

She put the quart of milk in the plastic bag so it looked like she had a reason for wanting it, and ran up to the checkout.

She bounced up and down on her toes while an old man counted out change to the grocery checker. He looked at her out of the corner of his eye.

"In a hurry, young lady?"

"Yes, sir. I am."

"Well, at least you're polite when you address me."

He took his receipt from the checker and stepped out of her way.

The checker rang her up and took her money, giving her back thirty-five cents in change. That was now all the money Abby would have until her next allowance.

She waited to be offered a paper bag, still bouncing impatiently on her toes, but it didn't seem like something that was about to happen.

"Excuse me. Ma'am?"

"Yes, hon?"

"Can I have a paper bag, too?"

"But you have it in a plastic produce bag. You can carry it in that."

"But I need a paper bag, too."

The woman sighed deeply and audibly. As if Abby was getting on her last nerve. "I'll have to charge you a nickel for that, then."

Abby wanted to sigh deeply and audibly, too, to express her disgust, but she figured only grown-ups were allowed to do that. She dug the change back out of her pocket and gave the woman a nickel.

She put the paper bag and the milk in her backpack and ran out the door.

The woman on the bus bench was gone, and hadn't bothered to holler. Or maybe she just hadn't hollered very loudly. That's a hard thing to know about a stranger—whether they'll holler loudly enough to get the job done.

Abby counted puppies, not breathing until she got to seven. They were all there. In fact, they were sleeping, chins resting on neighboring puppies' backs. Two of them woke up as she picked up the box. They looked up at her adoringly, and wagged. It took her breath away, the adoration in their eyes. They adored her. They had gotten attached to her already. They depended on her.

She shook the feeling away again, to better do what needed to be done next. She began the long, difficult uphill walk to the abandoned cabin.

"I just need a place to keep you overnight," she told them. At least, the ones who were awake. "And I guess also while I'm in school tomorrow. And then I'll take you someplace like the post office parking lot and see if I can find you good homes."

But her heart sank as she said it, remembering Linda's words. About the ten Aussie puppies, pure looking, with blue eyes. And only one had found a home.

She shook the thought away again, because she had no better plans.

———

When she left the river path and began the uphill slog, her circumstances ganged up on her. It was hard enough to walk steeply uphill without the extra weight. Her arm muscles seemed to be shrieking at her with pain. And her discouragement rose up and overwhelmed her. It was just all too much. It was more than she could do.

She plunked down onto the deserted road and just sat, trying not to cry.

The puppies were all awake now, and had returned to squirming. Which was good, in a way. It reminded Abby that they all had legs, and could probably get places on their own.

But would they follow her?

She lifted them out one by one and set them on the rutted dirt, and they immediately assaulted each other in play, tumbling over one another. The little black one with the white tail tip seemed least interested in being play-attacked, and yipped in fear when a larger puppy bowled him over.

Abby could see it was going to be hard to keep their attention.

She rose to her feet and carried the empty box up the road, looking back over her shoulder. It took them several steps to realize Abby was moving. But, when one did, he bounded after her. And when he ran, the others followed.

They made the long climb up to the cabin together. It was not without its unexpected detours, and there was herding involved. But the puppies stayed with Abby, because they had no one else. She was their world now.

It was a crushing sense of responsibility.

She nearly cried with relief when the cabin came into view.

She led them through the yard to the shed and opened its door. The lock had been cut close to the lock body, leaving a nice loop of shank that held the door closed. She hung the lock on part of the hasp and stepped inside, waiting until all seven puppies had followed.

Then she took the quart of milk out of her backpack. She folded the sides of the paper bag down. Three turns. Then she used the plastic produce bag as a liner. Finally she poured in the whole quart of milk.

The puppies dove into the treat, knocking each other aside, sticking their paws in as they drank. Covering their muzzles in white. Then they managed to knock the bag over, but it didn't matter as much as Abby had feared. They just continued to drink the milk off the concrete floor.

Abby wasn't entirely sure about the wisdom of feeding milk to puppies. Kittens, maybe. But she had never heard of puppies drinking milk. She had arrived at the idea because they needed liquids to keep from getting dehydrated overnight, and they needed some kind of nutrition. Plus she wasn't sure if they were old enough to be on solid food yet.

There was so much she didn't know. But she comforted herself by noting that they seemed fine with the plan.

"Okay," Abby told them. "You just need to stay here. I'll come back for you. It'll seem like a long time. But I promise I'll come back. It's better than . . ."

She never finished the thought.

She watched them lap up the milk and worried about them having only a concrete floor. They shouldn't have to sleep on a concrete floor. But it was only one night. And besides, there was nothing she could do about that.

Then she worried about cold. But it was the second day of June. Even in the foothills it wouldn't get cold enough to be a problem. And they were out of the wind and the elements here, and safe from coyotes and other wildlife.

It was all she had to offer them. It was the best she could do.

She stepped out and closed the door, securing it with the cut shank of the lock. The puppies didn't seem to notice. They were too busy lapping up the spilled milk.

She walked ten or twenty steps toward the road, then stopped.

She didn't figure she had any right to go into the cabin. But she thought again about the concrete floor. The cold, hard concrete. She walked back to the cabin door and untied the rope. Swung the door wide.

The big leather sofa had two throw pillows on it. Just as she thought she remembered.

But they didn't belong to her.

But maybe the place really was abandoned.

But maybe somebody would show up and be furious that she had used their throw pillows.

Maybe she could replace them if she needed to. Buy new ones out of her allowance. And besides, it might never come to that. It might never happen.

She quickly grabbed the two pillows, retied the door, and carried them to the shed.

When she opened the door, the puppies came bounding out. There was no more milk, and Abby had seriously miscalculated how hard it would be to keep them all inside without that distraction.

She placed the pillows in the corners of the shed, then began rounding up the dogs. But she could only get three or four inside at a time. The rest did not come when called. They bounded around the yard, their attention absorbed by epic mock battles. If she closed three or four in to go get the rest, when she opened the door again, they would race out.

For what was probably the better part of fifteen minutes she struggled with them. A voice in the back of her mind said it was almost funny. Or, at least, that it could have been funny. But Abby was exhausted, and the sun was nearly down. Which meant she was very, very late, and in a great deal of trouble at home. And she couldn't find it in herself to feel amused.

In time she simply sat down inside the shed, her back against its inner wall. It was an act of surrender, not a tactic. But a minute or two later she looked up to see that all seven puppies were swarming her, drawn like a magnet to the fact that she was down at their level.

"See you tomorrow," she said, patting two available heads.

She bolted out the door and closed it behind her before they could get out.

They scratched at the inside of the door, and whimpered pitifully. And yipped in protest. And it broke Abby's heart. Literally, from the feel of it—a pain in her chest that felt as though she were being torn in half from the inside.

But she had to get home. It was nearly dusk, and she was starving and filthy and exhausted and in trouble. And she had to go home now.

So she just kept walking.

In time their little cries faded in the distance, replaced by beautiful silence.

———

"Where the hell have you been?" Abby's mother shrieked at her. Shrieked. Full volume. It was unlike her. She was normally the quiet and balanced one. "And what happened to you?"

Abby sank onto a dining room chair, relieved to be off her feet. Her father didn't seem to be home, which was a blessing.

"I'm sorry," she said.

"What happened? You scared the life out of me! Start talking."

"Can't I eat something first? I'm so hungry."

Abby's mother sighed, and seemed to return about halfway to her usual moderate self. It struck Abby that her mom had been more scared than angry. Or, at least, that all that anger had been born out of fear.

Abby watched her march into the kitchen, pull on a hot mitt, and take a plate out of the oven. She had been keeping Abby's dinner warm. Abby was so grateful it almost brought tears to her eyes.

She watched as the plate was set on the table in front of her. Homemade macaroni and cheese with ham slices on the side.

She dug in immediately.

Her mom allowed her to take five bites before demanding the story.

"You look like somebody tried to drown you," she said. "What happened?"

"Somebody tried to drown this bag of puppies. And I saved them."

"You mean . . . in, like . . . a bucket?"

"In the river."

Abby watched the alarm explode in her mother's eyes. "You jumped into *the river*? You could've been killed!"

"I'm too good a swimmer. Where's Dad?"

"Out."

"Good. Don't tell him, okay?"

"I think it would be better if we don't. But you mustn't ever do anything like that again, Abby. It was reckless and dangerous."

"Okay," Abby said, and stuffed her mouth with another huge bite.

She was thinking she'd probably never see another bag of puppies thrown into the river. She was not thinking that if she ever saw it again she would ignore it. Because that scenario was never going to happen, no matter what she had promised her mother.

Then her mind ran to a hot bath. Normally she hated to take a bath. In that moment, it sounded like heaven.

"What did you do with the puppies?" her mom asked, pulling her back to the moment.

"Took 'em to the county pound," she said, her mouth ridiculously full.

And that was true, as far as it went. At least, Abby thought it was true enough to pass.

"Well, good. That was nice of you. Just never do it again."

———

Abby tucked herself into bed at last, her body fairly buzzing from exhaustion and the heat of the bath.

She thought about their pitiful whimpers.

She thought about how she wouldn't be able to go get them and try to find homes for them until after school.

She thought about how attached she was to them already, and they to her. How much it would hurt to watch them carried away in the arms of strangers.

Then she wondered if it was even possible to find seven strangers to take them.

She drifted at the edge of sleep for a time. Then she was struck by a thought so disturbing that she sat up in bed, suddenly wide awake.

She couldn't take them to the post office parking lot to give them away. She couldn't take them anywhere. She had told her mother she'd taken them to the pound. She couldn't be seen in public with them at all.

So what would she do?

Abby had no ideas. None.

She sat awake for hours, worrying.

The following afternoon they would need food. They would need water. They would have made terrible messes on the concrete floor, and she had no idea how to clean it all up. She didn't figure there was a hose. But it would need to be cleaned, because it wasn't her shed, and, besides, you can't leave puppies sitting in their own filth.

And she remembered Linda telling her that the adoption fee was so high because it covered shots and spaying and neutering. They would need shots and spaying and neutering.

They would need so much. And they would look to her for all of it. And what could she offer them? What did she even have?

Abby got very little sleep that night, much as she needed it. Two or three hours at most.

# Chapter Five

## How It's Done

**Elliot**

The memorial, which Elliot had been entirely too devastated to plan himself, was held on the outdoor patio of the church, and involved a great deal of food.

Elliot sat on a metal folding chair, in front of a metal folding table, feeling the sun on his scalp in a way he could not remember feeling it before. He wondered if that meant his hair was notably thinner on top. He knew he should have worn a hat, but his preparation for attending had been hampered by the fact that nothing felt real.

He had brushed his teeth, of course, and combed his hair. And put on a tie, because Pat would have wanted him to wear one. In fact, she would have selected one for him, because she had an uncanny sense of what went with what, clothing-wise. And he thought he had tied a decent Windsor knot, but he couldn't remember now if he had bothered to look in the mirror to check his own work.

Even now, mulling over silly thoughts about ties and sunburned scalps, Elliot was vaguely aware that he was lost. That he had come unmoored, and was drifting on an inner sea, utterly disconnected from the reality of the moment.

But realizing it changed nothing.

He loosened the knot of his tie slightly, because he had been focusing on it, which made him aware that it was vaguely uncomfortable. But the moment he did, he knew what Pat would do, if she were here. She would gently straighten it again, and snug it up about half as tight as it had been. Not enough to negate his wish to be comfortable, but enough to make it look neat. Then she would touch his face and tell him he looked handsome in it.

But Pat wasn't here. Pat wasn't anywhere. She did not exist anywhere on the planet now, a fact Elliot found nearly impossible to fathom. It stretched his brain until the poor organ collapsed back on itself and shut down almost entirely.

He snugged and straightened the tie himself.

One of the women from Pat's book group sat down next to Elliot, and set a plate of food on the table in front of him. He glanced at it without truly understanding its purpose. It was stacked with fried chicken and ribs, along with coleslaw and potato salad. But Elliot didn't want to eat chicken or ribs, because they reminded him of death, and he had no appetite for the salads. They didn't look bad, or unappetizing, and he didn't feel sick to his stomach. He didn't feel anything, as far as he could tell. He just didn't care to eat.

The woman, whose name Elliot did not know, leaned in closer to him, and placed a hand on his arm. Elliot wished she wouldn't, but couldn't find the words to say so. It was a chaste enough gesture, but it made Elliot feel found, which made him feel vulnerable and exposed. He was drifting out to sea on purpose, and did not like the feeling of anyone getting too close. It anchored him. He did not want to be dragged back into the moment.

"You should eat something," she said. "It might make you feel a little better."

Elliot looked up to see another woman standing over him. She was on the other side of the table, and the sun hung in the sky almost directly behind her head. Elliot had to squint uncomfortably to look at her, and he couldn't look long. He had no idea who she was, and no idea if he might have identified her in better lighting. Moreover, he couldn't bring himself to care.

"I'm so sorry for your loss," she said.

Elliot tried for a sad smile, but it might have come out looking more like a grimace. It felt like a grimace.

The woman kept talking, and it all raced downhill from there.

"Such a terrible disease. Thank goodness she was gone before all that awful stuff happened, like before she couldn't breathe or swallow." She leaned over the table and squeezed Elliot's forearm. "It's a blessing," she added.

Elliot opened his mouth for the first time in as long as he could remember. "It's not a blessing," he said. It came out too loudly, and the quiet conversations all around him stopped. Maybe everyone was listening. He wasn't sure, and did not feel inclined to check. "It's a damn tragedy."

"I just meant—"

"I know what you meant, but it's the wrong thing. It's just the wrong thing to say. You don't go up to somebody whose wife just died and say it's a blessing. I'm sorry. You just don't. I can see if you'd said, 'It's a tragedy, but it could have been an even more heartbreaking one. So for that one tiny little saving grace we can be grateful.' But don't try to tell me the worst time of my entire life is a blessing."

"I'm sorry," the woman said. "I didn't mean to upset you."

She hurried away.

A few silent seconds passed. Then the people around him seemed to resume their conversations, and life moved on.

*That's the thing about life,* Elliot thought. *Whatever just happened, good or bad, it always moves on.*

The woman from Pat's book group placed a hand on his arm again, and spoke softly to him. "I don't think she meant any harm."

"I'm sure she didn't. But people do plenty of harm when they didn't mean any. It happens all the time." He stopped talking for several seconds, and she did not reply. So he added, "I suppose I should go apologize."

"It's fine," she said. "Stay. This is one day in your life when you get to think about your own feelings more than anyone else's."

It sounded like something Pat would say, if Pat were here. That put Elliot at ease.

"Thank you," he said. "That's the first helpful thing anybody's said to me since Pat died. It's just . . . I have trouble with people like that. Like that woman who was just here. They come up to you in a time of grief, and they can't seem to accept that it's grief. They can't just be in that moment of grief with you. They can't just say, 'Yeah, this is some pretty awful stuff.' They have to try to fix it. They have to solve it for you in a couple of sentences, which is ridiculous, because it never solves anything. But they suggest something to get you out of what you're feeling, or they find some reason why it's all for the best. I don't understand why people can't just join you in your grief for a moment."

"People don't like to hold still with grief," the woman said. "Their own or anybody else's. If they can't sit in their own grief, they're not likely to spend any time in yours. You're not eating. Which is okay. I understand. Maybe a glass of wine is what you need."

"I would try a glass of wine," he said.

The woman got up and walked away, presumably to get him one. Not two seconds later, someone else plunked down in the chair she had vacated. Elliot looked over to see that Roger had joined him.

"Oh, hey, Roger."

"Really sorry, old boy. She was a hell of a woman. A real class act. It's such a loss."

"See, that's how it's done," Elliot said.

"What's how what's done?"

"Never mind. You had to be there."

"I should have gotten myself some food before I sat down."

"Here, take this. I literally haven't touched it."

He slid his plate over to Roger, who unfolded a paper napkin on his lap and dug in.

"This looks great," Roger said, and filled his mouth with an enormous bite of fried chicken.

It took Roger quite a while to chew up all that food so he could speak again. Meanwhile Elliot tried not to think of the food on Roger's plate as charred dead bodies, but it was hard to avoid.

Finally Roger swallowed, and continued. "So, not to rush you at all, but when do you think you'll come back to work? Have you thought about it?"

"I need a couple of weeks at least. I feel all . . . disconnected. Like my head is not screwed down at all. Meantime I thought I'd take your advice and drive back up to the cabin."

"How soon do you think you'll go?"

"I don't know. Soon, I think. I can't imagine going to sleep in that empty bed every night. But I also need a little time to clear my head enough. You know. Even enough to pack. To figure out what I'd have to bring up there to last me for a week or two in the middle of nowhere like that."

"Bring your rifles. Just in case you change your mind."

"I sold them," Elliot said. He had spares in the shed, but he wouldn't use them.

"Oh."

They fell silent, and Roger continued to bolt down the food as if he hadn't eaten for days.

"I know you don't understand that," Elliot said.

"I really don't," Roger replied, with his mouth full. "But I guess I don't need to. It's you, not me. So as long as *you* understand it, I think we're good."

"There was a poem. I don't remember most of it. But it was by Edna St. Vincent Millay. I remember the title. And the first line has been going through my head a lot. Over and over. The poem is called 'Conscientious Objector.' Do you know it?"

Roger laughed out loud. It struck Elliot as a foreign sound, and definitely out of place.

"I guarantee you I don't know any poems by Edna St. Vincent Millay." He sounded almost pleased about it. It struck Elliot as a strange thing to be proud of. Or even satisfied with. "But go ahead and tell me. What're the lines?"

"It goes, 'I shall die, but . . . that is all that I shall do for Death.'"

"Hmm," Roger said.

"Can you elaborate on 'hmm'?"

"Sounds hard."

"Most good things are," Elliot said.

The woman from the book group came back, and brought Elliot a glass of wine, and sat in a different chair. Elliot drank the wine quickly, and it made him feel a little better, because it made him feel even more disconnected.

Nobody else approached him, probably due to his outburst. Elliot liked it just fine that way.

———

He arrived home at nearly six that afternoon.

He unlocked the front door with his key, then pushed it wide open. That part seemed to go fine.

But after that he got stuck.

Over and over he sent signals to his legs to step across the threshold. Or at least he thought he did. He tried. But they never went through, or they went through but were ignored or overridden. He just stood there on the mat, trying to fully absorb his new reality.

Eventually he knew he had to step into the house, because he lived there. Trouble was, he didn't live there with Pat, and he never would again. Never. Not one day, for the rest of his life. He was only fifty-two, which felt plenty old enough to him in that moment. But he might have forty years of life left. How many days was that without her?

He did the math quickly in his head, still standing helplessly on his own welcome mat.

It was 14,600 days. And there was nothing he could do to change any of them. Well, he reminded himself, he could change some things about them. Just not the most important thing.

Elliot sighed deeply and stepped inside, closing the door behind him.

*There,* he thought.

He had done it. That nearly impossible thing. And that was the hardest part. People didn't realize it, but Elliot knew. The hardest part is not the moment when you have to call the ambulance. It's not even the part when you have to call the mortuary. Granted, those moments are hard, but they're also utterly absorbing. They pull you through them, and all you have to do is put one foot in front of the other. And they send you into shock, and that shock cushions everything you might otherwise feel.

No, the really tough bit is when you find yourself dropped on the other side, and you have to find a way for your life to go forward from there.

—

He pulled his two olive-green duffel bags down from the closet shelf. He had other, better luggage, but he wouldn't take them up to the cabin. He wouldn't take anything nice up there. It was too dirty a world.

He threw them onto the bed and began to fill them with clothing. First he packed underwear and socks. Then shirts for warm weather—for the days. A jacket in case it got cool at night, which it would, even in June. Then his good hiking boots, and a brand-new pair of trail runners that he had never used because Pat had been diagnosed the week after he bought them.

Then he stopped. And had no idea how to proceed.

He didn't know what his purpose was in going up there, so he had no idea how to pack for it. And besides, his brain wouldn't fully engage.

He just stood there over the bed, every bit as stuck as he had been on his welcome mat. It felt as though someone had just rousted him out of sleep and he wasn't awake enough to focus on the task at hand.

Eventually he gave up and ran himself a hot bath. And soaked in it, purposely thinking nothing.

He put himself to bed on his own side, without ever moving the half-packed bags.

He would go up to the cabin. As soon as he could. But that was not now.

Surprisingly, he slept.

# Chapter Six

*Swimming Upside Down*

**Abby**

Abby snuck a hammer off her father's tool bench in the garage. She slipped the handle of it into the waistband of her shorts, then pulled her shirt over it. Just in case she ran into him.

She trotted into the kitchen . . . and ran into him.

He was sitting at the kitchen table, drinking coffee, his face buried in the Fresno newspaper. He did not look up, or seem to notice her.

She froze, in more ways than one. She stopped dead, and felt her blood and belly grow colder. And not just because she was holding his hammer. It was a normal reaction to seeing him.

She hovered for a moment, unsure of her best move.

"What?" he said, not looking up from his paper. He sounded irritated.

It was just like him, she thought, to take in every sound and movement around him while pretending not to notice or care.

"What?" she said back.

She hadn't meant to mimic him. It might make him angry. It just slipped out.

"What are you doing here?" he asked, still sounding perturbed. "Other than getting on my nerves?"

She draped one arm casually over the lump of hammer. At least, she hoped it looked casual. "I'm just walking through the kitchen," she said. "I don't see why that should get on your nerves."

"No, you're not walking through the kitchen. If you were walking through the kitchen, your feet would be moving. You're just standing there staring at me."

*If you know what I'm doing,* she thought, *then why ask?*

Apparently he grew tired of waiting for an answer.

"You're ruining my morning," he said. "I'm going to count to ten. And when I get to ten, I'd better be alone in this kitchen."

"Fine," she said, a little too loudly.

She trotted through the kitchen and down the hall, then took the stairs two at a time up to her room. As she trotted, she felt a burning sense of disgust toward him. Something almost at the borderline of hatred, but it was a line she had always tried not to cross. And it was nothing new.

Only the day was new.

———

Her piggy bank was out on the desk in front of her. Right in the middle, where she never kept it. Until that morning. Normally she hid it on the closet shelf, not entirely trusting one of the two people who lived there with her. But she had taken it down. And it sat awaiting slaughter.

She pulled out the hammer. Raised it high. But for a moment she couldn't bring herself to do it.

She let the hand with the hammer fall to her side again.

She was so proud of that bank.

As her resistance toward the act moved through her, she reached out and touched its piggy back, as if stroking it. She had purposely bought the one with no plug in the bottom. The kind you can only put money *into*. That never lets you take it out. The plan was to be brave and adult about saving. And she had been. She had put in half of her allowance on any week that she could manage it, and half her birthday money on the rare occasions when she'd received any.

She had no idea how much she had in there, but she liked to think it was over a hundred dollars.

But she had no choice, she realized. Puppies have to eat.

She brought the hammer down hard. Harder even than she had meant to. The bank shattered into dozens of pieces, some of which flew across the room and landed on various parts of her floor, skittering across the hardwood before coming to a stop.

She gathered up the money and counted it.

Sixty-two dollars.

That was it. That was all of it. Sixty-two dollars.

After all those lessons from grown-ups about saving. About discipline. About showing a bit of dedication to something, and how it would pay dividends and add up to a better future for her. And that's what she got for her trouble. Sixty-two dollars.

She stood a moment, looking out the window onto the overgrown backyard, entertaining an entirely new thought. If one lesson from grown-ups had been proved wrong—and it had—maybe everything they had told her was bull. Maybe grown-ups had no idea what they were talking about.

Maybe she'd be better off trusting her own judgment from now on.

The door of her bedroom flew open. Abby held the hammer close to her leg, where it could not be seen from the door.

Fortunately, it was only her mother.

"Honey. What happened? It sounded like something broke."

"Yeah," Abby said. "I dropped my piggy bank. But it's okay. I got all the money gathered up. I'll get a new one."

"You're in your bare feet. You'll hurt yourself. Stand right there and I'll bring you your slippers. And then you can go downstairs and eat your breakfast while I sweep it up."

"Okay. Thanks."

She was already trying on the idea in relation to her mother. The idea of not really listening to her mother anymore. Not really trusting her advice. Granted, her mom didn't give much advice. It was her father who was constantly telling her what to do. How to live. And a couple of her teachers, though to a lesser degree.

Still, there was something heady about the new plan.

It was surprisingly liberating.

"I'll be late coming home from school today," she told her mom as she took the slippers. "We have extra swim practice."

It wasn't a very good fake excuse, because there were only a couple more days of school. And why would the team have extra practice right before summer vacation? There would obviously be no meets coming up.

But her mom asked no questions, and gave no indication that she was thinking it out too thoroughly.

———

She marched up and down the dog food aisle at the market, trying to decide how much she could bring herself to carry, and which was the least expensive for its size and weight. They had spill-proof plastic dog dishes, too, but they cost almost ten dollars.

That seemed a bit extreme.

It was before school, and she would be making herself late by walking all the way up there to see them and tend to them. She had planned to make them wait until after school, but then she couldn't. She just couldn't. They were probably hungry. And they needed to go out. And how did they even know that anybody was coming back for them . . . ever?

No, if she was late, she was just late. They could punish her any way they saw fit.

She picked up a ten-pound bag of kibble, even though she didn't know if they had been started on solid food. But, if not, they would have to start now. She decided they could eat it off the concrete floor as a cost saver.

Halfway up to the checkout station she stopped, realizing the flaw in her plan. They could eat kibble off the floor, but they had to drink water. And the lined paper bag hadn't worked out at all. Not only had they knocked it over immediately, but if left alone with it, they'd tear it to shreds.

Was there even water up there at the cabin? Abby had no idea. If not, she'd have to walk all the way down to the river and haul it up into the foothills. Every day. Every time.

She sighed, walked back to the dog food aisle, and picked up one of the pricey spill-proof dishes. She still had no idea what to do with the dogs in the long run, or even the medium run. But they needed food and water today. Now.

She carried both items to the cashier.

Her total with tax was over twenty dollars. After saving that money in her piggy bank for years, about a third of it was gone in one grand gesture.

She waited for a bag, but once again none seemed forthcoming.

"I need a bag," she said.

"The dog food is *in* a bag. That's why they call it a *bag* of dog food."

A feeling solidified in Abby's gut. She didn't like this grocery checker. The woman was rude, and she condescended to kids. But that was not the problem. Not in and of itself. The problem was that it was not a unique experience for Abby. In fact, it was not all that unusual. Everywhere she went, grown-ups treated her like this. Not all of them, but far too many. All over the world people were speaking to kids in a voice and with an attitude they would never use with another adult.

And then those same rude and condescending people told her what to do, as though she had no choice but to obey them. Because she was a kid and they were in charge of her, even if they weren't teachers or family. Even if they'd never seen her before in their lives.

Abby was done with that. She was just done.

"I also bought this expensive dish," she said, just a bit louder than necessary. And she had no intention of walking down Main Street carrying a clearly identifiable bag of dog food after telling her mother she'd taken the puppies to the pound. But of course she didn't share that information with the checker. "And I want to carry both together, and I'm a customer, just like the grown-ups who come into this store. My money is just as good, and I should be treated the same."

The store manager, an older man with short gray hair, stepped up behind the cashier and asked, "Problem here?"

"I just want a bag," Abby said. "I bought two things and I just want to carry 'em together in a bag and I want to be talked to like I count."

The manager shot his employee a truly withering gaze, and she handed Abby a bag. She did not charge Abby a nickel for it.

"Have a nice day," the manager said.

"Thanks," Abby said.

But as she walked out of the store, she couldn't help getting the sense that the day was off to a truly miserable start. As if to underscore that conclusion, she ran smack into Jamie Veitch as she stepped onto the sidewalk. Nearly bowled her over.

"Oh, there you are," Jamie said. "I called your house a bunch of times but you were never home. Are you avoiding me?"

"No. I'm just out . . . staying in shape. I have to stay in shape for swim team in the fall."

"But the whole idea of summer is to take a vacation."

But Abby didn't want to take any of her vacation with Jamie. Which is why she had been avoiding her. She had always found Jamie a bit silly—in what she liked, in what she thought was important. Now that Abby had something really important to do, time with her old friend would feel unbearable.

Besides, Abby couldn't tell her about the puppies. Because Jamie was the worst secret keeper in the history of the world. Tell her anything, and it would be all over town in minutes. If this town had managed to have even a whiff of cell phone reception—even one distant tower—those minutes would have shrunk to seconds.

"Gotta get these groceries home to my mom," Abby said.

She hurried away while her friend was still trying to answer.

———

She fumed all the way up into the foothills. The sun was hot already, and the bag was heavy. But that was not what troubled her. It was the grown-ups. It was the world.

Here she was in a world where grown-ups tied innocent puppies up in a sack and threw them into the river. And yet all her life she'd tried to play by their rules, believing they must know best. But what if they didn't? What had she been doing all her life if they didn't know any more than she did?

It reminded her of a time she'd gotten disoriented swimming underwater in the big pool at school. She had held her breath and pushed and pushed to get to the top. And then, just as she'd expected to break out into the air and gasp a breath, her fingers touched the concrete bottom.

Granted, she had been much younger. And she hadn't liked to open her eyes underwater at that age. Still, the feeling was unforgettable—to suddenly find out that everything you thought you knew was exactly upside down. And when you'd been so sure about it, too.

That's how dramatically she felt she had reversed her attitude toward the grown-ups all around her. Their rules and advice were exactly upside down, like a mirror image of what she'd always believed she could trust.

She chewed it over and over in her head like a dog worrying at a bone.

Then she looked up to see that the cabin had come into view. It surprised her. She'd had no idea she had come so far. The trip had flown by while her mind was elsewhere.

She walked through the yard, and they heard her.

They had the funniest reaction to hearing someone coming. They barked at her. With these tiny little puppy voices they barked serious warnings, like guard dogs. One of them howled. But mostly they barked the message that they were tough, and she'd best stay away.

Abby didn't realize dogs defended their territory at such a young age. Then again, these little guys had been thrown into scary circumstances.

It was all Abby could do not to laugh. Because they sounded so tiny and helpless as they tried to sound tough and dangerous.

She lifted the cut lock out of the hasp and opened the door. And they swarmed her, their tails—their whole bodies—swinging in joy and relief to see her.

She looked inside the shed. And smelled the inside of it.

"Newspapers," she said. "I should have brought newspapers."

There would have been a stack of them at home next to the out-door garbage cans, but it had not occurred to her to bring them. But she would definitely need to line the concrete floor of the shed with newspapers as a way of keeping it clean.

Today it would be a big job to clean it. Even if she did have water up here.

Meanwhile the puppies were swarming and jumping and yipping. Abby looked down at them, overwhelmed by how cute they were. How alive and guileless and perfect. And she decided that she deserved to simply enjoy them for a moment. She was working at keeping them properly, and most of the work was hard. But the puppies themselves were fun, and she had been robbing herself of that fun so far.

She dropped onto her back in the pine needles and dirt and allowed them to climb all over her. They nipped her with their needle-sharp puppy teeth and thumped her with their tails. Their little paws on her belly tickled.

It made her laugh.

Not just the ticklish part. All of it. Them. They made her laugh.

Her terrible morning—smashing her piggy bank and finding so little money inside and getting into an argument with the grocery store clerk and running into Jamie, who knew Abby was avoiding her—vanished. All of a sudden it was a good day and Abby was in a good mood.

She lifted them one by one as they swarmed near her face, and held them up over her, and looked at each close up. Their pudgy bellies felt warm. They all had different reactions to being held. The black one with the white tail tip was the shyest. Abby was able to see from that angle that she was a girl. She mostly froze, as if she could make herself safe by acting invisible until she was set down again.

The spotty one with the black ears, the one who looked most like a Queensland, was also a girl. But she was the boldest one. She yipped and barked in Abby's hands, aiming little nips at her nose and thrashing.

She continued to pick them up one by one and study them.

Though she couldn't quite put it into words, she resented having been thrust into a world where such perfect little beings could be treated as worthless. She knew she had been living in that world all along, but she resented having been forced awake. Forced to recognize it.

But the puppies themselves . . . they were perfect.

They would never tell her how to live her life. Or mistreat her mother. Or refuse to give her a bag. And they would absolutely, definitely never try to drown anybody.

"I'll have to give you names," she said. "Just to be able to tell you apart in my head."

She remembered something her mother had told her when she was six. She'd tried to bring home a stray cat as a pet, but her father had made her give it away. She had named the cat Elsie, but her mother had told her you should never name any animal you don't plan to keep.

Then Abby remembered something even more important. That grown-ups can be wrong. And maybe mostly are. And that she wasn't going to listen to them anymore.

She lifted the little boy with the tan ears and tan patches over his eyes.

"I'm going to name you Patches," she said, and he wagged hopefully and shyly. "I'm going to name each and every one of you. But I'm going to do more than just that. I'm going to keep you. All seven of you. And nobody gets to tell me it's a bad idea."

—

Abby arrived back at the cabin after school, and the puppies seemed ecstatic to see her. Positively ecstatic.

She had brought a big stack of newspapers to help keep their floor clean. And she had poked around at the cabin that morning and found a hose. It didn't reach as far as the shed, but there was a plastic bucket to haul the water over. And she'd found a broom on the cabin's back porch. Her main purpose in being there was to clean. And then, of course, to feed and water the dogs.

All those thoughts dropped away when she saw them.

They chased each other around the unfenced yard, growling and yipping and hitting each other with flying tackles and knocking each other down—until Abby decided to lie down on her back and look at the sky. Then they all seemed to land on her at once, climbing her like a small mountain, making her feel like Gulliver in that story about the one big guy in the land of tiny people.

She picked up the pup with the black ears. The bold one who looked most like a Queensland heeler, though not a pure one. The only other girl besides the tail-tip one, so far as Abby could tell.

The puppy was able to hold her ears straight up in attention. And they were huge, those ears. They seemed to dwarf the rest of her head, making it look petite and almost ladylike. She was the first puppy to show the ability to hold her ears erect. And her eyes were small and dark, perfectly round, showing just the tiniest bit of white at the corners. They looked eager, those eyes. She didn't yip, or snap at Abby's face in play, as she had that morning. Just stared raptly into Abby's eyes, as if trying to read her thoughts.

"You are so *cute*!" Abby's voice came up to a near-shriek on the final word.

The puppy took it as a sign of play, and struggled mightily to get back onto her paws.

"I'm going to name you Queen, because you look like a Queensland."

She set the puppy down and picked up the next one she could grab. It was the black one with the kite-shaped white marking on his chest.

"And your name is Kite," she said.

She set him down and grabbed another. It was the black-and-tan one. The only one that looked like a shepherd mix.

"And you're Shep," she said. "Okay, I know. It's not very original, but I need names that'll help me remember all of 'em and help me tell you apart."

She set him down, but was not able to grab another. Somehow the volume of their energy had been turned up, as if by an invisible hand, and all they could do was swarm her. And nip her face, and lick her nose.

And all Abby could do was laugh.

She sat up after a time, and looked at them, and they at her.

"I just figured something out," she said. "It's impossible to not be happy with seven puppies climbing all over you. It literally can't be done."

Amazingly, they held still and held her gaze. As if they wanted to understand her message and were concerned because they couldn't.

"Well," Abby said, and pulled to her feet. "I guess I'd better get this cleaning over with."

She gathered the broom and the bucket. Filled the bucket with water and left it by the shed door.

She walked inside with a stack of newspapers to pick up solid waste and absorb as much urine as she could. The smell was overwhelming and the shed had only one small window that did not seem to open. And Abby was overcome with a terrible thought.

*They shouldn't have to live here. They need a better home.*

But she pushed the thought away again by reminding herself what Linda—the animal control lady—had said. She'd said puppies weren't getting adopted fast enough. She'd made it clear that they would be killed if Abby left them.

*So I saved their lives twice. This is better than what they'd have had if I hadn't saved them.*

She balled up the dirty papers and realized she had no trash container to put them in. What could she do with them? Burn them? Too risky. She might burn down the whole forest. No, her best bet was to bring a trash bag up here and haul them down the hill. Sneak them into a dumpster in town.

For the moment she simply wrapped them up snugly in some clean papers and stashed them behind the shed.

Then she carried the bucket to the hose and filled it. There must have been a well. Abby realized she was lucky because it had not run dry or had its pump freeze up after all these years. She had no idea how she would have been able to do this without water.

She threw the bucket of water onto the floor of the shed, then swept it out the door. Then she did the same again. And again, and again, and again. Until she was satisfied that the concrete was clean.

She kept an eye on the puppies as she worked, but she was beginning to trust that they would not wander far from her. Especially since she was smart enough to hold off feeding them until it was time to leave.

She swept and swept and swept the water out the door until the shed floor was only damp—not really wet.

"We'll leave that to dry," she told the dogs.

Then she got down on her back and let them swarm her again while it dried. And let herself laugh. And laugh. And laugh.

———

She woke suddenly, surprised that she had ever fallen asleep. She was lying on her back in the pine needles and dirt, and the puppies were sleeping on and all around her—three on her chest and belly, three on her arms. The shy one, the tail-tip one—Abby had named her Tippy—was asleep on Abby's legs, separate from the group, as was her habit.

The sun was nearly down.

"Holy . . . I have to go home!"

She sat up, holding puppies to her chest, waking them all.

She set them down and ran to the shed, happy to see that the floor was nearly dry. She lined it with papers, filled their water dish and set it inside. Set the throw pillows in the corners again. She added the box Mr. Barker had given her, on its side, in case they liked its sheltered feeling. Then she spread kibble on the clean papers, and they raced inside to eat.

Just before she closed them in, she looked around at the inside of the shed and got a very different feeling about it. It was clean and dry. It had food and water. It had comfortable places to lie down. It was safe.

Considering where they had been headed, it was good enough.

She counted puppies, then swung the door closed and secured it with the curve of the lock's cut shank.

"It'll be better when school gets out in a couple of days," she told them through the door. "I can be here all day then."

They didn't whimper or yip or make her feel terrible, probably because they were too busy eating.

Abby jogged downhill, running all the way home.

# Chapter Seven

## Don't Break Her

**Mary**

"I'm worried about Abby," Mary said.

She had gone to Viv's house so she couldn't be observed meeting her friend. Stan had run out of sick time and gone complainingly back to work, but Mary didn't trust it. Didn't trust him. She had parked in the back, behind Viv's garage.

"Worried about her why?"

Viv was hovering over the kitchen table, ladling homemade gazpacho into two cobalt-blue bowls. It was a warm June day, and the cold soup sounded just right to Mary. It looked like something that would hit the spot.

"She's been gone a lot lately. A *lot*. It's not like her."

"Did you ask?"

"The first day I did. She said she'd seen somebody throw a litter of puppies into the river and she'd gone in and fished them out."

"She jumped into the river? She could have been killed!"

"She's a pretty darned strong swimmer. But, also . . . yes. Exactly. That's exactly what I told her. Then the next day she said she had an extra swim practice after school. I didn't think much about it at the time, but that was one of the last school days of the year. So why would the swim team need to practice? Their season is over."

Viv sat across the table and unfolded a paper napkin in her lap. She dug in, so Mary dug in, too, even though she was more interested in talking than eating.

She glanced around the kitchen and into the living room. It was the first time she'd seen Viv's house. Viv kept it clean, but cluttered. It was obvious that young children lived here. There were crayon drawings secured to the fridge with magnets, and a plastic big-wheeled trike parked next to the coffee table.

"This is good," Mary said.

"I like it in the summer. Go on with what you were saying. You're worried about Abby."

"Right. So that day, the day she said she'd be late because of swim practice, she was also late getting to school in the morning. By over an hour. The school called me because they thought it was an absence. And I asked why there would be a swim practice so close to summer vacation. Nobody knew a darn thing about it, Viv."

"Saw that one coming," Viv said.

"She didn't get home till nearly dark. And I didn't ask. I feel bad about that. Like I was being cowardly. Like one of those mothers who're afraid to draw a hard line, like maybe their kid won't like them anymore if they do. I'm not saying it's impossible for me to fall into that. But I sure try not to. The main reason I didn't ask is because it's obvious that she's willing to lie to me now, and so what's the point of asking, really? She won't tell me the truth. It's hurtful to me, though, because I thought we had a better relationship than that. I didn't think she would lie to my face."

"Any kid'll lie if the truth is far enough from what her mother wants to hear. So what's your guess?"

"I think she has a boyfriend."

"She's only thirteen!"

"I know it! Why do you think it worries me? It could be someone older. Someone who . . . you know . . . knows how to manipulate a young girl. Anyway, she was late again the next day. Or maybe it was the next two days. I've lost track. And then on the last day of school . . . well, granted it's only a half day and nothing very important goes on. But she didn't bother showing up at all. I got another call about it. She's never absent without permission, so maybe she didn't know that the school would call me. That's the only thing I can figure, because she's a bright girl. That was yesterday. Then this morning she just ate some cereal and disappeared."

"And that's unlike her?"

"Totally unlike her. She's always been such a good girl. I've gotten to count on that."

"She's a teenager, Mary. Kids change when the teen years hit."

"I know it. I mean, neither one of us really knows that parenting nightmare firsthand. Yet. But that's what everybody says. But here's another thing. She comes home really late and then . . . she seems . . . different."

"Different how?"

"Happy. Like . . . weirdly happy."

"Is that really so unheard of?"

Mary felt deeply ashamed of the answer. Ashamed to say, "Yes. It's unheard of. We're not happy at my house." So instead she just said, "If she's seeing a boy, I feel like I need to know about it."

"I agree," Viv said.

They sipped at their soup for a minute or two without speaking.

"What would you do if you were in my shoes?" Mary asked.

"Probably follow her."

"Oh, that'd never work. She'd spot my car in a heartbeat. It's bright yellow."

"I've seen your car, Mary. Yes indeed. *So* yellow. So here's what you do. Trade cars with me for a day."

"What if Stan notices?"

"Oh, to hell with Stan," Viv spat.

It surprised Mary. It hurt her feelings a bit as well. "Easy for you to say."

"Wait till he goes to work. Pick a day when Abby sleeps a little later. Drive over and trade cars while she's sleeping in."

"I guess I could do that. It makes me feel sneaky, though."

"I think you have to do it, Mary. What if it's not a boy she's seeing? What if it's a grown man? That happens to girls her age."

"You're right, Viv. You're right, of course. For Abby's sake . . . for her safety, I have to figure out what's going on."

—

Mary woke at a little after five and crept down the hall to Abby's room, moving as quietly as possible. She opened Abby's bedroom door slowly, anticipating the tense moment when the hinge would squeak. She didn't want to wake Abby, because she had no good explanation as to why she was spying. At least, none that she was prepared to share.

Abby's bed was already neatly made, and her daughter was gone.

She wandered downstairs, made coffee, and waited until Stan left for work.

Then she called Viv to tell her she wouldn't be coming by for the car.

"Not today," Mary said. "I already missed her."

"What time did she go?"

"Before five. It must've been barely light."

"We can try again tomorrow. But . . . before five o'clock on one of the first days of summer vacation? We know one thing for sure. Wherever she's going, she really wants to get there."

It made Mary's stomach hurt, but she didn't say so. All she said was "We'll try again tomorrow."

———

As it turned out, Mary didn't need to wait that long.

Abby turned up at the kitchen door at about noon, sweaty and dirty, but positively glowing.

"I'm surprised to see you," Mary said. "I figured you'd be gone all day again today."

Abby avoided her mother's eyes. "I have to go again. I mean, I don't have to, but . . . I like being outside. I've been walking up in the foothills. It's good conditioning for swim team in the fall. But I got hungry, so I wanted to come home for lunch."

"Okay," Mary said. "Sit down at the table and I'll make you a sandwich and warm up some soup."

Mary worked with her back to her daughter for a few minutes, thinking and deciding. She couldn't take Viv's car up into the foothills. She couldn't take any car up there. You would need a Jeep or a four-wheel-drive truck to get up there.

If that's really where Abby was going, the whole surveillance idea was pointless. It was a plan that had flopped before it ever started.

She spread two slices of wheat bread with just the amount of mustard she knew Abby liked, then added Swiss cheese and sliced turkey—and made up her mind.

She would have to have it out with her daughter, and she would have to do it now.

Her heart seeming to beat in her throat, she turned around and sat across from Abby, setting the sandwich in front of her.

Abby dug in immediately.

"We need to—" Mary began.

But then she looked at her daughter—really took her in, not just fussed and worried and half looked away. She gathered everything that was visually presented to her, and suddenly nothing was a mystery anymore.

"We need to what?" Abby asked, a little warily.

"Nothing," Mary said. "Never mind."

Abby's hands and arms were covered in tiny red bite marks. Not like insect bites. Little scratches made by little teeth. And on the shoulder of her T-shirt, where it was unlikely Abby could see it herself, Mary saw one perfect paw print. Puppy size, not dog size. As though a puppy had stepped in something wet before jumping up to reach her daughter's face.

Mary sat a moment, nursing her relief. Actually feeling it flow away from her, like a wave sucking back out to sea.

There was no boy. Or man.

There were puppies.

Abby had told her the truth about the puppies in the river. Which made a degree of sense, since it would have been an odd story for a girl Abby's age to make up. The only lie was that she had taken them to the county pound. She had stashed them somewhere, and kept them.

It might have been a disturbing revelation at some earlier time in Mary's life, yet it seemed so natural and so innocent compared to everything she had been picturing.

She watched her daughter eat and tried to decide what to say.

Abby looked up at her after a time. "You said soup, too."

"Coming right up."

Mary opened a can of soup, poured it into a saucepan, and added milk instead of water. Just because it was a little richer and nicer that way.

She didn't even have to think very hard about the dilemma. The answer was just there, in her head. In her gut and heart.

She would say nothing about the situation. She would not even let on that she knew.

Of course Abby could never bring them home. Stan would have a fit. But if she was managing to keep them somehow . . . if she had some place for them . . . who was Mary to step in and break her heart? Finally Abby was happy, with someplace exciting to go. Enjoying life in a way Mary knew she never could in this house.

It would be harder than Abby probably thought it would, but maybe Mary could trust her to face those challenges on her own.

It might not work out at all, and Abby might get her heart broken, but it still seemed better to let it run its course. Abby would grow up some. Learn something. Life might break her heart, but it seemed better than Mary breaking her heart prematurely, before she was even able to understand why the project was so untenable.

Mary didn't want to break her.

She stirred the soup on the gas burner, and felt around in the moment. Felt what it changed, and what it left the same. It was a strange comfort, to simply trust her daughter to experience the world for herself. To learn on her own, instead of being force-fed lessons from jaded adults who thought they could predict the outcome of any situation.

She poured the soup into a bowl and set it, steaming, in front of Abby's face.

"What kind?" Abby asked, sniffing.

"Cream of chicken. Your favorite."

"Oh, good. Thanks, Mom."

Mary didn't move away at first. She only stood, looking down at her daughter.

Finally Abby looked up and said, "What? Why are you looking at me like that?"

"No reason. I just love you."

Abby rolled her eyes at the corniness of the sentiment.

Mary trotted upstairs and dug around in the back of her top dresser drawer. When she found the loaded pink sock, she counted out two twenties and a ten, and slipped them into her skirt pocket.

Stan would never know if she had spent three hundred dollars on him or only two hundred and fifty. Let him think she was bad at bargain hunting. What did it matter? He deserved this money less than anybody.

Abby was trying to do something important. She was trying to be happy.

Mary trotted back downstairs to the kitchen.

Amazingly, Abby had already managed to bolt down all that food. In fact, she was halfway out the door.

"Abby. Wait."

"What? Why? I'm in a hurry."

"I want to give you something."

Abby hung in the doorway just long enough for Mary to sweep the money out of her pocket and hold it out where her daughter could see.

"You're giving me money?"

"Yeah. I am."

"Did I do something right that I don't know about?"

"You always do right. That's one of the things I really appreciate about you."

Abby reached out and took the money, then spread the bills out and counted them quickly, her eyes almost comically wide. "You're giving me *fifty dollars*? *Why?* I mean . . . I'm not complaining. I'll take it. But . . . why?"

"Oh, I don't know. Your dad never gives you much, and it's summer, and I just thought you might have something to spend it on. You know."

A strangely long pause.

Then Abby said, "Thanks, Mom!"

She jumped in Mary's direction, suddenly awkward and unable to organize her own limbs. And she gave Mary a peck on the cheek.

A second later she darted out the door and she was gone.

Mary sat at the table for a minute or two, feeling the ghost of that little kiss.

Then she got up and phoned Viv to tell her the news.

"You found out something?" Viv asked immediately.

"I did. And it's a lot more innocent than what we were picturing."

# Chapter Eight

## Mutually Exclusive

**Elliot**

When the cabin came into view, Elliot immediately saw that the lock had been cut—saw it, in fact, from the road. He was a few dozen yards away, just ready to pull his truck into the dirt driveway. It wasn't that he saw a cut lock from so much distance. He saw no lock at all.

He parked the truck and jumped out, cursing under his breath. He ran closer to the front door, which seemed to be tied shut by means of a short, thin piece of rope securing the two sections of the hasp.

He walked up close enough to touch the rope, then untied it and pulled it away.

It made no sense, he thought. Why would you cut the lock off a cabin's door, do whatever you had intended to do inside, and then carefully secure the door again? It didn't fit the pattern of a burglary.

Elliot pushed the door open and stood still on the stoop, looking inside. It was a wincing kind of looking, his eyes narrow, as if he could see the bad news but at the same time not see it.

The first things he noticed were the two missing throw pillows from the couch. Not that they really mattered. It was just visually obvious, and struck his eye first.

Then he saw that they had taken his little mini fridge.

"Damn it!" he barked out loud to no one.

He stepped inside and began to check the inside of cupboards and drawers.

A few of the dishes and glasses were gone, but not all of them. It was as if two people had just wanted two place settings. Yet they took all the flatware, an inconsistency Elliot's brain could not process.

He opened the pantry and found it completely empty. No flour, no pasta, no canned goods. No salt. They had taken the salt and pepper. Who takes a person's salt?

None of it would likely have been good by now anyway, with the possible exception of the canned goods and the salt. But it was the principle of the thing.

Elliot sat on the couch for a few moments, perched on its edge, his hands clasped and his forehead pressed against them. Eyes squeezed tightly shut.

Though he might not have been able to put it clearly into words, life had just crossed a line for him. Yes, Pat had died, and that was huge, but he could hardly blame life for it. People died. It had always seemed a bit immature to him when people wailed "Why me?" in the face of hardship. "Why not you?" he wanted to say. "Why not me? Why not any of us?" He was fully prepared to face life on its own terms.

But to come up here to feel better and be met with this? Now it just felt as though the universe was picking on him. It was more than he was able to dismiss as fair.

"The shed," he said suddenly, out loud.

Had they cut the lock on the shed and emptied it, too? That's where most of his valuable belongings had been stashed. His snowmobile for the winter. His big generator, and the cans of gasoline to run it. Tool kits and winches and fishing rods and extra rifles.

He sat a few seconds longer, not quite ready to find out. Then he sighed deeply, walked out of his cabin and around to the shed, and made himself look.

The lock had been cut. It was still on the door, its shank holding the hasp in place. Keeping the door closed.

He thought he knew what he would find when he looked inside: nothing. Just a concrete floor. Still, he had to look.

He removed the cut lock and opened the door—and did not see what he had expected to see at all.

Everything he had stored in there was gone, but it wasn't just an empty concrete floor. The floor was covered with layers of newspapers, a cardboard box on its side. The two throw pillows from his couch were being used as beds. There was a water dish near the door, mostly full, and a partial bag of kibble up on a high shelf.

And in the far corner, a litter of puppies huddled behind one another, watching Elliot over one another's backs. They had initially moved in his direction, all at once like a wave washing up on shore. But he had seen the moment when they realized Elliot was not who they'd been expecting. Now they hovered with their heads down, one whimpering, one growling. Two of them barked at him, and the barking seemed to spread as if contagious, until they were all barking at him. On his own property, they were telling him to keep back.

He stepped inside and closed the door so they couldn't get out.

"So somebody violated my place and stole from me," he told the puppies, "and then left me all of you." They stopped barking, as if to listen. "Well, that's not going to work."

He moved to the box and set it upright, and they skittered out of his path.

He reached for one, an all-black one, but the puppy evaded him. They all started up barking again.

Elliot sat cross-legged on the floor to consider his situation. The papers were clean where he sat. Apparently the puppies had learned to hold their bladders and bowels while in confinement, at least to a point. There was one far corner where it seemed they had urinated on the papers and then gotten as far from their own urine as possible.

"I'm going to put you all in this box and take you to the pound," he said in their direction. "Might as well get used to that idea right now. You can't stay here. But I'm not going to hurt you. I'm not that guy. I know you didn't rob my house. Whatever happened here, you're definitely not suspects. And I'm not going to take it out on you."

He reached a hand out to the one that seemed boldest. A little black-and-white Queensland-looking mix with black ears. A female. She approached cautiously, and sniffed his hand. Then she jumped back into the corner and growled.

It was almost funny, coming from puppies so small and so young. Elliot probably outweighed them forty times over, but here they were, bravely standing up to him.

He didn't reach out again. Just sat.

In time they began to come to him, hesitantly. One by one. He lifted them with a hand under their plump bellies and set them inside the box. Then, after the first couple had been placed in the box, the siblings tried to climb in as a way of staying together. All Elliot had to do was scoop them up from behind and set them inside.

He carried them out the door and loaded the box into the cab of his truck. Then he started the engine. Buckled his seat belt.

As he drove down the rutted road toward town, Elliot made the mistake of glancing over at them.

They were staring at him. Every one of them. Fourteen bright little eyes, fixed on him. Drilling through his hard exterior. As if they thought they could shame him into telling them what was going to happen to them next. There was no doubt that they understood a change had been made to their situation.

"Don't look at me like that," Elliot said. "None of this is my fault."

———

He stepped into the outer office of the county pound, where a uniformed animal control officer lifted up onto her tiptoes to get a look inside his box.

"Oh no," she said, sounding genuinely disappointed, "she couldn't find homes for them, huh? I guess I'm not surprised. She seemed like such a determined kid, though. I thought she just might pull it off against all odds. Are you her father?"

Elliot only blinked for a moment.

"We don't seem to be on the same page," he said. "I don't know who this person is that you're talking about."

"The little girl who found them. Well, not little. She said she was thirteen. She seemed little to me, but I guess everybody kind of does when we start to get older."

"That last part I can relate to. Everything else might as well have been Greek. So you've seen these puppies before?"

"Yup, I have. A few days ago a girl brought them in here. Said she'd seen somebody throw them in the river to drown them. Tied up in a sack. Doesn't happen as much as it used to in the olden days, but it does happen. Well, obviously."

"So how did they get here if they were in a sack in the river?"

"She jumped in and pulled them out."

"From *the river*? I'm not even sure if *I* could do that."

"She said she's on the swim team at her school, and that she's just a real strong swimmer. She wanted to surrender them but I think I broke her heart by being honest about their chances. I hated to do it to her, but what was I supposed to do? Lie?"

"People don't adopt puppies around here?"

"Not as regularly as they surrender and dump them."

That was when Elliot realized he couldn't leave them here. Surrendering them would be the same as killing them.

"So where did *you* find them?" the woman asked, knocking him out of his thoughts.

"They were being kept in a shed on my property. Up in the foothills."

"I guess she couldn't bring them home."

"Wait," Elliot said. "Just wait now. You seem so sure it's this same girl keeping them in my shed, but you don't know that. After all, you said yourself that she was looking to give them away."

"Doesn't seem likely she found someone to take all seven. Does that make sense in your head? Doesn't in mine. The only person I know who might want seven puppies all at once is a person who's already attached to them."

"But . . . ," Elliot began.

There was nowhere to go with the thought, though. So he just stopped talking, placed the box on the counter, and stood silently. And felt dejected, because his anger had abandoned him. He hadn't wanted to let go of it, because it was temporarily powering him through the exhaustion of his ever-present grief. That's why he'd been arguing with her.

He had brought the puppies to the pound because he had assumed they belonged to his burglar. He was no longer sure why he'd assumed it, but he had. And it had been a satisfying act of defiance on his part, to gather them up and take them away.

*There, go pay the fine on all of them if you want them back. Serves you right. How dare you think you could keep them in my shed after what you did?*

But all that lovely, satisfying anger had abandoned him now.

They belonged to a little girl who had risked her life to save them from drowning. And who sounded like an unlikely burglary suspect.

Now the only person Elliot could be angry with was himself.

"You want to surrender them?" the woman asked him.

"No. I can't do that. I mean, if she's just a girl. I'd better talk the situation over with her first. You know her name?"

"I don't."

"Well, it hardly matters. We'll meet soon enough. She'll come back for the dogs and there I'll be."

———

"Well," Elliot said out loud as he pulled up to the cabin again, "that didn't take long."

The girl was standing in his yard, arms crossed over her chest. Pitched forward some, as if leaning into the fight she expected to come along and find her. He knew she must be the girl in question because it was just too much of a coincidence if she wasn't. And because she looked mad.

He stepped out the driver's side door of his truck, and looked at her. And she looked back at him.

She was presenting herself as almost . . . fierce. It reminded Elliot of the puppies, barking and growling warnings at him in the shed, even though he outweighed them forty times over. It had a humor to it at one level. The surface level. Under that, Elliot felt a strong sense of admiration. It made him wonder how differently his life might have turned out if he could have mustered that level of fire toward adults when he was thirteen.

Elliot moved to walk around the truck. To get the box of puppies out from the passenger's side.

The sun beat down on the crown of his scalp as he walked, and the wind blew his shirt around. The air had that fine charge, that mountain thinness—somehow more alive than city air. He had been too busy earlier to notice. To reflect on how much he had missed it.

"Did you take my dogs?" the girl asked.

Elliot kept walking, and did not look back at her. "Yes," he said.

"Did you take them to the pound?"

"Yes and no."

"That's terrible! You're a terrible man! How could you do that to me? How could you do that to *them*? What kind of a person takes somebody else's dogs to the pound?"

Elliot opened the passenger door. He picked up the box and plunked it firmly on the warm hood of the truck.

"What kind of person keeps their dogs on somebody else's property?"

He watched her face change. Watched all the fight drain out of her. It might have been a harsh thing to say, but he hadn't meant to hurt or upset her. He had simply made an error. She had presented herself to him as invincible, and he had made the mistake of believing her.

"I'm sorry," she said, and for a second she looked as though she might cry. "I thought the place was abandoned. I didn't expect anybody would notice or care."

"I guess we can pin that on me. I haven't come up here in years."

"I'm sorry about the couch cushions. The pillows, I guess I mean. I just felt bad about making 'em sleep on concrete. I know they've been chewing on 'em. I'll buy you new ones out of my allowance."

"It doesn't really matter," he said. "They're not particularly expensive or special."

They both stood in the sun a moment, considering each other. It struck Elliot that all the anger, all the conflict, had been stripped from the moment. And he wasn't even sure why, except perhaps that there was something charming about her determination. Wasn't that the word the woman at the pound had used?

"Such a determined kid."

The determined kid must have noticed the shift in mood, too. She seemed to want the conflict back.

"That's still a terrible thing to do. Taking my dogs to the pound. You could've just waited till I got here and told me to take 'em someplace else. But that was just mean."

Elliot looked down into the box. He was holding it with both hands so any movement inside would not send it tumbling off the truck's hood. But they were not moving. They couldn't see the girl over the high side of the box, but they seemed to be following her voice. One of them looked up into his eyes. The all-tan one. It was a look that seemed to say, "The world is beyond my understanding."

*You and me both,* Elliot thought.

Instead he turned his attention back to the girl. "Are they *at* the pound?" he asked her. "Or are they right here?"

He honestly didn't know if she understood that all seven dogs were right there on the hood of his truck. It was hard to tell. She might not have been able to see them over the cardboard sides, or she might have been too caught up in fighting with him to notice the box at all. Or maybe she knew but she chose to call him mean anyway.

"You brought 'em back?"

"They're right here. Yes."

"Why did you bring 'em back?"

"Because the lady at the pound told me about you, and how you were only thirteen. And how you jumped in and snatched them out of the river before they could drown. And then I started figuring you're probably not the person who cut my padlocks and robbed me. I don't know a lot of thirteen-year-old burglars, though I suppose anything's possible. But I decided the two things were mutually exclusive."

She twisted up her face in confusion. Or maybe it was just the sun in her eyes. "I don't know what that means."

"It's when something can't be two ways at the same time. Like . . . the person who rescues puppies is not the person who breaks into people's cabins. Or at least I'd like to think not."

"Like the way Superman and Clark Kent can't be in the same room together?"

*Not really,* he thought. If she had been an adult, he might have dissected the comparison. Superman and Clark Kent were always in the same room together. They were the same person, not two things that can't coexist.

But she wasn't an adult, so he only said, "Something like that."

"So you're giving 'em back to me?"

Elliot lifted the box and swung it off the hood. He carried it over to the girl and set it at her feet.

"Thank you," she said. "I'm sorry I yelled at you."

"That's not so important right now. I'm more interested in who stole my snowmobile and my generator. Do you have any ideas? Did you see anything?"

"No, sir," she said, lifting puppies out of the box, one by one, and setting them in the dirt on their paws. "I don't know anything about it. My friend Jamie was the one who first noticed that the lock on the cabin door'd been cut. But I think she would've told me if she knew who did it."

"Will you ask her?"

"Sure."

"I'm going inside now," Elliot said, suddenly feeling how much the struggles of the day had left him drained. He had no energy since losing Pat. "I'm tired, and I'm going to lie down."

He got all the way to the door thinking the conversation was over. But before he stepped inside, she called to him.

"Wait," she said. "What do I do now?"

"About what?"

"Do I have to find a new place to keep 'em?"

"Of course you do," he said. "This is my cabin."

It seemed like something that should have gone without saying. But the look on her face suggested that he had overestimated her toughness. Again.

# Chapter Nine

## *Glass*

### *Abby*

Abby was still in his yard, sitting with the puppies, when he came out the door again and walked to his truck. She hadn't left, because she'd thought he was going to take a nap or something, and that she had plenty of time.

And because she had nowhere else to take them.

He stopped when he saw her. She thought he might yell at her, because he didn't seem to be in the best mood. Or maybe he never was. How would she know? She had only just met him.

"You're still here," he said. He was squinting down at her. He didn't seem particularly happy, but he wasn't yelling. Nothing even close to it.

"I thought you were taking a nap, so it wouldn't matter."

One of the puppies, Patches, dared to approach him. He reached up and put his front paws on the legs of the man's jeans. The guy leaned down and scratched the dog behind the ears. He seemed to scratch in a distracted way, as if he hadn't noticed himself doing it. Still, it seemed like a good sign to Abby, who desperately wanted the puppies to win him over.

"I was going to. But then I realized I have food with me that needs to be kept cold. So I have to go into town and get a cooler and some ice or it'll go bad."

Abby waited, saying nothing. Watching more puppies swarm closer to him. She wanted to ask why he hadn't stopped at the market on his way through town. It wasn't as though his having brought food was any surprise to him. After all, he was the one who'd brought it. But she thought it might be rude to ask, and she didn't feel she could afford to be rude.

"I had a little refrigerator," he said, seeming to note that more explanation was needed. "But it's one of the things that was stolen."

He began to walk toward his truck again.

Abby felt as though she'd better talk fast. "Wait," she said. "Don't go for just a minute. How long are you staying at the cabin?"

He stopped walking. Turned around and gave her that squinty look again. But now the sun was at his back, so it was definitely about her. Or her dogs. Or both.

"I don't think I want to answer that question," he said.

"Why not? People ask each other questions like that all the time. Small talk, you know? 'Where you from? How long you plan to stay?'"

"I don't want to answer, because I have a bad feeling you're planning to use the information to move those puppies right back into my shed when I'm gone."

Abby climbed to her feet and dusted off the seat of her jeans. Took a step or two closer to him. "But if you're not here, what difference would it make? It's not like you're keeping anything in there right now. I mean, I'm sorry your stuff got stolen. I really am, too—I'm not just saying that. You didn't deserve to be robbed, I know you didn't, because nobody deserves that. But it happened, and now the shed is empty."

"But I'm going to have to start replacing what I stored in there. Maybe not the snowmobile, because I don't know if I'm still sportsman enough to come up here in the winter. But I definitely need to buy a new generator. The solar panel is small and I don't have much battery storage for it."

He paused. Looked into her face as if trying to figure something out about her. But she didn't know what, so she didn't know whether to mind.

She started to open her mouth, but he never let her get that far.

"Look, I'm sorry," he said. "You seem like a nice enough kid, and I know this is important to you. I understand that you're attached to them. And I know you think I'm mean and terrible—"

"I don't think you're mean and terrible."

"You already said both about me. But never mind that. You were upset. Whatever. The bottom line is that I'm going through a miserable time in my life, and I'm unhappy, and I just need to be alone. I need some time to get to feeling better. And I'm just not handling things well right now. Extra commotion like this . . . well, I'm sorry, but I can't cope with one more thing on my plate. No offense to you."

He waited for a second or two. Maybe in case she had something to say. Then he dug his car keys out of his pocket and opened the driver's door of the truck.

"Wait," she said. "Why are you unhappy?"

She knew it was none of her business to ask, but it felt like her last chance to engage him. Maybe make him like her better. Maybe change his mind.

He leaned on the roof of his truck for a second, and Abby knew he was trying to decide whether to tell her to get lost, or whether it was easier to answer. She wasn't sure how she knew that about him, but she did. The guy seemed to have these emotions that Abby could almost see. Maybe because he was having such a hard time.

"My wife just died," he said over his shoulder. He more or less threw the words back to where she was standing. He didn't turn around or meet her eyes. He didn't deliver them personally.

"Oh no. I'm so sorry. Wow. That must really suck."

"See, even a thirteen-year-old can do it," he muttered to himself.

"Do what?"

"Never mind. You had to be there. Yes. It sucks. Now if you'll excuse me."

He plunked down into the driver's seat, started up his truck, and drove away.

—

Abby walked down the road for several minutes, the puppies more or less following. She was carrying their box with the bag of kibble and the empty water dish inside.

She had left the pillows behind because they were too much to carry. And because they weren't really hers—though she expected they were close enough to ruined that the man would only throw them away. Maybe she would go back later and ask.

She stopped in the road and counted puppies, as she had been doing every few yards along the way. She was worried about coyotes, even though it was abnormal to see them in broad daylight. It was not, unfortunately, unheard of.

In time the old, broken-down barn came into view.

Now this, Abby knew, was an abandoned property.

The roof of the house had literally collapsed, taking down most of the front wall of the place. The barn was more or less in one piece, but it was very old. And it looked fragile.

Abby called them into the yard with her, and they walked all the way around the structure, through the weeds and junk lumber. It had four walls, but that's about all that could be said for it.

When they arrived at the front of the barn again, Abby counted puppies, then pushed the barn door. It swung in easily. Abby saw a single shaft of light coming down at a slant from a huge hole in the roof. It was about a quarter of the roof missing, she estimated. *That* huge.

Still, it would allow her to close them in.

She walked around on its dirt floor, looking up at the piles of . . . well, once upon a time it might have been something. Now it was all garbage. Metal garbage that might have been tractor parts, now rusted beyond recognition. Wood garbage that might have been stored lumber, or might have been the rest of the roof. It was hard to tell after so much decay.

"I guess it's better than the pound," she said, and several of the puppies cocked their ears to listen to her. One tilted his head in that heartbreakingly sweet gesture that dogs sometimes use when trying to understand.

Her biggest fear was that a strong wind would come along and the whole structure could literally collapse on them.

"Then again, it's been here all this time," she said.

A shriek of a sound pierced her midsection. It felt as though it literally cut through her, like a bayonet. It was the cry of an animal in pain.

She looked down to see Patches hopping along with one back paw held raised. Trailing blood. Then she focused on the dirt floor in the beam of light through the missing roof. The floor of the barn was littered with broken glass. Brown, curved shards. Somebody had apparently been drinking beer in here, and then smashing the bottles. One of the corners was littered with it.

"Oh no! Patches. Wait!"

She ran to him, hoping that broken glass couldn't penetrate her sneaker soles. She picked him up and turned him over in her arms. He had sliced a pad of one back paw. It was a deep gash. It was a lot of blood.

"We have to get out of here!" she shouted to the puppies. "Come on!"

She ran for the barn door, braced to hear another shriek of pain. Amazingly, they all came out into the light without additional injuries.

She took the water dish and kibble out of the box and set Patches inside. Just so the gash would stay clean for a moment while she took time to think. She needed something to wrap around that paw to slow down the bleeding. And it had to be fairly clean. But Abby had only the clothes on her back.

She sat in the weedy dirt and pulled off one sneaker, then the white sock underneath, and put the sneaker back on without it. Then she lifted the poor injured Patches and gently wrapped the sock around his paw, causing him to yelp again with pain. The sock immediately soaked through with bright blood.

"Come on!" she called to the puppies.

They more or less followed her. That is, they followed the way puppies follow. With detours, and play fights. And moments when they forgot to follow entirely and Abby had to remind them.

She could feel her heart pounding.

The sock was not holding back the blood the way she had hoped, but she was afraid to squeeze more tightly. Red dots began to drip onto her legs, and onto the road.

How would she herd them through town? *There are cars in town.*

At almost the exact moment she thought the word "cars," a truck came up the road. She wanted to wave wildly to stop the driver, so he wouldn't hit any of her puppies. But she couldn't raise either hand. One hand was cradling Patches, the other was holding pressure on his bloody paw.

Fortunately the driver saw her situation and stopped.

She ran closer to the truck, realizing as she did that it was the man from the cabin. He was coming back up from town with his cooler and ice.

He powered his window down and leaned out.

"What happened?"

"He stepped on some glass," Abby said. She moved close to his truck window, puppies at her feet. "It's bad. It's deep. I have to take him to the vet, but I . . ." She couldn't quite think how to sum up the impossibility of her situation. Then again, maybe it was obvious.

"Can I see?"

He asked it as though she might be exaggerating. As though Abby would show him the cut and he would say, "Oh, that's nothing. He doesn't need a vet for that."

Abby would have liked to hear such words.

She pulled the sock away and they looked at Patches's sliced paw pad together. Watched it ooze blood at an alarming rate.

"Get in the truck," the man said. "Wrap it up again as best you can and get in."

"But the other—"

"Just do it," he said, stepping out of the still-running vehicle.

Abby did as he had said. Because he sounded like he had a plan. He spoke as though he was willing to take charge of the situation. And Abby desperately wanted—needed—someone to take over.

She walked around to the passenger side, and he held the door open while she climbed in.

Then she watched as he walked around in the road, picking up her puppies. Sometimes one at a time, sometimes one in each hand, he reached through his open driver's side window and placed them on the bench seat.

"How many are there again?"

"Seven."

"Who's missing?"

"The all-black one."

"I don't see . . . oh. There he is."

He scrambled after the last puppy, scooped him up, then climbed into the truck. It was hard for him to sit down without sitting on puppies. And Abby couldn't help, because she had no free hands.

When the man got settled, he shifted the truck into gear and drove up the road.

"Where are we going?" Abby asked him. "The vet is the other way."

"It's faster to go up to the next driveway and turn around. A three-point turn on this road is more like a thirty-point turn."

She decided to shut up and let him be in charge.

The next driveway was the property with the run-down, glass-filled barn. He swung into the driveway, shifted into reverse and backed into the road, then took off driving at a good clip toward town. The truck's tires bounced in the hard ruts, jarring her and kicking up a cloud of dust that trailed out behind them.

Abby watched the old barn in the side-view mirror. Watched it get smaller in the distance. It looked evil to her. Like something from a horror movie. It looked like a half-living building-being that only existed to lure people and animals in and then hurt them.

She wondered why she hadn't seen that from the start.

When it faded into a point in the distance, she looked over at the man. He had gray at his sideburns, and a furrowed brow.

"Thank you for helping me," she said.

"I'm not a mean man."

"I never said—oh. Sorry. I guess I did say that, didn't I? But I shouldn't have."

They rode in silence for a time. Until the river came into view.

"Can I tell you something?" she asked. Because the emergency of the moment felt as though it was bringing them together. Like soldiers in a foxhole. Or what they always say about them, anyway.

"I suppose you can say whatever you want."

"I had this bright idea that grown-ups don't know much. And I was just going to use my own judgment. You know. Ignore them and do what I thought was best. But now I think . . ."

She didn't finish the thought. She didn't quite know how.

He waited for a while, as if to give her time.

Then he said, "Now you're in over your head."

"Yes, sir."

"Please don't call me sir. It makes me feel old."

"I don't know your name."

"Oh. It's Elliot. Elliot Colvin."

"Mr. Colvin, then."

"Elliot would be better."

"I was taught not to call grown-ups by their first name."

"But I'm asking you to."

"Oh. Okay, I guess."

They drove over the bridge together. The bridge that could so easily have been the scene of the last moment in these seven precious lives.

He surprised her by speaking. He also surprised her with what he said. It was the last message she had expected from a grown-up.

"In one way you were right. Adults don't know as much as we want you to think we do. We're faking it a lot of the time. So not only was that true, that feeling you got, but it's a necessary part of growing up. Somewhere along the line, every kid has to realize that adults are fallible. That they're not the ultimate authority you thought we were. Then again, the second part—the part where you figured you knew better—that was going off the rails some. Grown-ups have it over you in sheer day-to-day life experience. I'll be the first to admit that we don't know everything, but you at least have to be open to the idea that we might know a few things you don't."

Abby just sat a moment, absorbing his words. Absorbing the way he was speaking to her. Not as though she were an idiot. Not as though she were an enemy to him. Just as one human being speaking to another human being.

And it helped, too. It was helping to clarify her thinking.

"That's good advice, sir."

"Elliot."

"Right. Sorry."

They didn't speak for an odd length of time. As if that had been too much getting to know each other, and too quickly.

"I'm worried that we're getting blood on your nice truck seat," she said.

He shrugged. "It's only vinyl. It cleans."

"Oh. Good." Then she took a deep breath and said, "Thanks, Elliot."

# Chapter Ten

## Try This

**Elliot**

Elliot stepped back out of the vet's office and onto the street, leaving the girl sitting alone with the injured pup. He spent quite a bit of time looking for a parking place in the shade, because he was worried about the six puppies waiting in the truck's cab. Unfortunately, he never found one. He had to settle for parking the truck in a spot near a big street sign that threw shade into about a third of the truck's bed.

He transferred the puppies two at a time into the bed of the truck, where they yipped and fussed, somehow knowing they were about to be left.

He poised there for a long time in the hot sun—possibly several minutes—to be sure they couldn't jump out. But they were small puppies, and it was a deep bed.

Still, Elliot walked only halfway to the door of the vet's office before stopping again. To double-check.

"Stay. Right. There," he told them.

Then he felt foolish, because they had received no training and clearly understood no English.

He stepped back into the vet's outer office, but there was no one waiting.

"Your daughter is in an examining room with the vet," the assistant said. "You can go in if you want." She pointed toward a door.

Elliot opened his mouth to correct the woman's assumption that he was the girl's father. He almost said he didn't even know her name. He closed his mouth again and said nothing. Because it was a long and fairly complicated story, and he wasn't even sure he understood it himself.

He opened the door to the examining room and stepped in. Once inside he saw no vet and no puppy. Just the girl, sitting alone in a chair and crying openly.

"What happened?" he asked her.

She looked up. Her face was dirtier than Elliot had realized. He could see clean tracks left by her tears. "They had to take him back and . . . what do you call it when they have to put him to sleep?"

"*Euthanize him? Why?* It's just a cut!"

"No, no. Not that. Not put him to sleep *forever*. Just while they put the stitches in. He wouldn't stop squirming. There were four of us, like, sitting on him, but he wouldn't stop squirming. They took him in the back to do that thing . . . it sounds a little like that word you said. But not quite."

"Anesthetize?"

"That's it!"

Elliot sat in the only other chair, which was fairly close by the girl's side, feeling his alarm drain away. It puzzled him that his reaction of alarm had been so sudden, automatic, and enormous. He barely knew this girl and her brood of pups. Why had he been so devastated to think she had lost one?

Thinking it over, he realized he might know the answer. But, as with any thought connected to death, he didn't think it through for long.

"I forgot to ask your name," he said.

"I noticed that. I figured you didn't care."

Elliot didn't know what to say in response to that, so he said nothing.

"It's Abby," she added.

"Abby," he repeated. "So why are you sitting here crying if he's just in the back room getting some anesthetic, Abby?"

"Because now I think it'll cost more. I had some money, but it was for feeding them and stuff. But now it has to be for the vet, and I thought it might be enough, but now I don't think it will be. What if I can't pay them? Maybe they won't give him back until I can pay them, and then I'll never get him back."

They sat quietly for a moment.

Elliot looked up and around. On the walls he saw photos of horrific pathological conditions in dogs. An advanced case of mange, or some other severe skin disease. A dog's heart infested with heartworms that made Elliot's blood run cold. He couldn't imagine why anyone would frame and display such images. Unless the point was to scare people into buying more preventive veterinary care.

He looked back down at the black-and-white linoleum again.

"How much do you have?" he asked her.

"Eighty or ninety dollars. Think it'll be enough?"

"I doubt it. No. Sorry. I'm not trying to be discouraging. I don't have pets, so I can't say for sure. But if he had to have a general anesthetic . . . no. I don't think it'll be enough."

For a time, all he heard from her was a deep sigh.

Then Abby said, "They didn't ask me how I was going to pay. I think the reason they didn't ask is because they thought you were my dad. They didn't know I'm kind of in here all by myself. They probably figured you'd just take out your credit card and take care of the whole thing just like that, like it was nothing."

Elliot looked briefly over at the girl. He had seen her looking at him in his peripheral vision, so he looked back. She obviously needed help, but she wasn't going to come right out and ask for it. But she had a look in her eyes that said she hoped Elliot would be her savior.

But Elliot didn't want to be anybody's savior. He barely felt able to save himself. And he needed saving, too.

It was like that woman had said. That woman from Pat's book group who had talked to him at the memorial. "This is one day in your life when you get to think about your own feelings more than anyone else's." Only it had stretched out into more than just a day.

He opened his mouth to tell her this truth.

Before he had managed any words, a door swung open and a young man Elliot thought must be the vet came in. He looked hardly more than twenty-five. But he was wearing a name tag that said "Dr. Prieczek."

"Okay," Dr. Prieczek said. "We put four stitches in that little paw pad. It wasn't easy. Not much room to work, but we managed. But I can't let you take him home yet. We have to monitor his situation for a bit. Until he's fully awake. And he'll have to wear one of those awful cone collars everybody hates—people and dogs both. Nobody likes a clown collar. But without it he'll rip those stitches out in no time flat. And he'll have to be on a round of antibiotics."

"So how long do I have to stay?" Abby asked.

"Oh, you can go home. You can pick him up at six, or you can call and see if he's ready earlier. I'll just get his paperwork up to Janice at the desk and you can settle up now, or when you come to get him. Whichever is easiest for you."

Elliot was on his feet now—though he had no conscious memory of standing—and the girl was standing by his side. And he could feel her gearing up to tell the vet the truth about her situation. To throw herself at his mercy. And he could feel how hard this was for her. He wasn't sure how he knew all that, except that it was all right there in the room to be felt.

She opened her mouth, but Elliot stopped her. He draped an arm around her shoulder and turned her toward the door.

"We'll settle up *now*," he said over his shoulder.

He guided Abby out into the waiting room in silence. Her eyes looked huge and round, and her mouth was slightly open, as if her jaw had half dropped with the shock. She looked as though she wanted to know what he meant. But apparently she didn't dare ask.

Janice was on the phone.

They waited, side by side in front of her desk. Elliot pulled his wallet from his back jeans pocket and searched around for the credit card with the highest limit. He set it on the desk.

"I'll pay you back," Abby said quietly.

"Yes you will."

"I don't know how, though. I only get ten dollars a week allowance, but I'll pay you back somehow. I could give you that almost ninety dollars I have."

"Then how will you feed the puppies?"

"I have no idea."

They waited a while longer. Elliot began tapping his foot. They did not discuss finances again until Janice got off the phone and presented them with Patches's two hundred seventy-seven-dollar bill.

———

"There's a lot of work to be done up at the cabin," Elliot said. "If you wanted to work it off."

"Like what?"

They were leaning on the bed of the truck together, staring at the six puppies. Who, fortunately, had not jumped out.

"Obviously the front door was open for some time. So everything is covered in dust and grime. It all needs to be cleaned. Even the walls. And it's all wood, so it's all dried out now. Everything will have to be oiled. Floors, walls, cabinets. It's a big job, even though it seems like such a small place."

"Doesn't sound like two hundred seventy-seven dollars' worth."

"And the windows need to be cleaned inside and out."

"Still doesn't sound like two hundred seventy-seven dollars."

"Whatever. We'll figure it out. Jump in."

"I can't leave. I have to wait here with Patches."

"It might be hours."

"But I don't want to have to walk all the way down here again."

Elliot didn't know how to give her six dogs back. The box had been misplaced in all the confusion. He opened his mouth to say what he would do next. Though, oddly, he didn't know what he would do. He just started talking, as if he were as curious as anyone to hear.

"I'll take them back, then," he said. "And when Patches is ready to go, you can bring him up."

"Back?" There was a tension in her voice. Again, she seemed to want to know what he meant. Again, she didn't dare ask.

"You have to have someplace to keep them. For now. Patches needs someplace clean and dry. At least until he heals."

"Right," Abby said. "For now. Thanks, Elliot." She walked toward the vet's office door. Then she stopped and turned back to him. "Hey. Try something when you get back up there."

"Okay. What?"

"Put them all down on the ground. And then just . . . lie down."

"Lie down?"

"Right."

"Why? Then what?"

"You'll see. Just try it. You said you were unhappy, right?"

"I did say that."

"Well, turns out it's impossible to be unhappy when you're lying on your back with a bunch of puppies all around you, doing what puppies do. Trust me. I know. I may not know everything, but I know all about this."

Elliot didn't figure he'd lie down with the puppies. It seemed like a thirteen-year-old's version of how not to be unhappy, and Elliot knew he needed stronger medicine.

He opened the passenger door of his truck, then stopped. He had been seized by a thought.

"Wait," he said.

Abby was halfway through the door to the vet's office again, but she waited. "What?"

"Were you the one who tied my door closed?"

She looked down at the pavement, as though embarrassed to have been caught. "Yeah. That was me."

"Why? You didn't even know who owned it."

"No. But I knew somebody did. And I knew whoever owned it must care something about it, because why would you own a place if you don't even care that you do?"

"That was nice of you."

"Just what anybody would do. I mean . . . I think."

"That's worth something to me."

"I don't know what that means."

"There should be some sort of reward for that. I could take some off what you owe me."

She paused in the doorway a moment longer. Then her face changed into something akin to a miniature smile. Or at least the closest thing to one that he had seen from her.

"Thanks, Elliot," she said.

She let the door swing closed behind her.

———

Elliot drove back up to the cabin carefully. Uncharacteristically slowly. He eased over the bumps, because the six puppies were still in the bed of his truck and he didn't want to jostle them too much.

He glanced at them from time to time in his rearview mirror. They were sitting, heads pointed upward, noses to the wind. As if the air was filled with fascinating and relevant information and they were reading the scents the way a person might read a newspaper.

Oddly, it wasn't until he parked his truck by the cabin that he realized he had no idea what he was supposed to do with them. Not even in the short run.

He stood for a time by the truck bed, looking down at them. They sat looking back up at him.

"You probably want something to eat," he said.

They wagged furiously at that. Elliot had no idea if they knew what the word "eat" meant. Maybe they were just thrilled that he had broken his silence and spoken to them.

"I don't have any dog food, though. Sorry."

Their tails slowed. Maybe Elliot was telegraphing too much emotion with the words. Tipping the puppies to the difference between good news and bad news with the tone of his voice.

"Abby took it with her when she went, and I don't know where she . . . Oh, what am I doing? I'm explaining this to you like you speak English."

The little all-tan puppy tilted his head questioningly. Elliot found it almost shockingly appealing and sweet.

"I guess I can give you some water, though. You're probably hot."

He reached for his recently purchased cooler, which was in the corner of the truck bed with them, its ice inside. Elliot lifted the lid to see that half of the ice was melted already. And he hadn't even put his food inside it yet.

He sighed and carried it into the cabin, saying nothing about the fact that it was chewed at the corners—not even to himself.

He found a metal mixing bowl that had not been stolen, and filled it with water at the sink.

He carried it outside to them, and they nearly knocked each other over to get to it. They drank it almost dry in a matter of fifteen or twenty seconds.

While he watched them lapping, Elliot pressed a hand against the metal of the truck bed, and determined that it was too hot to leave them there.

"Let's put you back in the shed," he said.

He lifted them down two at a time, then walked to the shed. Three followed. Three did not.

Half keeping an eye on the stragglers, he opened the door and looked inside. Abby had cleaned its floor and taken up all the papers. The only things on the empty shelves were his two chewed throw pillows.

"Well," he said, looking down at the two puppies who had followed him inside. "It's not quite set up for you. But I don't want you out in the road, so I'm going to close you in until she gets back. Jeez. There I go again, explaining things to you in English."

He stepped out quickly, closing them inside.

He rounded up three more and scooped them into his arms, trying to ignore the pitiful whimpering and scratching from the other side of the shed door.

He carried the three to the shed, opened the door—and immediately lost the two that had been inside. He dumped the three inside and closed the door as quickly as he could. But it wasn't quick enough. Two of the three escaped again.

Elliot sighed, opened the door, and left it open.

He sat with his back up against the shed and watched them run and play.

"Well, this isn't working," he said out loud, to no one.

He decided the only really workable arrangement would be something like a baby gate inside the shed. Some barrier that would allow him to drop them on the other side of it. But of course he had nothing like that to work with.

The little black-and-white Queensland-looking mix galloped back in a big loop and raced across his legs, which made him laugh. Just one short burst of laughter. It sounded strange to his own ears, like some remnant of such a deep part of the past that he barely recognized it as himself.

Then the laughter abandoned him and he realized he had been placed in an uncomfortable situation. He still hadn't had that nap. He still hadn't put his food on ice. That is, what ice there was left. And he couldn't even go inside, because he didn't want to leave them unsupervised in an unfenced wilderness.

He stood and gathered them two at a time, setting them back in the truck bed. It was the only place he knew to put them without them dashing right back out again. When he had them all gathered, he climbed into the truck, started it up, and pulled into a very awkward parking space between two trees. He could barely open his door to get out again. But at least it was in the shade.

He stood looking down at them, and they up at him.

Then he jumped up onto the bumper and stepped over the tailgate, joining them in the now-shady bed.

"What the hell?" he said out loud to them. "What do I have to lose?"

He lay down on his back with his long legs draped over the tailgate. They did exactly what one would expect a gang of puppies to do. They swarmed him, all at once. They dashed onto his belly and chest and made sudden turns there, pushing off like leaps off a diving board. They licked at his face and nibbled at his nose. One of them grabbed a piece of his shirtsleeve and began tugging. And showed no signs of stopping.

Elliot lay, half protecting his face and half laughing, for three or four minutes. Then he sat up.

"Well, that was fun while it lasted," he said. "But . . ."

But he wasn't going to fall into that pit a third time—carefully explaining the world to puppies. In English. Elliot knew what the "but" was. They didn't, and wouldn't. And they didn't need to.

It had been fun, yes, and had provided a fleeting sense of happiness. Like a miniature vacation from the sorrow. But the problem with a vacation is that it always ends in a return trip home. Abby's recipe for happiness was interesting and fun, but it was all too temporary.

"I'm going to go in and take a nap," he told them.

He climbed out of the bed.

They yipped and cried for him, but he ignored them as best he could and went inside without them.

He put his food on ice and lay on the couch without folding it out into a bed. But he could still hear them crying. He tried for sleep for a few minutes, then gave up and joined them outside again.

They appeared nearly ecstatic to see him.

He lifted them out two at a time and set them in the dirt on their paws. Then he settled in the pine needles and dirt and took another, much longer, vacation.

# Chapter Eleven

## Hunter Green and Deep-Sea Blue

**Mary**

It was after 1:00 in the afternoon when the phone jangled on the kitchen wall. Mary was sure it was Viv, because hardly anyone else called her. She grabbed up the receiver.

"Hello, Viv," she said.

Silence on the line.

"Hello?" It was a question this time.

"Oh. Sorry. Hi. It's not Viv. It's Cara Masterson. You know. Paula's mom?"

"Oh. Yes. Of course. How are you?"

Mary had no idea why Paula Masterson's mom would be calling her, unless Abby had gone and gotten herself into some kind of trouble. But to ask "Why are you calling?" might have sounded rude. So Mary just waited.

"Oh, fine, fine. But I just . . . this is probably nothing, Mary. I'm not even sure if I was right to call you about it."

Mary felt her belly go icy cold.

"What? What is it? Tell me."

"You know any reason why Abby would be talking to a guy in his fifties who's not from around here? Steve was going back and forth through town to the hardware store, because he's doing that home remodel. The one on Tank Street. You know? And he saw Abby talking to some guy. Leaning on his truck. And they were having what he said was . . . I think the word he used was *intense*. Like an *intense* conversation. Like they knew each other. But does Abby even know a guy his age who's not a townie?"

Mary opened her mouth to answer, but she never managed to get a word in edgewise.

"It's probably nothing. I mean, it might be nothing. Maybe he was just asking her for directions. But even that feels a little bit off, because, things being what they are these days, he should ask an adult. Not strike up a conversation with a thirteen-year-old girl. People can get a wrong impression real easy. Steve wasn't sure what to think, so when he saw the guy driving back through town, he followed him for a bit. Not all the way up there, because he took off up that road that turns to dirt and goes up into the foothills. You know, over the Tank Street Bridge and then up into the middle of nothing, up near the state park land. That's such a deserted road, so he didn't feel like he could follow him up there. He said it would've been too obvious. You know. That Steve was tailing him. But that road dead-ends, so he figured he must be staying in one of those old hunting cabins up there. But he says you can't miss the guy if you see him again because the truck he was driving was green. Like a dark hunter green. Nobody drives green anymore. Nobody drives any colors, really. Steve and I were just talking about it the other night. Have you noticed that?"

Once again, Mary opened her mouth to weigh in. Once again, it did no good.

"Everybody drives silver or black these days. Or if it's any color at all it's fire engine red, which is a big mistake because you're only going to get pulled over more in that. But I'm sorry. I didn't mean to go off on a tangent. Maybe it's nothing. I feel bad calling you and getting you all riled up if it's nothing. But what if it's not nothing, and I didn't call? Then how bad would I feel?"

"You did the right thing to call me, Cara."

"You think it's nothing?"

"I don't know what to think."

But she remembered something Abby had said to her. When she had popped into the kitchen unexpectedly for lunch. *I like being outside. I've been walking up in the foothills.* That made it far less likely that she had only just run into this guy the one time in town.

It filled Mary with a sickening sense of dread. And guilt. Guilt because she was a terrible, terrible mother. Because she had been too quick to dismiss all of Abby's time away from home as innocent fun.

If something bad happened to Abby, she would never be able to forgive herself. Never.

You just don't forgive yourself for a mistake as big as that one.

———

Mary puffed uphill for several minutes in the hot sun. It was hard going.

Years ago, when Stan had first moved them here, Mary had walked all the time. Half the day sometimes, trekking as far up into the mountains as her legs would carry her. But the sad truth, she realized, was that she was no longer in shape for that kind of exertion.

She stopped often, leaning her hands on her thighs and panting until she was ready to take a few more steps. But she didn't stop for long. Because she couldn't.

Abby's safety was at stake.

She passed locked gates, most overgrown with vegetation, obscuring . . . well, it was impossible to know what was hidden back there. She couldn't see if anyone lived behind those gates, or if the places were even habitable.

She passed an old tumbled-down house with a spooky-looking barn that gave her slight chills. It reminded her that this was not a suitable place for her daughter to be wandering. She had thought of it as clean and safe, because it was the fresh air. The great outdoors. But a young girl could get in trouble anywhere, and any deserted area carried its own dangers.

She passed propane tanks, and water tanks, and solar panels mounted on posts, but they all looked old and dirty and rusted and unused.

She began to wonder if there was anything or anyone up here at all. Or if she was only wasting her energy and time.

Twenty minutes later she collapsed onto the road, sitting in a hard rut and nearly crying from the pain of the exertion. But she knew she had to get up and move again. Still, she took a couple of minutes this time. A genuine rest.

In time she forced her exhausted legs back into action. She pushed to her feet with the help of her hands and began to trudge again.

Not ten steps later she came around a bend in the road and there it was.

A dark hunter-green pickup truck, pulled into a strangely tight spot among the trees, as though someone were trying to hide it. A man in his fifties, lying on his back in the dirt. And a litter of puppies.

Maybe they weren't Abby's puppies at all, she realized with a jolt to her exhausted gut. Maybe they belonged to this stranger, and Abby had been up here playing with them because she was too young and innocent to register the danger in such a relationship. Wasn't that just the sort of ploy predators used to lure innocent children?

He saw her, and sat up quickly, holding two of the puppies against his chest.

Mary's heart thumped so hard it made her dizzy. But she stood up to him, because that was what she'd come here to do. It was what she had to do.

"Where's my daughter?"

He set the puppies down, stood, and walked closer. Mary could hear the pounding of her own pulse. It echoed inside her ears. He looked directly into her eyes. His own eyes were an unusual color of dark blue. Almost navy. Like a stormy sea. There was something guarded about his energy, as if he were wearing a suit of armor that Mary could sense without seeing.

"That's a strange question," he said, "coming from someone I've never met or even seen before."

"Are you denying you know her?"

"Is your daughter Abby?"

"Then you do know her! I demand to know where she is! How do you know her? *Why* do you know her? What are you even doing around a girl her age?"

"I don't even know which one of those questions to answer."

"Answer all of them!"

The man sighed, and looked down at the dirt, and Mary was filled with a strange sensation that she was scaring him. Maybe even hurting him. As though she were the bully. Not the other way around.

"I only met her this morning," he said. "She needed a ride into town."

"Why couldn't she walk into town? She walks everywhere."

No answer.

"That's a really bad sign," she said. "That you won't even answer a simple question. I can feel you hiding something."

Still no answer.

"Okay. I'll just go get the sheriff."

She turned to walk back down the hill, a renewed sense of panic rising up into her throat. Why had she said that? What kind of fool tells a dangerous person that she's about to call the sheriff on him? And out in the middle of nowhere like this?

Mary had just been reading a book in which the heroine was alone in the house with the murderer and told him all about what she knew— how she knew he'd committed the crime. And then of course he had to come after her and try to kill her, too. Mary had set the book down and not finished it because it seemed so preposterous. She had actually said out loud to the book, "No one would ever be that stupid!" But now look what she had just gone and done.

And he was behind her, too. She could hear and feel him, catching up to her.

"Wait!" he said.

He sounded . . . pathetic. Helpless, almost. As if the world was simply too much for him in that moment. So she stopped and turned. And waited. To see what he had to say.

"I thought the puppies were a secret," he said. "You know. Something she wasn't telling her parents. I didn't want to rat her out."

She looked at his eyes again. He didn't look back. He was staring down at the dirt.

"Why were you trying to hide your truck?"

"I wasn't trying to hide it. I had the puppies in the bed, and it was too hot in the sun. I was just trying to get them in the shade."

"If they're her puppies, what are you even doing with them?"

"She was keeping them in my shed. I just drove up this morning. I hadn't been up here for a long time, so I guess she thought the place was deserted. I told her to take them somewhere else. But then one of them got hurt. There was a lot of blood. She was trying to get to the vet on foot, and I gave her a ride because I saw how much trouble she was in."

Mary only stood a moment, her head swarming with thoughts. It all made perfect sense, really. Of course it did. She knew the story about rescuing the puppies was something Abby would not have made up. If nothing else, Abby wouldn't have told Mary about jumping into the river if it weren't true—if she hadn't *had* to tell it—because she had to have known Mary would be horrified. Why make up a story that would only get her in trouble? And yes, she knew Abby had been keeping them somewhere . . .

Still, there was a missing piece here. Something that didn't quite add up.

"So then why did you bring them back up here?"

His face took on an embarrassed expression. Mary actually thought she might have seen him flush just a little bit red.

"Turns out I'm a huge sap," he said.

To her surprise, Mary laughed out loud. It was partly the way he'd said it, and probably partly a necessary release of her built-up tension.

"You're okay," she said, almost as though telling herself and him at exactly the same moment. "Thank goodness."

"Would you like a cold drink? You look so hot and tired from the walk."

She wanted to say no. To leave as quickly as possible. But she *was* hot and tired. And thirsty. She was also feeling guilty and embarrassed over the things she had said to him.

"I think I might take you up on that. I'm so sorry about everything I accused you of. I feel just awful now."

"It's okay."

"How can it be okay?"

"She just seemed so . . . Your daughter, I mean. Granted I've only known her for a few hours. But it seemed like she was so . . . on her own in the world. I'm kind of relieved to know she's got someone who's ready to burn down the world to make sure she's okay. It's a relief. You keep an eye on the puppies, please. I'll go inside and get us a couple of sodas."

—

Mary leaned in the open doorway of the cabin and looked around at the inside of the place. And watched him work. And intermittently looked around to make sure the romping puppies were okay.

It was nicely furnished inside, but dusty and dirty. Mary couldn't imagine how someone could live in all that dirt. Then she remembered that he'd said he had just driven up that morning. And he had mostly been dealing with Mary's daughter and her emergencies since then.

She looked at the animal heads on the walls, and they gave her a shiver because she was not a fan of hunting. She looked at him again, trying to make the killing of animals fit with what she saw. He was filling plastic glasses with ice from a cheap supermarket cooler. He wore a gold wedding ring on his left hand. But after noticing that, Mary quickly looked away again, not sure why she had even checked.

"You hunt?" she asked him.

"Not anymore."

He joined her at the open doorway and handed her a can of soda and the plastic glass of ice. They stepped outside together.

"I'm sorry there's nowhere to sit," he said. "I used to have those folding camp chairs for sitting outside, but they got stolen."

"That's too bad," she said, and settled cross-legged in the dirt. A puppy immediately ran across her thighs, startling her. "A person should be able to leave a couple of folding chairs outside without anybody helping themselves."

"They weren't outside," he said, settling a more than respectful distance away. "They were in the locked shed."

"Somebody broke into your shed?"

"Shed *and* cabin. And took most everything that could be carried out and left the door hanging open. That's why it's such a filthy mess in there."

"Abby would never do that."

"No, I know she wouldn't. She just came along afterward to make use of the empty shed. She's the one who tied my door closed to keep things nicer in there. Unfortunately it'd been standing open for quite some time by then."

Mary popped the top on her soda and poured it over ice. She was so thirsty that she felt almost as though she were drooling, watching it fizz. She took a long gulp and closed her eyes, savoring the icy feeling as it made its way down.

"I like your daughter," the man said. "But not in any way that should concern you. I just like her because she's so . . . fiery. And determined."

"Yeah, that's my Abby all right."

She took a few more sips with her eyes closed and noticed that they had fallen into an awkward silence.

"Your wife must be a very patient woman," Mary said, surprising herself. She had not realized that she was about to say anything, not to mention such a rude and ridiculous thing.

"What do you mean?"

"Well, you know. The hunting thing. They talk about football widows. And golfing widows. Having a husband who goes up into the mountains to hunt must be the same sort of thing."

She purposely did not look at him as she spoke. She had not shaken her sense of embarrassment. In fact, it seemed to be growing. She wanted to leave, but she felt compelled to finish her cold drink first.

"Oh," he said. "Yes. She was. Very patient."

"Was? Oh, that's right. You said you don't hunt anymore. So one of the puppies got hurt, you say? Not badly, I hope."

"Nothing life threatening. Just a cut. But it needed stitches. And look. I hope this is okay. She didn't have enough money for the vet. And, like I told you . . . I'm a big sap. So I put it out and told her she could clean the place for me as a way of paying me back. It never occurred to me that her parents might not want her around me. But I get it. Young girl, middle-aged man. If you want me to withdraw the agreement . . ."

Mary looked at him closely. Right into his face. Right into those dark-blue eyes. It wasn't easy, but it was just another one of those things she had to do. She measured what she saw there for an extended moment.

"No," she said, sounding firm and feeling sure. "Don't withdraw the agreement. I know now that she's okay here. I'm sorry for thinking otherwise. You're a nice man and you were just trying to be helpful. And it'll be good for her. She wants to stand on her own two feet and raise all these puppies. I don't know if she can or not, but I know she'll learn a lot by trying. It'll be good for her to learn that they get hurt, and that vets are expensive, and that debts take time to pay off. But, do me a favor. Please. I knew about the puppies. She told me about rescuing them, but she told me she took them to the pound. But I knew she didn't."

"She actually did," the man said. "The lady at the pound told me so. But they would've been put down if she'd left them there. So she didn't. Leave them there, I mean. But it was half true, anyway."

"Well, you hope for better than half truths from your daughter, but I guess that's something."

"How did you know she still had them?"

"All of a sudden she was out of the house all day, and then she'd come home with little bite marks on her hands and muddy paw prints on her clothes."

"I guess that would tip you off, yeah. But what was it you were going to ask? You said, 'Do me a favor.' But then you never said what the favor was."

"I was going to ask . . . just don't tell her I was even here, okay? I want her to feel like she's really doing this thing on her own. Not like I'm sneaking around checking up on her. So just maybe don't even mention you met me. Speaking of which, I need to get going. I don't want to bump into her on that road home."

She gulped down the last of her soda and rose to her feet. He stayed down in the dirt. A puppy ran up and nipped her calf through her pant leg, and she yelped. Then they both laughed. Mary and this man. Laughing at something together. It felt decidedly odd.

It also struck her that if Stan were witnessing this scene, he'd have an absolute meltdown.

"Thank you for helping my daughter," she said, and stepped away. "You seem like a very nice man."

Then she hurried down the road before she could hear what he had to say in reply.

# Chapter Twelve

## The Temporariness

**Abby**

When she got back up to the cabin, Abby still had Patches under her shirt, holding him close against her bare belly. He was sleepy, and only had three good paws, and besides, she hadn't wanted to be seen with him in town. It was unlikely she would have run into anybody on the upper part of the road, but Patches was warm and soft against her and not ready to walk on his own. So she carried him all the way up the same way she'd carried him through town. Hidden.

The terrible cone collar was rolled into a tight little coil in her back pocket, with her shirttail down over it.

Elliot was sitting on the ground with the puppies, who swarmed her gleefully when they saw her, jumping up and scratching her legs with their little claws.

She pulled Patches out into the light and he blinked miserably.

His back paw was bandaged, the bandage then covered by a tiny rubber sleeve to keep it clean and dry. And the vet was right—it wouldn't last long without that cone collar.

She pulled it out of her pocket and tried to position it around his neck, but she only had one hand to work with because she was still holding him. And Elliot was watching all of this with mild curiosity.

"You want help with that?" he asked after a time.

"Yes, please. I don't want to set him down until it's on him, because he might run off faster than we can catch him."

She held the puppy with his butt firmly pressed into her belly while Elliot snapped the tiny collar in place and then tied the soft strings that made it just snug enough.

"Set him down and let's see how he does with that," Elliot said.

She carefully balanced Patches on three paws in the dirt and then straightened up. The other six puppies swarmed him, knocking him down. He struggled to his feet again and tried to lope forward, still holding the injured paw aloft. He immediately banged the edge of the plastic cone collar against Queen's face, bounced backward again, and fell into a sit. Queen stood, looking a little stunned, and blinking the eye that had been hit. Patches struggled onto three paws again and just stood with his head down, seeming too intimidated to move.

Abby sat in the dirt to watch. Elliot sat not too far away. They stared at the puppies together. Patches still showed no intention of attempting to navigate the world in that contraption.

"Wow," Elliot said. "That's really going to be a trial for him, isn't it? How long does he have to wear it?"

"At least ten days. Until the stitches come out."

"That's going to be a hard ten days for him."

"I know, right?"

They sat and stared a while longer. The puppies milled around Patches, but did not run or play. Seeing him half-anesthetized and injured seemed to have taken the wind out of everyone's sails. Human and canine alike.

"This is all a lot harder than I thought it would be," Abby said.

She looked over at Elliot to see him nodding thoughtfully.

"Even one puppy is hard. Most people think they know how hard it's going to be to raise one. But then, after they do it, they pretty much have to admit that they'd really had no idea. It's one of those things that's always more involved than you imagined going in. And most people don't take on seven at once. In fact, I don't know anybody who ever took on seven puppies at once."

"Well, you know *me*," she said.

"True. I meant *before* I knew you."

They watched as Patches took two or three steps forward, then dropped his head too far. The bottom edge of the plastic cone snagged in the dirt and he tripped on it, falling almost face-first into the dirt, then over sideways because the cone prevented a fall onto his face. He seemed to give up in that moment. He settled into a sphinxlike position, testing the weight and clumsiness of the thing. Then he dropped over onto his side and resigned himself to napping in the warm afternoon sun.

"So did you try it?" she asked.

She expected him to say, "Try what?" He didn't. He seemed to be on the same page with her thinking.

"I did."

"And . . . ?"

"It was nice while it lasted. It was just so . . . you know. Temporary. Once you sat up and it was over, I mean . . . that's it. It wasn't a lasting happiness."

"Nothing's a lasting happiness," she said.

It seemed weird to Abby that she should have to explain such a basic fact of life to him. Elliot being a grown-up and all.

"Not sure why you would say that."

"Well, think about it. When's the last time something made you happy, and then even when that something was gone, the happiness just lasted forever? There's no such thing, right? If there was, I think I would've heard about it. It'd be pretty famous, a thing like that, if it existed."

He didn't answer for a strange length of time. If Abby had been called upon to guess, she'd have said he really was thinking about it, just as she had asked him to. If so, that was revolutionary behavior coming from an adult.

"My wife made me happy on an ongoing basis," he said after a time.

"Yeah, but . . . no offense, but now she's gone, and now you feel terrible. So it was still just something that made you happy while it was there. It still wasn't permanent."

"I suppose you're right," he said.

"I mean . . . you just make the best of happy while you've got it, right?"

"I would say that's probably good advice."

Two of the puppies, Queen and Kite, began climbing around on Abby's legs and biting at her hands. At first it was a fun sort of nibbly biting, but their little teeth were razor sharp, and it was only a matter of time until one bit down too hard.

"Ow!" she yelped, and pulled her hand up out of their reach. "Watch it. That hurts." She lowered her hand to look at the damage Queen had done. The bite was bleeding.

Elliot lifted himself up out of the dirt and walked back into his cabin. He didn't say anything like goodbye, so Abby didn't know if he was coming back or not. She began to go over in her head what she'd said to him. Maybe she had offended him somehow.

She probably should have kept her mouth shut about his wife. Yeah. That was it. What had she been thinking, saying anything like that to him?

A minute later he reappeared, carrying a red plastic first aid kit. Abby knew what it was, even from a fair distance, because it had the red cross symbol on it. Everybody knew that symbol. It was practically an international language.

"Thanks," she said, taking it from him.

She opened it and set it on the dirt. It had adhesive bandages inside, in different sizes, and little plastic packets of antibiotic ointment.

She set about dressing the bite.

"You shouldn't let them bite you like that," he said. "It's a normal enough thing for a puppy to do. Until they know better. But it's the kind of behavior you'll want to discourage."

"I don't know what I'm supposed to do about it."

"Train them. You're supposed to train them. Even one puppy can be a real disaster with no training. Seven untrained puppies . . . well . . . I hate to even think."

Abby sighed, and found herself overwhelmed by that feeling again. That sense that this was already too hard, and getting harder by the minute.

"I don't know how to train dogs," she said.

"Nobody knows anything until they know it. Until they take the time to learn. Get a book out of the library about dog training. There's a library in this town, isn't there?"

"There's a branch. Yeah." Shep climbed into her lap and began chewing on her elbow. "Ouch. Down, boy. Jeez. How much first aid you think Elliot's got in here?"

She lifted him off her lap and set him down in the dirt. He jumped back onto her lap and began biting her little finger.

"This doesn't have to be that hard," Elliot said. "Some of it is just common sense. Here. I'll show you."

He climbed to his feet again and walked to his truck. She watched him open the driver's side door and pull a coil of rope out from under the seat. He dug a pocketknife out of his front jeans pocket and opened out the blade. Then he cut off four lengths of rope. Abby figured them to be about two feet apiece.

He folded up the knife and threw the rest of the coil back onto his truck seat. Then he carried the pieces back to where Abby sat. He settled cross-legged in the dirt again and tied a single knot into each end of one of the ropes.

He handed it to Abby.

Now that it was knotted, it looked like one of those dog toys that were made to be vaguely bone-shaped. Like an expensive tug toy you'd buy for your dog at the supermarket, only not expensive. And not all the way down the hill in town.

Elliot knotted the ends of the second length of rope.

Queen ran up to Elliot and grabbed the end of it, and pulled, and Elliot held tight and allowed her to tug. Abby was surprised at how strong she was for such a little pup. Then she dropped the rope and went for Elliot's fingers instead.

"No!" Elliot said.

It was loud, and sharp. It was said in a deep and serious tone. It startled Abby. It startled Queen, who jumped back and planted her butt in the dirt. She looked up at Elliot curiously—testingly—her head slightly tilted.

Elliot held the rope toy out for her, encouraging her to grab it.

She did, and they began tug-wrestling again.

"Good girl!" he said, and then looked over at Abby. "See? A lot of it is pretty simple. 'No, don't do that, I don't like it when you do that. Here, this is what I want you to do instead. Good girl for doing what I want. I'll always praise you for doing what I want.'"

"I get it," Abby said, feeling her sense of overwhelm drain away. "Thanks."

She offered Shep her rope toy, and they tugged against each other for a minute. Abby was wishing they had found a spot to sit in the shade. It was hot out in the sun. But she wanted to sit by Elliot because he knew so much. She wanted the benefit of everything he knew.

It struck her for the first time that people had fathers who were like Elliot. Abby wondered how that would feel. It would be nothing like the life she had now. That much was clear.

"Hey," she said. "How do you know so much about dogs? You said you didn't have any pets."

"I used to," he said. "I had dogs for years. But then I met my wife, and she was allergic. To dogs and cats both."

"Oh. That's too bad. Are you going to get a dog now?"

For what seemed like a long time, he didn't answer. Abby had to go back over the conversation again in her head, in case she had said something she shouldn't have.

"I was thinking about it," Elliot said, knocking her out of her thoughts. "Today, while you were gone. I was thinking about just that."

"Good. You *should* get a dog. It'll be good company for you. So your house won't get so lonely."

"Are these guys still up for adoption?"

Abby looked over at him, then quickly away again. "Oh," she said. "*My* dogs. I didn't know we were talking about *my* dogs."

"Well, we don't need to be. I could go to the pound and look around. But I thought the idea was that you wanted to find good homes for these guys."

"Yeah," Abby said. "That *was* the idea."

"But then you got attached to them."

"I sure did. But still. Seven puppies *is* an awful lot. I don't know. I have to think how I feel about that. Which one do you think you'd want?"

"I was actually thinking of two. That way when I go back to work, and they're alone during the day, they'd have each other."

"Oh," Abby said again. "Two." It was making her feel a little sick to her stomach to think about it. Still, five puppies would be easier than seven. Not to mention cheaper. And Elliot would be a good home for her pups. "Which two were you thinking?"

They both looked at the puppies, who were standing still. It was almost shocking to see them all holding still, except for poor Patches, who really didn't have much choice. They were looking at the two humans, as if they understood the seriousness of the talk. As if they understood the language. Or at least as if they could, if only they listened hard enough.

"Tell me their names again?" Elliot said.

It seemed like an odd thing for him to say, because Abby hadn't told him their names in the first place.

"That's Queen," she said, pointing. "That's Shep. You know Patches already. The one with the white chest marking is Kite. Tippy is the one with the white tail tip. The tan one is Buffy, because he's buff colored. And the all-black guy . . ."

"Don't tell me, let me guess. Midnight."

"Nah. That was too not original even for me. I named him Noche. That's Spanish for *night*."

"So I've heard," Elliot said.

They stared at the puppies for a few moments longer, and the puppies continued to stand like statues and stare back.

"I think I'd probably want to take Queen and Patches," Elliot said.

"Oh," Abby said.

"Unless you didn't want me to."

"Well . . . the only thing is . . . those are kind of my favorites, too." But then Abby couldn't help wondering . . . what if he'd said he wanted Tippy and Shep? Would Abby have said—and felt—that Tippy and Shep were her favorites? "No, never mind," she said, quickly. Before he could answer. "Forget I said that. I don't have favorites. I love 'em all the same. And I want 'em to be happy and have a good home. So if you want Queen and Patches, you should take Queen and Patches."

"We have a little time to think about it. Both of us."

"How long are you here?"

Abby flashed back on having asked him the question before. It had been earlier that morning, but it didn't feel nearly so recent. It felt like a conversation from months ago. So much had happened since then. So much had changed.

He hadn't answered her then. He had been too suspicious of her motives in asking the question. Would he answer her now?

"I'm not sure," he said. "I didn't have a clear length of time in mind. I used to come up for a week at a time. Sometimes even ten days. But I had something to do back then. I came up to hunt, and that kept me busy all day long. If I got nothing, I'd be out all day trying. If I got something, I'd have work to do with it. But now that I don't hunt anymore, I really had no idea how long I could stand to be up here. I mean . . . doing what? Sitting out in the yard and watching the sun move across the sky? I figured I'd be bored to death and ready to jump out of my skin, and I'd probably climb in the truck and head right back home again. But, I've got to tell you, Abby . . . I sure haven't been bored so far."

Abby smiled, almost in spite of herself, because it seemed as though he was saying something good about her. And maybe even about her sea of puppies.

"Well, we'll both think about it," she said. "For however long you're here. But if you decide you want 'em, you should take 'em. I'm supposed to want good homes for 'em. Right? I'm supposed to not be selfish."

"You don't strike me as selfish. Not at all."

For the second time in less than a minute, he had said something nice about Abby. Something that made her feel as though he liked her. As though her company was more of a blessing than a curse.

She tried to count how many times her father had made her feel that way, but she couldn't even come up with one time. She literally couldn't count to one.

"Thanks," she said. "I better get home now. I'm starving, and my mother'll be wondering where I've been."

"Good idea," he said. "Go home so your mother knows you're okay."

There was something odd about the way he said it. As though he knew something about the importance of that situation. But Abby couldn't put her finger on it, and, besides, she decided it was probably only her imagination.

"Oh, wait," she said. "I can't just get up and go home. I have to get the puppies all set up. And I have to clean your cabin."

"Clean tomorrow. It's late. You can leave them out with me if you'll tell me how you get them back in the shed again. All at the same time, that is. I had no luck with that at all."

"There's really only one way I know of. You have to wait till they're hungry and then put a bunch of kibble on the floor, and then close the door real fast while they're eating. Oh. I just thought. The dog food and the water dish are still down by that old barn. I had to ditch 'em when Patches got hurt. I'll go get 'em and bring 'em back up."

"I'll line the floor with papers while you're gone."

"Oh," Abby said, standing and brushing off the seat of her jeans. "That's really nice of you. Thanks. Try to get the edges real nice and flat, or they'll rip it all to shreds. Think a dog training book'll teach me how to stop 'em from doing that?"

"Probably not."

"No," Abby said. "Probably not. That's what I thought, too."

She set off walking down the hill, thinking about how it would feel to have a father who not only let you keep the puppies, but who spread out the newspapers while you went to fetch the kibble. She quickly put the thought out of her head again, because that was not the hand she had been dealt in this world, and there was nothing she could do to change it.

Why waste time thinking about a thing like that? Abby figured she would never know how that would feel.

# Chapter Thirteen

## Fatherhood, or Lack of Same

**Elliot**

Elliot woke in the morning and lay still for a split second in that state of bliss, the one in which he did not remember what he had so recently lost. Then it all came crashing down, crushing him. As it had done every morning since Pat's death.

He rose slowly, a bit grumpily, and made a cup of the instant coffee he had bought at the store the previous day. He hated instant, but his burglar had taken the coffee maker.

He sat looking out the window toward the mountains, and took several sips of the horrible stuff.

Then he remembered the puppies.

He walked to the cabin door, his mug of coffee still in hand, thinking they would like to be let out. He threw the door wide and saw that they were already out. They were playing with Abby, who was sitting in the dirt on a small rise. She had one of the knotted rope toys in each hand, with more than one puppy hooked on the other end of each of them.

They all looked around at Elliot, and the puppies ran to the door and swarmed him in greeting.

"What are you doing up there?" he called to the girl.

"I came to clean."

"Okay, right. But . . . what are you doing *up there?*"

"I didn't know if you were awake yet. I didn't want to wake you."

"Oh. Got it. Well, that was considerate of you. But I'm awake now. Obviously. So come on in."

———

Elliot felt bad sitting on the couch while she worked, so he leaned in the cabin's open doorway and sipped the terrible coffee. The morning air felt cool and fresh, welcome and invigorating on his face. And he could keep an eye on the pups that way, which made him feel he was doing something useful.

Abby was sweeping. She was digging deep into the corners with the broom, careful to gather up all the grime, plus some old dried scat from some kind of small wild animal who had sheltered here in his absence.

"I'm sorry," she said. "I didn't mean to make it your job to watch them. I could bring them in here and close the door."

"Except they're not housebroken yet."

"Oh. Right."

"It's fine. I'm just kind of enjoying the morning here."

He watched Patches climb to his feet and try to run after one of his brothers. But the puppy's front paws kept hitting the plastic cone collar. In time he gave up and sank into the dirt again in defeat.

Elliot opened his mouth to say something about it. Express some sympathy for the poor little guy. But Abby spoke first.

"You have kids?" she asked.

She never stopped sweeping, and the swishing sound of her broom punctuated her question.

"No. No kids."

"Why not? Didn't you want 'em?"

"I'm . . . not sure. It's a complicated question."

"I'm sorry if it was rude. I didn't mean it to be rude."

"It's okay. I guess. I had a career that meant a lot to me. And Pat had a career that meant a lot to her. And neither one of us wanted to put everything on hold. I think we both might have liked kids at some point, but we kept pushing the idea down the road. And then after a while we just ran out of time."

The sweeping noise paused. Elliot looked away from the puppies. Looked to Abby, who stood leaning on the broom. It took his eyes a minute to adjust to the relative dimness of indoors.

"That's really too bad," she said. "Because you would be an awesome father."

For a minute, Elliot didn't answer. Possibly a literal full minute. He was busy feeling her statement move around in him. Waiting for it to find a spot to settle.

Abby seemed to give up on getting an answer from him. She went back to sweeping.

"I'm not sure why you say that," he said after a time. "But it's a nice thing to say."

"It's just obvious. I mean, don't *you* think you'd be an awesome father?"

"I don't know. I guess I *hoped* I would be. If I ever got the chance. But it's hard to judge a thing like that about yourself."

"Well, trust me," Abby said. She scooted him out of the way to sweep a load of dirt and other nasty stuff out the door. "I have the world's worst father, so I know."

For a few seconds, Elliot didn't respond. He wasn't sure what to say in reply. He wasn't sure it was wise to say anything, but it was hard to leave a statement like that lying where she had dropped it.

"Why is he so terrible?" he asked after a time.

"I have no idea. You'd have to ask *him*."

"No, I mean . . . what's so terrible about him?"

"Everything."

"Does he hit you?"

Elliot dreaded the answer. Because, if yes, he felt he would do something. It was a strange thought. But it was a thought he had all the same, though it almost felt more like the thought had him.

"No. He doesn't even really notice me. He kind of acts like I'm not even there."

"Does he hit your mother?"

An image of Abby's mother filled Elliot's head. Sitting in the dirt with him, outside the cabin. Having trudged up the hill to bravely defend her daughter against a perceived enemy. She had seemed so vulnerable to Elliot. So good. So determined, like her daughter. He felt as though he might have to go down the hill and beat Abby's father to a pulp if the answer was yes. Even though that wasn't genuinely a thing Elliot would do. But, same as he would have if Abby had been endangered, he felt as though he would need to do something.

"No. He doesn't hit her. He's just so mean. I think he's really unhappy, and he just sort of always has been, and I guess for some reason he figures it's better if everybody around him is miserable, too. So he just always makes her feel bad about herself."

"Why doesn't she leave him?"

"And go where?"

"I don't know. Anywhere."

"Hard to explain, I guess. She never had a job. She got married young. So she went from living at home with her parents to living with my dad. I guess she doesn't know what she could do to support us if she left. For a while she was saving money. You know, like out of her household budget, so maybe she could leave with me. I wasn't supposed to know that, but I heard her talking to her friend Viv about it. But then she gave me fifty dollars. And I didn't think about it at the time, but now I'm thinking about it, and now I'm figuring she must've given up and stopped saving, otherwise she wouldn't've been giving money away. So I guess that's it for that."

Elliot looked out at the puppies again, blinking into the light.

"That's too bad," he said.

He wasn't sure how—or whether—to say it genuinely hurt him to hear it. Because it shouldn't have. It shouldn't have hit him so hard. It shouldn't have been close enough, relevant enough to his world, to cut deeply. So he only said what he said. Only made the mild statement that seemed socially acceptable.

"It kind of is," Abby said. "Yeah. Okay, I'm done with the sweeping. Show me what comes next."

———

It was barely an hour later when Abby approached him with an empty bottle of the leather cleaner and conditioner he had bought for the sofa and armchair. He was outside playing with the dogs, and she had it behind her back, so it took Elliot some time to know what had gone wrong.

"Uh-oh," she said.

"Uh-oh what?"

"I think I messed up." She pulled the empty bottle around to show him. "I must've used too much. I feel really bad about it."

"Let's go take a look," he said.

He walked into the cabin with her, expecting to see the leather furniture fairly dripping with the stuff. But if anything it still looked a bit dry.

"You didn't use too much," he said.

"But it's gone."

"It's my fault. I didn't buy as much as I should have. It's really soaking it up. I'll tell you what I'll do. I'll just drive into town and get another bottle. And maybe some lunch while I'm at it. At some point you'll need to take a break and have something to eat."

———

He was driving alongside the river—just above the spot where the road curved around and crossed over the bridge—when he saw her. At first he wasn't sure it was her. After all, he had only met her once. But it sure looked like Abby's mother.

She was on foot, just stepping onto the bridge. There was no sidewalk, so she turned to look all around her before stepping out. But she didn't seem to notice him or his hunter-green pickup.

He pulled onto the bridge and slowed beside her, powering down his passenger-side window.

"Hey," he said, wishing he knew her name. But he hadn't thought to ask for hers, or to tell her his.

"Oh, hey," she said.

She did not stop walking.

"You need a ride?"

"No thanks. I'm fine."

He allowed the truck to roll slowly beside her as he spoke.

"Out walking for exercise?"

"Not really. My car wouldn't start. I think the battery is dead."

"Then you *do* need a ride."

"I'm fine. I just need to go to the market. I can walk."

"And then carry all those groceries all the way back uphill?"

"I'll manage. Thanks all the same."

Elliot put his foot on the brake. The truck stopped. Abby's mom stopped, as if wondering why *he* had.

He was about to say something that might upset her. But it had to come out.

"Because you're worried about what your husband would say if you took a ride from a male neighbor?"

He watched her brow furrow. She turned to glare through the open window at him but ended up mostly squinting into the sun. She marched the two steps to his truck and leaned her forearms on the door.

"What do *you* know about my husband?" she asked. Her voice sounded terse, but barely above a whisper. As though everyone in town might hear.

"Abby told me a little bit about him."

"Well, she shouldn't have."

She took her arms back and began to walk again.

"I'm sorry if I upset you," he said, allowing the truck to drift forward. "Don't get mad at Abby for it. She wasn't trying to tell secrets. At least, I don't think she was. It just came up naturally in conversation." She didn't answer, so he rolled along in silence for a couple of seconds. Then he added, "Oh, right. You can't really get mad at her, because you're not even telling her we've met."

She stepped off the far end of the bridge and onto the dirt shoulder. Elliot pulled over and stopped, cutting his engine. He wanted to make it clear that if she really wanted to walk away from him and his offer of assistance, she could.

Instead she walked to his open window again.

"I don't see how 'My father is a terrible, terrible person' can just come up naturally in conversation."

"Well, we were discussing fatherhood," he said. Elliot sat and she stood in silence for a few beats. Then he said, "I have jumper cables. We could go up and get your car going. Maybe I can even figure out how it ran down. Unless you just need a new battery."

"The battery is only a year and a half old," she said.

"Something could be draining it." They endured another brief silence. Then he added, "He's at work, right?"

"You don't know how it is in a small town. Everybody sees everything. Everybody talks to everybody else."

"If he's as bad as Abby says he is, I would think they'd keep quiet out of respect to you. And to keep your life from getting even more difficult."

"Some might," she said. "Not all." He expected her to either get in or walk on. But she did neither. "Abby loves her father," she said.

That was when Elliot knew that it hurt her, knowing that Abby had talked her father down to someone outside the family.

"I'm sure she does, down deep somewhere. But she doesn't have a single positive thing to say about him. Look. The bottom line is, you deserve better. You don't deserve to have to walk all the way into town and haul groceries back up the hill manually just because you're afraid of his reaction if you take a ride from a neighbor."

She sighed. Then she opened his truck door and climbed in.

Elliot made a U-turn and crossed the bridge again, headed uphill.

"How do you know what I deserve?" she asked quietly. "You don't even know me."

"You don't know me, either. But five minutes after meeting me you announced that I was okay and that I was a nice man who was only trying to help your daughter. Or words to that effect. So how did you know?"

"It was just obvious. It's something that was right there for me to see."

"Exactly," Elliot said. "That's how I know you deserve better than this."

———

"Well, that's your problem right there," Elliot said. He hadn't even stepped out of his truck cab when he said it. He hadn't even set the hand brake or turned off the engine.

"You haven't even gotten out of your truck yet."

"I know. I didn't need to."

He set the hand brake and turned off the engine.

"You know it's the yellow one, right?"

"Oh yes," he said. "It's very yellow."

They stepped out into her yard together. Elliot couldn't help looking past the car and on to the house. He figured you could tell a lot about people by looking at their houses.

It was a small box of a house with faded wood siding, and years' worth of pine needles moldering on the roof. The problem in Elliot's mind was not that it was modest, or small. He would never judge by factors like that. Elliot had one judgment and one judgment only regarding people's houses: Does the house look as though someone takes care of it? In other words, does it reflect a pride of ownership?

This house did not. This house seemed to have been built a few decades earlier and then pitched immediately into a state of decline.

It didn't change his feelings about this woman, so much. It just made him like her husband even less, if such a thing were possible.

"So what's this thing you can see from your truck?" she asked, bumping him out of his thoughts.

"Your brake lights are on."

"Huh. That's odd. Why would my brake lights be on?"

"Not sure yet," he said.

He opened the driver's door of the very yellow vehicle. He reached his right foot inside, placed his toe under the brake pedal, and pulled upward.

"They just went off," she said.

"Pedal is sticking."

"What do I do about that?"

"Not sure. Might help to spray some lubricant under there. Might be something's corroded and needs to be replaced. But in the meantime, you can just do what I did. Lift up on the pedal. You can check before you go into the house each time. Make sure they're not on. If lifting up on the pedal doesn't help, you could always disconnect the battery cables. That way it'll still be drivable in the morning so you can take it in to the shop."

"I wouldn't know how to disconnect the cables."

"I could show you."

"Is it dangerous?"

"Not if you don't bridge from one terminal to the other with something metal like a wrench."

Elliot walked back to his truck, climbed in, and started the engine. He drove it up as close as possible beside the woman's disabled car. Then he took his jumper cables out from behind the seat.

"Go ahead and pop the hood," he said.

"I really appreciate your doing this. Probably saving me a lot of money."

"It's no problem."

He raised the hood of his pickup and hooked up the cables the way his grandfather had taught him, decades earlier. Positive, positive, negative, ground.

"We'll just let it run for a minute," he said. "Before you try to start her up."

He leaned back against the grille of his truck, crossed his arms . . . and had no idea what to say.

"Mary," she said.

"Excuse me?"

"It's my name. Mary."

"Oh. Sorry. Seems I have a bad habit of forgetting to ask people's names. Elliot."

"Thanks for helping out, Elliot."

"What does Abby like to eat for lunch?"

"Oh, she's not a picky eater at all. She'd be happy with just about anything."

"But . . . say I'm going into town. And I want to bring us back some lunch."

"She's up at the cabin cleaning?"

"She is, yes."

"She likes the submarine sandwiches they make at that place called the Sandwich Port. On Main. She likes the salami one best."

"Good advice. Thank you."

They didn't talk for a time. Two or three minutes, maybe. They just leaned, and stared at her very yellow car. As if it might be about to do something interesting.

"Go ahead and try to start it," he said.

It started on the first try.

Mary stepped out of it again with a whole different look on her face. A whole different energy. As if everything didn't have to be as difficult as possible, every day of her life.

# Chapter Fourteen

## The Option

**Mary**

She leaned on the grille of his truck beside him, just a foot or so from his right arm. Her car was running now. And his truck was running. She could feel the slight rumble of it against her lower back. He had carefully, neatly coiled up his jumper cables and put them back behind his seat. But it was his advice that they let her car run a little longer before Mary took off in it. Just to be sure it wouldn't stall before it was charged enough to start up again on its own.

Mary found herself hoping that was real advice, based on real facts. Not just a chance on his part to pin her down here longer and make further comments about what he thought she deserved.

The whole thing was making her a bit uneasy. *He* was making her uneasy. In fact, the more time she spent in his presence, the less comfortable she felt.

Though it was not her usual tendency, she decided to hit the problem head-on.

"I know what you're thinking," she said.

She could tell she had knocked him out of some kind of deep thoughts. He looked as though she had wakened him from a half sleep. He looked over at her with a furrowed brow, but, at the same time, a half-amused look on his face.

"Do you? I'm surprised. I don't even know what I was thinking."

"You think I should leave him."

"Oh," he said. The half-amused look evaporated. The furrowed brow stayed. "Well. I hadn't been thinking that just now, no. I hadn't been thinking much of anything. But I do think so, yes."

"It isn't any of your concern."

"Right. I know that. That's why I didn't bring it up again. *You* did."

"Oh," she said. She could feel a wave of deep embarrassment rise in her. It made her face feel hot. "I guess I did."

A movement caught the corner of her eye, and she turned her head to examine it directly. It was a curtain in the window of the home of her neighbor Effie Winger. It had peeked open just a little bit, as though drawn back by a hand. The moment Mary looked, it quickly swung closed again.

"Great," Mary muttered under her breath. "That's just what I need."

"I'm sorry?" Elliot said.

"Nothing."

But it wasn't nothing. Not to Mary. It was the genuine danger of a nosy neighbor, melding with the embarrassment of her conversation with this man. It was causing her to feel defensive, and it was not something she felt inclined to hold inside.

"It's for my daughter," she said, her voice brusque.

"What's for your daughter?"

"Staying. I stay for Abby. Teenage girls need things. Clothes for school and stuff like that. What would I have to give her without my husband and his income? It's not fair to ask her to live in poverty. I've never worked. I don't know what I would do to earn us a living, and it's just not fair to her. You know?"

For a moment, he offered no reply. The only sound was the dull rumble of both engines. Mary felt her car must have been ready to drive by then. She felt an overwhelming urge to jump into it and speed away. But she froze there with him, still feeling the slight vibration of his truck engine against her back.

"Well, it's really none of my business," he said at long last, "which is why I'm not the one who brought it up this time, either. But I would think there are more important things for your daughter than school clothes."

Mary waited, thinking he would go on to say what they were. But the moment stretched out. In time she decided he was purposely withholding his thoughts until he was sure she wanted to hear them.

"Like what?"

She *didn't* really want to hear them. But she asked anyway, because she knew she would wonder later, after driving away. And she knew that the wondering would be irksome, and that she would roll it over and over in her head until it became mentally exhausting. And that it would ruin her day.

"Bear with me here," he said, "because I'm really not trying to pry. I just need this answer to help me make my point. How was it when you were growing up?"

"How was it?"

Effie Winger's curtain flicked open again. Mary glared at it, and it dropped closed.

"Between your parents. What did you see growing up with your parents?"

Mary's face grew hot again. And she knew if she answered the question it would likely turn humiliatingly red. But she opened her mouth and answered. She wasn't even sure why she answered, except maybe that she wasn't good at saying no to people when they asked something of her.

"My father was a bully," she said. "He bullied my mother. So what? So what's your point?"

"So you grew up watching that and internalizing it. Thinking that love must look like that. And then when you got married . . . Well, the point I'm making is that maybe the best favor you could do for Abby is to let the pattern end right here. I'm just thinking that might mean more in the long run than new school clothes."

"I think my car is ready to drive," she said.

She pushed off from the spot where she had been leaning on his truck and moved fast for her open driver's door. For the freedom of driving away from him. From this conversation. From his observations about her life.

"I'm sorry if I upset you," he called after her. "If I was wrong to say any or all of that, I'm sorry. It's just that you kept bringing it up."

"Thank you for getting my car started," she called back over her shoulder.

She jumped in and slammed the door behind her.

Just as she was shifting into gear she heard a tap on the window. It made her jump. She calmed her startled reaction, shifted into park again, and sighed.

She powered her window down.

"What?"

He was holding what looked like a business card in through her open window. It was only about three inches from her nose. Grayish card stock with embossed burgundy letters. She didn't reach for it or touch it in any way. She wasn't even sure she was breathing.

"I have a guest room with two twin beds," he said. "In the city. If you're thinking you and your daughter might literally end up on the street, well . . . at least you could be there until you could get a job. Work out something better for yourselves."

Mary felt her blood quickly turning to ice. She felt her face begin to tingle. Her poor hot face was suddenly having to deal with icy coldness.

"I don't even know you. You don't even know me."

She shifted into gear and tried to leave. Or at least tried to make it clear that she wanted to. That she was ready to. But the hand with the card did not retreat.

"Take it and refuse to use it if you want," he said. His voice sounded quiet and almost . . . gentle. "But don't refuse to take it. It's an option. It's just an option. Everybody deserves to have an option."

Time seemed to freeze in Mary's world. It felt as though she spent many long minutes saying nothing. Doing nothing. Just trying to breathe and exist with that business card under her nose.

"If I take it, can I go now?" she asked when she had managed to force out words.

"Of course you can."

She took it.

The hand disappeared.

She powered up her window and drove quickly away, toward town.

As she drove, it struck her that if she decided to keep that card, she had better find a damn good hiding place for it. It would have to live in the last place on earth Stan would ever think to look.

But no. She wouldn't keep it. She couldn't.

She powered down the window and almost tossed it out into the wind. But her fingers, as if independent of her thinking, held tightly to it.

Maybe it would be better to talk it over with Viv before making any rash decisions.

———

"Okay, so wait," Viv said. "The part I'm not getting is why you're so upset."

"I would think it would go without saying."

"Sorry. I'm lost."

They were sitting in Viv's backyard, at a wrought iron table in the shade. Viv had poured Mary a glass of iced tea—real brewed iced tea, not the instant garbage Mary made for herself at home—even though her visit had been unscheduled and unannounced.

"Did you even go to the market?" Viv asked. "Do you have groceries sitting out in the hot car?"

"No, I forgot all about that. I just drove straight here."

"So tell me again why this is a bad thing."

"He's a married man."

"Isn't that the good news? If you ever took him up on it, there'd be a wife right there in the house. That makes it all pretty aboveboard. But, listen. Mary. You have a pretty good sense of people. Did it feel like there was something wrong with the offer?"

"No," Mary said. Without hesitation. "No, it felt like he just wanted to help."

"So what's the problem?"

Mary sipped her iced tea in silence for a moment. It frustrated her that her friend was not able to understand the situation. Normally Viv was quick to catch on.

Then it struck Mary that the problem might be on her end of the communication. Maybe she wasn't making herself clear about why it was all so upsetting.

She searched around inside herself and discovered, to her surprise, that she didn't know. No wonder she was doing such a poor job of getting her point across.

"I just feel very . . . uneasy . . . in his presence," she said.

"But you can't tell me why?"

"Not in any very precise words, no."

"We'll play a little game with it, then. Let's say you're on a quiz show, and the prize for a right answer is ten grand. Ten thousand dollars.

So you don't know. Fine. But you're not just going to say 'I don't know' and walk away. Because you might as well take your best guess. Right? At least that way you have *a chance* at the prize."

"Oh," Mary said. "That's a little strange."

"Humor me."

Mary briefly watched a dragonfly hover over their table. She had read somewhere that dragonflies undergo more than one metamorphosis in their lifetimes. It made her wonder if her own life was ever destined to change. It never seemed to.

"He's just kind of . . ." The pause dragged on. "I guess . . . handsome."

She glanced over at Viv, whose eyebrows seemed strangely arched upward.

"And we're faulting him for that?"

"I don't know. I'm just guessing, like you said."

"But that's what makes you uncomfortable about him?"

"I suppose."

"Are you trying to tell me that you feel uneasy around this guy because you're a little bit attracted to him?"

Mary started to answer but realized she had one hand over her mouth. She hadn't even noticed it going there. She dropped it into her lap again.

"I did sort of say that, didn't I?"

They sipped iced tea in silence for a minute or two.

"Just hang on to the card," Viv said. "You don't ever have to use it if you don't want. But it's an option. And you don't have enough of those in your life."

"That's almost exactly how *he* put it," Mary said, still awkwardly trying on this sudden new revelation regarding Elliot and her budding feelings about him. "But I could never do that. He's a married man. I'm a married woman."

A brief silence. Then, much to Mary's surprise, Viv reached across the table and rapped on Mary's forehead with her knuckles, as if knocking on a door.

"Ow," Mary said.

"Hello-o."

"What?"

"There is nothing wrong with having feelings for a married man."

"There most certainly is."

"No. There isn't. There's something wrong with *acting on them.* What you feel is none of anybody's business. Save the card. Use it if you have to. Keep your feelings to yourself."

"If Stan ever found it, there'd be hell to pay."

Mary was surprised to hear herself say it, because it meant she was considering keeping the card and hiding it. Maybe it even meant she had already decided to do so.

"It's a business card," Viv said. "What could possibly be easier to hide than that? Stick it in one of your books. Stan's not a reader, right?"

"He reads the newspaper, but that's pretty much it. He keeps these books about the Second World War around the house. I figure he read them. But not for years."

"You have any books you bought used?"

"Tons of them. I buy books at the thrift store all the time."

"Put it in one of those. On the off chance that Stan ever finds it, just tell him you never saw it before and it must've been in the book when you bought it. Something the old owner must've been using as a bookmark."

"Wow," Mary said, and drained her glass of iced tea. "You're good at this."

"Now go to the market before you forget again. And try to stop being so freaked out about all this. You can feel anything you want. It's nobody's business and nobody needs to know."

—

Mary arrived home with her groceries, and, as she put them away, was surprised by the feel of the card in the pocket of her blouse. Surprised because it shouldn't have had a feel. It shouldn't have felt like anything at all.

It wasn't a stiffness or a temperature. It just seemed to have a presence there in her pocket. Of course Mary knew it was only a small scrap of card stock with no magical powers, so she had to assume that the feeling was coming from her. From its significance to her.

She took it out into her hand and carried it to the living room, where she scanned the bookshelf, reading the titles on spines. Poetry would be best, she decided. Stan hated poetry with a virulent passion that he was never shy about announcing.

Her eyes settled on a collection by Emily Dickinson.

"That should do it," she said out loud to the empty room.

She pulled the book out into her hands and let it fall open. It settled on a page with the poem "A Prison gets to be a friend." It seemed almost painfully appropriate to Mary. Like a cosmic joke at her expense.

Careful not to read the poem, she placed the card between the pages, snugging it against the binding. Then she put the book back on the shelf and walked out her own front door.

She marched across the dead grass to old Effie Winger's house, and knocked.

Effie answered the door almost immediately. She had her hair up in curlers in the middle of the afternoon. It seemed strange to Mary, especially since Effie lived alone.

"What?" Effie said. "You never come over and knock."

"That was just a neighbor," Mary said.

"What was just a neighbor?"

"You know darn well what I'm talking about." Mary averted her eyes. Dropped them to Effie's scratchy welcome mat. It embarrassed her to speak so confrontationally. "I saw you looking." She waited, but heard only silence, so she plunged on. "My car wouldn't start. The brake pedal sticks and it was making the brake lights stay on, and it ran the battery down. So this neighbor saw me walking into town, and he gave me a ride and jumped my car battery for me. And that's all there was to that."

"I know all our neighbors," Effie said. "Never saw that guy."

"He's just a part-timer. He owns one of those hunting cabins up in the foothills. By the state park land."

"It's just interesting," Effie said.

"What is?"

"That you felt the need to come over here and tell me it was nothing. It just seems like if it was nothing, you would just assume that I would *see* that it was nothing. And you wouldn't feel the need to come say so."

"Oh my gosh, you're just as bad as Stan," Mary said.

Then, startled by her own frankness, she turned and strode back to the safety of her own house.

As she did, it struck her that she shouldn't have been rude to Effie, since Effie now held a weapon capable of bringing Mary down. If indeed she chose to use it.

# Chapter Fifteen

## The Oracle

### Abby

She was down on her hands and knees scrubbing dirt off his nice wooden floorboards. Or, at least, they looked like they had been nice at one time. Before raccoons and pack rats and whatever else had sheltered inside the cabin. Before the door had been left open to the combination of blown rain and dirt-road dust. And if Abby had anything to say about it, they would look nice again when she was done.

She owed him that much. She owed him a lot.

When he walked back into the cabin, Abby's eyes immediately fell on the bag in his hands. Not the brown grocery sack that probably only held more of the leather cleaner. He was also holding a white bag from the best lunch place in town.

"The Sandwich Port!" she said, her voice awed. "That's my favorite!"

Then she froze and wondered if she'd said the wrong thing. Maybe he had only brought lunch for himself. But . . . no, he'd said he was bringing lunch for both of them. Hadn't he?

If only she were sure enough that she was remembering correctly.

"Good," he said.

He took a paper-wrapped submarine sandwich out of the bag and set it on the very clean coffee table. Abby was proud of how clean she'd gotten it.

"What kind?" she asked.

She felt as though she could nearly drool if she let herself. She was suddenly aware of how hungry she was after the long morning of work.

"Salami," he said. And, much to her relief, he pulled a second sandwich out of the bag.

"Ooh. That's my very favorite one. But that one's probably yours."

"No. Actually I got egg salad and cheese for me."

"Seriously? You'd rather have egg salad and cheese than salami?"

"Seriously," he said.

"Wow. Thank you. Really. Thank you. I better wash my hands."

She washed up at his kitchen sink. By the time she had dried her hands and turned around, he was outside again, sitting in the pine needles and dirt with the sandwiches. And the puppies. Abby could see him through the open cabin door.

She walked outside to join him.

"I thought it would be better out here where we can keep an eye on them," he said.

"Oh. Good idea." She settled cross-legged in the dirt a few feet from his knees. "I mean . . . I think it is. Won't they try to get the food?"

"I'm not sure," he said. "But everything is an opportunity to train them."

He handed her the salami sub.

She unwrapped it, and immediately had two puppies—Kite and Noche—jump onto her lap and nip at it. She shooed them away.

"Wait here," Elliot said.

Abby stood up to wait, to keep her sandwich safe. She took three huge bites while he was gone, and it was the best thing ever. It nearly made her eyes roll back in her head; it was that good. Not that she had never had them before. But she had never had one when she was this hungry.

Elliot appeared again, holding a slightly dented-looking can of soda.

"How is having a drink with our lunch going to train 'em?"

"It's not a drink," he said.

He settled into the dirt again with his sandwich in one hand and the can in the other. The puppies swarmed him.

"Looks like a drink," Abby said, also daring to sit.

"It's just the empty can from one. I put some change in the bottom."

"Change?"

"Coins."

"Oh. What does that do?"

Before he could even answer—or maybe this was his answer—Queen jumped up and tried to bite at his sandwich.

"No," he said firmly. Then he gave the can one good, hard shake.

It made a huge noise. It even scared Abby. Queen jumped backward, away from it, and landed in the dirt on her rump, in a sitting position. Tippy ran almost all the way out to the road and then turned to watch the scene with wary eyes.

"Good girl," Elliot said, and patted Queen's head, a gesture she cautiously accepted.

The pup moved in again, tentatively, still locked and loaded on the sandwich.

"No," Elliot said again.

This time all he had to do was raise the can and she retreated.

"Wow," Abby said. "That's good. You're good at this. Where did you learn that?"

"I don't remember exactly. It was so long ago now, since I had dogs. Probably in a book on dog training or something."

Meanwhile all the puppies had turned away from Elliot's sandwich and set their sights on Abby's. Except Tippy, who was still purposely far away.

"Can I borrow that?" she asked him.

He handed her the can, and she held it high, like a threat, and they backed off and mostly sat. A couple of them stood staring at her. But a respectful distance away.

"That is so brilliant," she said.

They ate in silence for a minute or two. Abby made a mental note to go to the library as soon as she was finished with her work here. That is, if it was still open by then. She needed to read every book on dog training she could get her hands on. She'd had no idea you could do so much with puppies, and felt suddenly obsessed with training them.

"I used to have chairs," Elliot said, breaking the silence.

"You still have chairs," Abby said, her mouth rudely full of salami sub.

"Camp chairs, I mean. For sitting outdoors."

"Oh. That kind of chairs. What happened to 'em?"

"They were part of what the robbers took."

"Oh," Abby said. "That sucks."

"It does."

"But I'm saying that *really* sucks. Not just the chairs, I mean. The chairs were probably cheaper than just about everything else they took, but it still totally sucks. I mean, your wife dies, which is awful. And then you come up here to try to get some peace and quiet and feel a little better. And this is what you get. 'Surprise! We took your stuff.' That must've felt really, really terrible. You know. On top of everything else."

He didn't answer for a time. Abby looked away from the staring puppies. Glanced over at Elliot. He wasn't looking at her. But he had this expression on his face . . . almost as though what she'd said made him want to cry. He wasn't crying. But he almost looked as though he wanted to.

"I'm sorry if that was the wrong thing to say," she told him, quietly.

"No, actually I appreciate your saying it. It was a very hard day and I appreciate that you're aware of how that felt."

She chewed, swallowed, then was struck by a thought. A bad thought.

"Oh no. And then there was *me*. I must've been a really awful part of it, too, with everything I said to you. Going off on you and saying you were a bad person for taking my dogs to the pound, even though it should've been totally obvious by then that you brought 'em back and gave 'em back to me."

"Well, we worked that out," he said, his voice low and soft. Kind, she thought.

"I'm still sorry."

"Don't worry about it."

Another silence fell, and Abby used it to continue to stuff herself with lunch.

"You know . . . ," he said. Then he didn't seem anxious to finish the thought.

"What?"

"I was just thinking . . ." Another stall.

"What?"

"Maybe your mom would be okay if you told her about the puppies."

Abby stopped chewing suddenly. It was hard to talk around the huge mouthful. But she did anyway.

"Why would you say that?"

"I'm not sure. But . . . you have a good relationship with your mom, right?"

Still Abby could not bring herself to chew. "I guess," she mumbled.

"I know you don't like lying to her."

Abby swallowed the mostly unchewed bite. It hurt going down.

"How do you know that?"

"Well. I don't *know* it. I shouldn't have said I *know* it. I guess you just don't strike me as the kind of person who would be comfortable lying to a loved one. Am I right about that?"

Abby felt a bit queasy. Maybe from eating too fast. Maybe not.

"I'd be happier if I could tell her. But what if she makes me give 'em up?"

"I don't know, Abby. I don't have all the answers. It just seems like she's somebody you could trust."

"But you don't even know her."

"Call it a hunch."

They ate the rest of their lunch in silence.

Abby's mind whirled with thoughts. Mostly she was intrigued with Elliot's thinking. It seemed like he *knew* things. Like the advice he gave was . . . almost . . . above and beyond somehow. Better than everybody else's advice.

If someone else had suggested telling her mom about the puppies, Abby might not have considered it. But Elliot sounded strangely sure. And he seemed to know things that other people only guessed at.

If Elliot was what he seemed to be—what Abby was beginning to think he could be, a reliable source of knowledge about the world—Abby wanted to know it. She wanted to confirm it. See what she had in him.

So maybe—just maybe—she would try telling her mom. Just because she had to know.

It was a big gamble. One that might cost her the puppies. Then again, she could lose them in other ways. To having no place to keep them, or to being unable to afford them. If Elliot was right, maybe her mom would be a helpful ally. Maybe she had more money to contribute to the cause.

"I guess it's worth thinking about," she said.

It seemed to surprise him when she spoke after so much silence.

"I don't think you'll be sorry."

He sounded so sure. It made her believe him. Or at least want very badly to believe him.

"I should get back to work," she said.

"Aren't you exhausted?"

"Yeah. But I made you a promise."

"We never said you had to do it all in one day. You did a lot. Go home and rest. Talk to your mom. You can come back and do some more in the morning."

———

Abby had walked almost a quarter of the way home when she realized she'd forgotten to ask a very important question. Or maybe she just hadn't dared. It was hard for her to feel around in the missed opportunity and find the difference.

She turned around and trudged back up the hill, even though she was tired.

The puppies were still in the shed, where she and Elliot had put them so they wouldn't try to follow her home.

She rapped on the cabin door, and the puppies heard her and fell into barking and howling.

Elliot came to the door and blinked into the light, as though she had woken him.

"Forget something?" he asked.

"If I do decide to tell my mom . . . well . . . I was just thinking. She's probably going to ask me if I have a place to keep 'em. Because that's a whole big part of the thing—of her saying yes or no—having a place to keep 'em. And I don't even know what to tell her. You just said I could keep 'em in your shed while Patches has stitches and needs to keep that paw clean and dry. But we didn't talk about what would happen after that. So . . . this is sort of hard, but I decided I just have to ask you. Do I have a place to keep 'em?"

He stared over her shoulder and into the distance, as though listening to the dogs bark with a sort of curiosity. Abby thought maybe he was thinking hard about her request.

"Well," he said. "By the time Patches is all healed up, I will have headed home, most likely. And I guess it doesn't make much difference to my situation if there are still puppies in my shed while I'm not even up here. So long as you keep it nice and clean."

"You know I'll keep it super clean. It's just . . . you said you had to start filling it up with stuff again. Like another generator."

Abby hated to say it. She would have liked to avoid reminding him. But it would be even worse if he remembered later and changed his mind.

"I suppose I could chain the generator to the back porch," he said.

Abby rushed in and threw her arms around him. Too hard, she realized when it was too late to correct it. It seemed to knock the wind out of him. Abby could hear it go. A little "oof" sound.

Then she jumped back away.

"You're the nicest man in the world," she said, the words all tumbling over each other. "Thank you."

Then she trotted away before he could change his mind.

———

Abby arrived home with three library books on dog training. She held them close to her side, so the titles could not be read, and found her mom in the kitchen.

Her mom was stirring something in a pot on the stove. Abby's nose told her it was spaghetti sauce, which was disappointing. They ate spaghetti a lot. Abby would've preferred steak. Then again, if they ate steak all the time, her mother wouldn't have saved up fifty dollars to give Abby just when she needed it most.

"Hey," Abby said.

Her mother jumped as if Abby had startled her. As if she'd been so lost in thought as to be nearly asleep, and hadn't even heard Abby come in.

"Oh. Hey, Abby."

"I wanted to . . ." But then she couldn't force herself to go on.

"What?"

"Never mind. I'll be in my room."

Abby trotted down the hall a few steps, then stopped. Because she remembered Elliot's weird tendency to be right.

She turned and walked back to the kitchen again.

"So . . . ," she began.

Her mom turned to acknowledge her. To listen. But nothing more seemed to get said. Abby tried. But nothing more would come out.

"You want cookies?" her mom asked.

Abby felt her mouth fall open.

"You never let me have cookies before dinner."

"We'll make an exception."

Her mom took a plastic storage container down from the cupboard. Cookies at Abby's house were always homemade.

Abby plunked down on a chair at the kitchen table and watched her mother put three cookies on a plate in front of her. Chocolate chip. Then her mom moved to the fridge and took out the milk. Poured Abby a glass. Delivered it to the table.

"So why am I getting cookies before dinner?" Abby asked.

"Seems like you wanted to talk."

"Oh," Abby said. She shifted the books farther under the table and covered them with the napkin her mom provided. "Yeah. I guess I sort of did."

But for a minute or two she only nibbled on a cookie, weirdly slowly, as if she wasn't positive about actually eating it. And definitely as though she wasn't positive about having a talk, because she wasn't the least bit sure about that.

But maybe Elliot was right. She felt as though she had to know now. How could she just never know if he was right about something as important as this?

"You have to promise not to tell Dad," she blurted out.

"Oh, honey. I tell him as little as I possibly can."

"That's not exactly a promise."

"Okay. I promise. Whatever you say today is just between you and me."

Abby sighed. Fiddled with the napkin on her lap.

"I sort of . . . a little while ago . . . when we were talking about something . . . well . . . how should I say this? I didn't exactly lie. But I didn't exactly tell you all there was to tell, either."

Abby waited, wondering if she was visibly wincing. She felt as though she might have been. This was around the point where she figured her mom might get mad.

Nothing happened. She looked up at her mom's face. Her mom was looking down at the table. Listening. Or waiting to listen, anyway. She didn't look mad.

Abby took a deep breath and plunged on.

"Remember when I came home all wet and messy and told you I pulled those puppies out of the river?" Abby didn't wait to hear if she remembered. It was mostly a rhetorical question anyway. Who could forget a thing like that? "You asked me what I did with 'em and I said I took 'em to the pound. And I did. I did take 'em to the pound. That was true. I just . . . didn't . . . leave 'em there." She waited. No reply came. "You're not saying anything."

"I didn't know if you wanted me to."

"Sort of. At this point. Yeah."

She wanted to know if her mom was angry, but she didn't want to say so out loud. That might be too much like inviting the anger.

"I'm sure you had a good reason," her mom said. "I know you. And I know if you'd thought the puppies would get nice homes at the pound, you'd have left them there to get nice homes."

"They were going to *kill* 'em," Abby said in a near-whisper. Her voice dropped even lower on the horrible word "kill." Then she waited, saying nothing, for a time. Her mother also said nothing. "So you're not mad?"

"I was a little troubled because you didn't take me into your confidence. But now you have, so now I feel better."

A thought rushed into Abby's head. A huge, vivid, sudden thought. It came from nowhere and filled up everything. Occupied Abby's whole world at once.

*Elliot knows all about everything. He knows what all these other grown-ups don't know, even though they pretend they do. I wish Mom wasn't married to Dad. I wish she was married to Elliot.*

Abby closed her lips more firmly and said nothing.

She waited for her mom to ask a dozen questions about the puppies. Where was she keeping them? How was she going to feed them when the money she'd given Abby ran out? What if there were vet bills? What if her father found out?

None of those questions ever came.

"I want you to meet 'em," Abby said. Suddenly. Confidently.

But what she really meant was "I want you to meet Elliot."

"Okay," her mom said. "Sure. I could do that."

But her mom's eyes looked distant and worried, and Abby had no idea why.

She didn't ask. Things had gone infinitely better than she'd feared, and she didn't want to jinx it. She finished her milk and cookies and retired to her room with her dog training books. And left well enough alone.

Then, about a fifth of the way through the first book, she walked out and stuck her head in the kitchen again.

"Mom?"

"Yes, hon?"

"Aren't you even going to tell me all about how hard it's going to be? Taking care of all those puppies?"

"I wasn't going to, hon. No."

"Any special reason?"

"It's been a little while since you found them," her mom said. "So I figured you already knew."

# Chapter Sixteen

## *A Man*

### Elliot

Elliot was brushing his teeth at the sink when he heard the puppies barking in the shed. It was unlike them to bark unless they heard something very distinct. Other than a little soft whimpering now and then, they tended to be quiet. Or maybe some of their sounds didn't carry through the shed door and all the way to the inside of the cabin.

He quickly rinsed and spit and went to the cabin's front door, which he threw open.

Abby was standing on his stoop, one hand raised to knock. She was bouncing up and down on her toes, as if there were something inside her that she could barely contain.

"Oh, there you are," she said.

Elliot opened his mouth to speak but never got a word in edgewise. She was a tornado of words that morning. A sheer storm of verbal information.

"So wait till I tell you this, Elliot. You were right! You said I should tell her and you said if I told her she'd be okay with it and you were right. I wasn't sure if you'd be right so I was kind of scared to tell her about it but then I just made myself do it anyway and she was fine. She didn't even give me a bunch of advice about how hard it was going to be like grown-ups usually do. You know, like how there were going to be all these problems I wasn't thinking about because I'm just a kid and I can't think of all the bad things that might happen. Why do grown-ups do that, Elliot?"

Elliot paused a moment before speaking, to be sure she really did plan to allow a space for him to respond. "I'm confused," he said. "Why do they do . . . which part of everything you just said?"

"Lecture kids on all the terrible things that could happen. Like they think it's smart to imagine all the worst possible things that could happen and then make sure you imagine them right along with them. And I don't get that at all, because good things could happen, too. So why don't they lecture you on all the good things that might happen?"

"No idea," Elliot said. "Maybe I'd do better with the question if I hadn't just woken up."

"Oh, did I wake you up? I'm sorry."

"No, I was up. Just not for long." He paused, listening to the barking and yipping from the shed. "Maybe go let them out, since they know you're here."

"She's coming up," Abby said, not yet moving off his stoop.

"Not following."

"My mom. She's coming up. I asked her to come up and meet the puppies. And you. I hope you don't mind. Maybe I should've asked first, but it's not like you've got a phone or anything."

"It's fine," Elliot said. He opened his mouth to say, "Her car will never make it up this rutted dirt road." Then he realized he wasn't supposed to know what kind of car she drove and how low-slung it was. "Does she have a truck that can get up here?"

"No. She's walking."

"Long walk. Steep, too."

"I do it every day."

"You're thirteen."

"She said she'd do it. She just had to do a couple of things first. She's probably already left by now."

"Good," Elliot said. "I'll take the truck and pick her up on the road."

Good because it would not do to pick her up at her house. It might cause trouble for her. If he could meet her and offer her a ride on the deserted upper part of this seldom-traveled dirt road, that would be perfect.

He grabbed his keys and headed for the truck, still hearing the yipping of puppies waiting to be let out. Before he climbed in, he looked back over his shoulder at Abby, who was standing still and staring at him.

"What?" he asked.

"Don't you even need to know what she looks like?"

"Well, how many people walk up this road, really?"

"That's true. Anyway, she's wearing a red blouse this morning. Tell her you're the guy with the puppies. So she'll know you're not a stranger. And she won't be afraid to get in."

"Got it," Elliot said.

But actually the thought of even that simple task made him feel tired. Everything did. The grief made the simplest movements of life feel like more than he could bear, and he had no idea how long he would have to live this way.

She broke away then to go let the dogs out. Elliot drove away quickly before he had to worry about one of them dashing into the path of his truck.

—

He found her about a third of the way up from her home to his cabin, wearing a bright red blouse. Just as Abby had described.

He stopped and powered down his window, and looked at her. And she looked back at him.

It was hard for him to pin down what he saw in her eyes and on her face, especially since parts of her seemed to contradict other parts of her. She seemed glad and sorry to see him in nearly equal measures. Or maybe not sorry exactly. Maybe glad to see him but afraid to see him as well.

It was all very hard to sort out.

She was panting from the exertion of her hike.

"Going into town?" she asked him, her voice breathy.

"No. I came down to offer you a ride."

"Oh, thank goodness."

She walked around to the passenger side of the truck and climbed in. Elliot headed downhill toward town, keeping an eye open for a good spot to turn around.

"I'm not as young as I used to be," she said.

"Lot of that going around," Elliot replied.

They didn't speak for several minutes. Until he had turned around in an old, abandoned, weed-choked driveway and headed back uphill. Then they both opened their mouth to speak at exactly the same moment. And both fell silent at exactly the same moment, yielding to the other.

"You go," Mary said.

"I just wanted to apologize for yesterday."

"Oh. Which part of it, exactly?"

"I know I made you uncomfortable talking about your marriage, and it goes without saying that you're right—that it's none of my business. I shouldn't have been confrontational about it, and I feel bad now."

She seemed to wait for him to say more. He didn't.

"Well. Thank you. I do know you were trying to be helpful."

"That's almost never helpful, though, when we tell people to live more the way *we* think they should. When have you ever seen anybody's life turned around that way?"

"Even if it doesn't help," she said, "I can at least give you credit for wanting to."

She had her head turned away from him. Looking out the window. As if something amazing were going by out there. A red rock canyon or a herd of caribou. Something she couldn't take her eyes away from. Or maybe she just felt better when she wasn't looking at Elliot.

He watched her as much as he could without failing to watch the road for too long.

"It's just . . . ," he began, not even sure where he was going with the thought. Not even knowing what it just was. "I meet people like you from time to time, who just seem to have so much to add to the world, and I can't for the life of me figure out why they're not surrounded by people who recognize all that value."

She didn't answer. She didn't turn her face toward him. But he thought he saw her face redden, especially around the ear that faced him.

"But there I go again," he said. "I'll just stop talking now."

While he listened to the silence and watched the redness, he confronted himself regarding why he had said such a thing at all. He didn't know her. How did he know what value she added to the world?

The recrimination in his head, however, was not nearly so well thought out. It was just a frustrated statement along the lines of *What the hell is wrong with you, Elliot?*

Still, in the echo of that thought, Elliot figured he might know why.

It was because she reminded him a little bit of Pat. Just a little bit.

She really looked nothing like Pat. Her hair was finer and straighter, and a lighter color of brown. Her features were sharper and more defined. And she was smaller and more petite. More fine boned. But she had a look in her eyes that struck him as familiar. Something strong and clear.

He doubted himself briefly. Maybe the look in Mary's eyes just reminded him of Pat's eyes. Pat had certainly been strong and clear.

But, after all, if this woman was strong, why hadn't she struck out on her own?

Still, his gut told him that the look he saw in her eyes spoke for itself. It was not an error. It was exactly what it was, and he should trust what his own eyes told him.

He looked through the windshield and saw the cabin up ahead, which felt like a relief. He had made a mess of this. Again. To her, and even on the inside of his head. Everything felt like a mess. He was glad to arrive at a place where he and Abby's mother were supposed to know nothing about each other.

That would feel easy.

———

"Oh, they really are adorable, aren't they?" Mary said.

She was standing a few yards from his front porch, the puppies swarming around her feet, wagging their whole bodies with the sheer joy of meeting her. Elliot had been on his way inside the cabin to get them all something to drink, but he found himself leaning in the open doorway, silently watching the scene play out.

"Lie down," Abby said to her mom, her voice weirdly high pitched with excitement.

"Lie down?"

"Yeah."

"Why would I do that?"

"Just try it, Mom. Just trust me."

"I'll get my clothes all dirty."

"So? You were going to put them in the hamper at the end of the day anyway. Right?"

Mary just stood a moment, as if considering the request. Then she glanced over at Elliot. As if she had only just realized that he would be witnessing whatever happened to her next. If it was undignified or embarrassing, Elliot would see.

At least, that seemed to be her concern. That's what Elliot thought he saw on her face.

It was a shy, nervous glance, and it brought up something that Elliot had not consciously noticed before. It may have been there all along, but he only in that moment confronted it.

She was aware of him as a man. She reacted to him the way a woman will sometimes react to the presence of an interesting man.

It had been a very long time since any woman had reacted to Elliot that way.

Ever since Pat's diagnosis he had been heaped with respect. Buried in empathy. He had been treated as a pitiable figure, but not as an attractive man.

But Mary didn't pity him, because she didn't know.

And it felt good.

And the minute he realized it felt good, Elliot felt guilty. As if he had been caught cheating on Pat. Even though it was quite obvious that there was no cheating and there was no Pat. But a suitable amount of time had not passed, to phrase it mildly.

All of this ran through him like a mild jolt of static electricity in the second their gazes snagged on each other.

He quickly looked away.

Mary settled on her back in the pine needles and dirt and was immediately assaulted by the overly expressed love of seven puppies. Even Patches was feeling better enough to swarm over her, though he repeatedly struck her chin and his littermates with the edge of his plastic cone collar.

Mary's unfiltered and unrestrained laughter filled the morning air.

It was nice to hear someone laughing, Elliot thought. He hadn't been around a lot of laughter for as long as he could remember. He guessed that Mary hadn't, either, and that, even if she had, it probably had not been her own.

———

"I should go in and get started," Abby said.

She dashed into the cabin before Elliot could stop her. And he tried, too. He had already raised one finger in an attempt to get her attention, and opened his mouth to speak. Because he felt uneasy being left alone with Mary. He wanted to convince Abby to stay because her presence made the meeting feel emotionally safer. Less intense.

But it was too late. She was already gone.

He glanced over at Mary, who was staring down at the dirt, and who looked at least as uneasy as he felt. If not more so.

"Please don't be uncomfortable," Elliot said. "I promise I'm not going to talk about your life. I'm sorry. I don't know what got into me. Let's just talk about normal things like normal people talk about. Normally."

A long silence, during which she kept her eyes trained down to the dirt.

Then she said, "What do people talk about normally? I swear I don't remember."

Elliot laughed out loud. But a second later he realized she had not been joking.

He looked up at the puppies, who had tired of the humans and begun a series of epic play battles amongst themselves. All except Tippy, who sat by herself underneath a tree, watching the mock violence as if deeply relieved to be outside the sphere of it.

"Well," Elliot said. "When there are seven puppies nearby . . . I think people talk about puppies."

"Oh," Mary said, and looked up at them.

They both watched for a few minutes in silence. At least, he and Mary were silent. The puppies growled and yipped and sometimes shrieked if a tooth caught them a bit too roughly. But the humans said nothing.

"They really are cute," she said after a time, breaking the silence.

"They are," Elliot said.

"I worry about the situation, though. It's just so much responsibility for a girl her age. When your thirteen-year-old asks for a puppy, you have to think hard about whether she's ready for all that responsibility. But *seven*? *Seven* puppies?"

"If it helps any to know, I'm thinking about adopting two. Taking them home with me when I go. I guess that doesn't help much. Does it? I mean, five puppies. That's still an awful lot of puppies."

She looked at him—right at him—for the first time in as long as he could remember.

"No, it does help. I mean, that's a good start. Maybe she'll find homes for some of the others."

"Maybe. If she can bring herself to part with them."

"I just worry that she's going to get her heart broken."

Elliot offered no reply. He wanted to reassure her, but he couldn't. It did seem as though heartbreak was a possible outcome.

"You're not doing it just for her, are you?" she asked, her voice thin and unsure.

"Taking two of the puppies?"

"Yes. That."

"No. I'm thinking about it for the companionship. And I'll be going back to work soon, so I always thought two dogs would be better than one because they can keep each other company all day while I'm away."

She opened her mouth to speak, but didn't. Her eyes shot past him to the door of the cabin. Elliot turned to follow her gaze and saw that the door was now open again, and Abby was looking down on them as if they were doing something right. Something that pleased her immensely.

"You guys are talking," she said. "Good. What are you talking about? I *knew* you would like each other. I just *knew* it."

"I should probably be going," Mary said.

She jumped to her feet and took off toward the road before Elliot could argue.

"You want a ride?" he called after her.

She waved one arm but kept walking.

"I'm fine. Downhill is fine. Thanks anyway. I just have to get home."

# Chapter Seventeen

## *You Wouldn't—Would You?*

**Mary**

Abby barged in through the kitchen door at a little after noon.

Mary was at the sink doing up the breakfast dishes. It had been unlike her to leave them for so long. Then again, it had been a weirdly atypical morning.

"I came home for lunch," Abby said, talking fast and excitedly. "I hope that's okay. I figured Elliot shouldn't have to buy me lunch every day, especially since the whole point is that I owe him money anyway." She paused. Caught Mary's eyes. "Oh, but you didn't know about that part."

Mary did know, but not from Abby. She realized just in time—before she opened her mouth and said something she shouldn't have—that she wasn't supposed to know anything about the financial arrangement surrounding the vet visit.

She took cookies down from the shelf while Abby told her the story of Patches and his accident.

"I did notice that one of them had a bandaged paw and one of those plastic collars," Mary said when she was fairly sure Abby was done.

She set the plate of cookies in front of her daughter, who stared at them with wide eyes.

"I get cookies *before lunch*?"

"You've been working so hard," Mary said. "Working up a big appetite. I know you'll eat your lunch anyway."

She sat down across from her daughter and watched her shove a whole cookie into her mouth at once and attempt to chew it. Under normal circumstances, Mary would have let her daughter know that she found this impolite. But Mary had something on her mind, something that had been troubling her all morning, and Abby's lack of table manners only registered in a very distant way. Because Mary's attention was so thoroughly elsewhere.

"Honey?" she began.

"Yeah?"

Or something like the word "yeah." It was hard for Mary to tell around and through all that half-chewed cookie.

"When you wanted me to go up the hill and meet that man . . ."

"Elliot."

"Right. Elliot. You just wanted me to meet him because . . . I mean, you didn't . . . I guess what I mean is . . ."

Abby rolled her eyes slightly as she swallowed. "Jeez, Mom. Am I actually supposed to understand what you're getting at? Because I don't."

"You said you knew we'd like each other. But you just meant as friends, though. Right? You just figured he's somebody I might like as a friend?"

To her surprise, Abby shrugged.

"I don't know. How did I know how you would like each other?"

"But you didn't . . . I mean, you wouldn't . . ."

"Mom. You're doing it again."

"I just can't imagine that you would . . . I mean, he's a married man."

"No he's not."

"He wears a wedding ring."

"His wife *died*."

Mary sat in silence for a moment, absorbing this information. She could feel herself taking it hard, as if it were the death of someone she had known well. But she had no idea why.

She remembered him saying something about wanting two of the puppies for companionship, and it had struck her as an odd thing for a married man to say. As if he were casually and openly stating that he was lonely in his marriage. She had almost asked him about it. Called on him to elaborate. But something had derailed the conversation. And maybe she wouldn't have asked anyway, because, really, what business was it of hers?

"Oh, honey, that's awful."

"I'll say. He's really broken up about it."

"When did she die?"

"Like five days before he came up here. And he just came up a few days ago."

More silence as Mary tried to absorb the additional news. Tried to utterly reframe everything she knew about him. Every word, every glance, every impression she had gotten about him and his life and mood suddenly needed to be filtered through the lens of this new information.

"Now can I have lunch?" Abby asked.

Mary looked up to see that she had finished all the cookies Mary had given her.

"Yes. Of course. I'll make you a sandwich."

"Soup too?"

"I could heat up some soup. But all we have right now is tomato."

"That's fine. I'm really hungry."

"So I gather."

Mary got up and moved to the refrigerator, feeling slightly shocked. She felt too aware of herself and her movements, and the familiar kitchen around her seemed unreal. Like a dream kitchen.

Before she opened the fridge, she turned back to address her daughter.

"But honey . . ."

"What?"

"He might not be a married man. But I'm still a married woman."

"But you're married to *Dad*. Who would want to be married to *Dad*?"

"Be that as it may, honey—"

A sudden movement caught Mary's eye. She looked up to see Stan standing in the arched kitchen doorway, watching her with narrow eyes. Her gut turned to ice in less than a second.

She had no idea how much of that he might have heard.

"What are you doing here?" she asked.

"I don't get to come home for lunch?"

"Sure you do. Yes. Of course." In fact, she encouraged it, often, because it saved money. It was so much more economical than eating out at a restaurant. But he never seemed to take the hint. "I was just about to make Abby a sandwich and some tomato soup."

"I hate tomato soup. You know I hate tomato soup. How many years have you known me and you still don't know I hate tomato soup?"

"I'm sorry. It's all we have. I had no idea you were going to come home for lunch. You never come home for lunch. Just a sandwich then, I guess."

"Never mind. Forget it. I'll just go out. I'll just go to the Sandwich Port. Doesn't seem like asking too much. Just a decent lunch when I work hard."

Before Mary could open her mouth to answer him, he had banged the back door open with the heel of his hand and marched out, leaving the door swinging wide.

Mary hurried over to close it behind him.

She looked at her daughter, who looked back at her. Mary could tell that they were both thinking the same thing. Both worried about the same situation. But neither of them said a word. Maybe they didn't dare to. Maybe they both correctly perceived that they had said far too much already.

Mary made lunch for her daughter in absolute ringing silence.

———

Just before it was time to clear the dishes away, Mary managed to speak again.

"Headed back up there?"

"No. I'm done."

"Really? You did all that work already?"

"Two mornings. Seems like a lot of work to me."

"Do you still owe him money?"

"Nope. He said he's willing to call it even. It was a lot of work." Abby sat still while Mary collected her plate and bowl. Then, as Mary was rinsing them in the sink, Abby added, "He's a nice man."

"Yes," Mary said, without looking back at her daughter. "He *is* a nice man."

———

Mary marched all the way uphill to his cabin. Maybe it was only her imagination, but it seemed to get a little bit easier each time she tackled the steep hike. Maybe the trek was getting her in shape again, and that would not be a bad thing. That would be nice, she thought.

She glanced over her shoulder every few steps to be sure no one was observing. To satisfy herself that she was not being followed.

She expected to have to knock on his cabin door, which would have been hard for her. It would have felt like an intrusion. And she figured he would throw the door open suddenly, and stare down at her, and expect her to explain why she had come. All of that felt intimidating.

None of it happened.

As she rounded that last bend, she saw him out in the front yard playing with the puppies.

He had bought two of those white plastic outdoor chairs, which he had arranged in his front yard. But he wasn't sitting in either of them. He was down on his back in the dirt, lifting the puppies one by one and holding them over his face. Staring up at them as if memorizing the look in each one's eyes.

Mary watched their tails swing as they looked down at him. They liked him. And so did Mary. More than she wanted to. She liked him more now that she knew he played with the puppies when Abby wasn't around. Not just, as she had imagined, locked them in the shed until Abby came back to tend them.

She didn't want to like him more. But there didn't seem to be much she could do about that.

He saw her then, and sat up, holding one of the puppies to his chest. The wounded one, with the bandaged paw.

"Oh," he said. "Hello."

Mary felt her face heat up, and presumably redden, and it embarrassed her.

She walked closer, and sat in one of the plastic chairs. He set the puppy down and rose to his feet, brushing off the seat of his jeans and reaching around to shake out his shirt in the back. He sat in the other chair and said nothing. Apparently he was just waiting for her to explain why she had come.

"You have chairs," she said, ignoring one of the black puppies who was tugging ferociously at her pant leg.

"I do," he said.

And, unfortunately, he seemed to go back to waiting for her to explain.

"I wanted to warn you about something," she said.

"Okay."

And he waited again.

"My husband might . . . emphasis on the word *might* . . . have heard Abby and me talking about you. So he might be aware of the fact that we know you."

"And that would be bad."

It didn't sound to Mary like a question.

"With Stan, pretty much everything is."

"How would he know where to find me?"

"Well, just if he followed me or something."

"So you came running right up here to tell me that it would be bad if he followed you up here?"

His words rang in the air and vibrated through Mary's gut. They stung going through. She didn't think it out in these specific terms, but if called upon to name another time she had felt so humiliated, she likely would have come up blank.

"Okay," she said. "I'm an idiot."

"You're not an idiot. I just wondered why you didn't have Abby tell me next time she came up to see the puppies."

"Oh. Wow." Her face grew hotter, if such a thing were possible. And, she assumed, redder. "I'm *really* an idiot."

"Please don't say that about yourself."

"It's so true, though. In my own defense, I did do my best to make sure I wasn't being followed."

"And he might follow Abby up here, too. And she might not be as careful to look around. So you're not an idiot."

"I feel like one. I'm just really sorry if we put you in a bad position."

She was careful to look away from him as she spoke. She was watching the puppies and their play fights. They both were. It was so much easier that way.

"I don't care," he said.

"If you ever met Stan, you might."

"If he wants a fight, fine. He'll get one. That's a rare thing for me to say. I'm not a fighter. I don't relish using my fists with anyone, and I haven't since I was young. But a man who controls his wife so tightly that she's afraid to talk to a neighbor . . . whose own daughter thinks he's a terrible father . . . a guy who doesn't appreciate having you but feels free to be jealous that you'd talk to me, well . . . if he wants a piece of me, he'll get his chance at it."

Mary sat in silence for a time, unsure what to say. His willingness to defend her almost seemed like a sign of caring, but that felt too good to be true. They barely knew each other.

"Why would you want to do that for me?" she asked after a time.

He didn't answer for what felt like nearly a minute. A minute is a long time, she realized, when you're waiting for an answer. Especially if it's one that matters.

"I think you remind me a little bit of my wife."

His words fell hard into her stomach, like a meal she had forgotten to chew and would never be able to digest. She couldn't even tell if she liked them or not. It was too complicated. Everything was suddenly complicated.

"Abby told me about how you lost her. Just recently. I'm so sorry. I can't imagine how awful you must feel."

For a few seconds he didn't answer. Then he did.

"I hope you won't take this the wrong way . . . ," he began. Mary felt her gut tighten in anticipation of being wounded. A familiar feeling. ". . . but you probably *can't* imagine. Because it was a wonderful, equal marriage. A true partnership. And unless you've been married before, or have had some other relationship I don't know about, I'm guessing you don't know how that feels, or how hard it is to lose it."

"I married Stan young," she said. "There was nobody else."

They sat in silence for a few beats and watched the puppies frolic. The one with the plastic cone collar kept tripping on it and falling onto his chin. Mary was amazed that he didn't just give up and hold still. It struck her as an awful lot of determination. She found herself admiring him.

"I wonder which one of us is luckier," she said, surprising herself by finding the courage to speak. Maybe the wounded puppy had inspired her. "You had something that good and lost it. I never had something that good, so I can never feel that kind of loss. I just wonder who's luckier."

"I think I'm luckier," he said, without hesitation. "What do you think?"

"I think you're luckier, too," Mary said.

# Chapter Eighteen

*Nobody Feels Sorry for the Fish*

**Elliot**

He brought them each a soda, and they sat in the dappled sun and sipped for a long time without speaking. She was watching the puppies play. He was holding one of the knotted rope toys with a puppy gnawing and tugging on the other end. After a time a sibling would come along and ambush the tugging pup, who would abandon the toy to react in his or her own defense. Then another pup would come along and grab the rope.

This went on for a while. Elliot was feeling that familiar sense of fatigue fueled by grief, but, rather than wanting her to go home, he found himself relieved by the distraction of having someone around. He couldn't help wondering what she was thinking. She definitely did not seem inclined to leave as quickly as possible, as she had in the past.

A moment later she surprised him by speaking.

"So what do you *do* now?"

He opened his mouth to tell her all about his engineering degree and his job at Meade, where he hadn't set foot in so many months. It felt like a dream he'd had about a workplace. Not so much like a real part of his history.

But she was still talking.

"I mean, you used to come up here and hunt, I know, because you told me, and now that you don't hunt, I'm not sure what you do."

"I'm not sure what I do, either," he said.

She turned her head to regard him for a split second, and he was struck by the impression that it embarrassed her to look at him.

"Well, what have you been doing these last few days?"

"Pretty much being entertained by your daughter and her seven bouncy puppies. But that was unanticipated, of course. That was just one of those curveballs life throws you when you least expect it."

"So what did you anticipate that you'd come up here and do? Do you fish?"

"Fishing and hunting are pretty closely related," he said, and left her to work out the rest of the thing on her own.

"I guess. I guess because you end up with a dead animal either way. But a lot of people don't care as much about the fish—maybe they don't even really think of them as animals. Like they're a whole different . . . I don't know. Something. Sort of in a class by themselves. Because they're so . . ."

For a while she didn't seem inclined to go on.

"So . . . what?" he asked after a few beats. "I'm interested in your take on that."

"Well, they're . . . they're *cold*, you know? They're not warm-blooded. And they don't have fur. And I guess they *sort of* have faces, but they're not faces anything like mammals have."

"In other words, they're quite unlike us."

"I guess that's it," she said. "Yes."

"Seems unfair."

They sipped in silence for a minute more.

Kite dashed across Elliot's feet. Patches came bounding after him, caught his plastic cone collar on Elliot's shoe, and tripped, pitching himself chin-first into the dirt. Elliot helped him up, but he seemed not only uninjured but undaunted. He set Patches on his feet and the pup galloped back to the herd. He was using that bandaged paw fairly normally again. Favoring it slightly, but not much more.

Elliot turned his head to see Mary watching him. Approvingly. Actually "tenderly" was the word that sprang to mind, but he dismissed it.

"I don't mean unfair of *you*," he said.

"I didn't take it wrong."

He found that interesting. Because she had struck him as a sensitive woman, forced onto the defensive in life, and unfortunately inclined to take everything as a slight. He figured she must have been growing more accustomed to him, and feeling a bit more trusting in his company.

"I just think it's odd how we parse out our empathy," he said. "Why we only have empathy for those who remind us most of ourselves. I'm not saying I don't understand it. Sure, it's easy to have empathy for someone who's just like us. It comes naturally. I just think it's a shame we can't take it a bit further. I can't help wondering what the world would be like if our empathy muscle were a bit more developed."

"That's an odd way to put it," she said. "Do you think it *is* like a muscle, and the more we use it the more it can do?"

"Just anecdotally, from my own experience, I'm beginning to play with the idea. I'm starting to think it might be true."

"So you never told me what you thought you'd come up here to do."

"Oh. That. Just run away from my life and exist in the silence, I guess."

She let out a small, rueful laugh. "You sure didn't get much silence."

"True. But now I'm thinking silence might be overrated."

He waited for her to answer. She never did. So he jumped in again.

"A friend of mine suggested hiking. I guess I figured I'd do some hiking."

He was surprised to see her light up at the word. He saw it and felt it in the air between them. It brought her back to life in a way nothing else had in the short time he'd known her.

"Oh, I used to love to hike!" she said, her voice seeming to cradle the subject of her words, as though she were admiring a wild animal or a fine gem. "I was mostly just wanting to get out of the house at first, but it was so beautiful up here in the foothills. I used to go halfway up some of the mountains. There was wildlife, and the sky was this amazing dark navy blue, and I liked the way the wind made the leaves on the trees shudder. And then when I was home later, I was so tired that I felt like a different person. More relaxed, you know?"

"Endorphins," he said.

"Is that what it is?"

"That's a lot of it. But nature has an effect on people, and it's something that's hard to quantify. Our science doesn't quite reach to phenomena like that. In my opinion, anyway."

They watched the puppies for a few seconds more in silence.

"Come on a hike with me," he said suddenly.

It was not something he had thought out carefully in advance. It had raced into his head fully formed. There was more feeling behind it than careful thinking. Somehow he had been seized with the idea that if he could draw her away from this town and that awful man, he could find the part of her—or help *her* find the part of her—that would never want to go back.

He knew it was probably not true, and likely would not work. But he also knew it would do no harm, even in failure. *Actually,* he thought, *it would only be dangerous if it worked.*

He watched the look in her eyes. She was looking partly away from him, staring at the constantly moving targets of flying puppies. She wanted to go. He could see that in her eyes. The only question remaining was whether she would dare.

"Can we take them?" she asked.

"I think they're too young for that. I think they should stay in the shed while we go."

"Okay. Yes. I'd like to. But I have to be home on time. I have to be there when Stan gets home from work, or he'll have a fit."

Another idea came into Elliot's head, also fully formed and also more sense impression than thought. Maybe he could display her own fear to her, so she could see it through his eyes. Anything that's been with you every day for years begins to feel normal, he knew. It's more that moment when you see it through someone else's eyes. That's when you truly see it.

It was a tall order. But, again, he had nothing to lose.

"Okay," he said. "I'll put some kibble down for them in the shed and then we'll go."

———

They reached a section of tumbled boulders on the path around the base of the mountain. He reached out his hand to help her, but she had already scrambled up. Quite ably, from the look of things. So he moved forward, feeling her just a step or two behind his right side.

Scrubby trees seemed to grow here out of solid rock, utilizing whatever tiny amount of dirt hid in the cracks. Elliot admired their tenacity. He watched the leaves to see if they shuddered. He had never thought to look before. But there was no wind. The air stood perfectly still. And it was hot.

He had only brought one small bottle of water for each of them. So that would limit how far they could climb.

He shaded his eyes with one hand and looked up, noting that the sky was the exact color of dark navy blue she had described.

He looked over his shoulder to see if the town was visible from this section of trail. It wasn't, but in looking he accidentally caught her eye. She quickly looked away again.

He slowed to allow her to pull level with him.

"Rest stop," she said.

He didn't know if she meant she needed to find a private place to relieve herself, or if she just needed a moment to breathe. He waited with her, looking down into a small valley of boulders between mountains. Her situation appeared to be the latter. She leaned her hands on her thighs and puffed. He watched waves of heat rise over the boulders, skewing and distorting his view of the base of the mountain behind.

"You know," she said, "when you go back to the city, I'll miss these talks. I don't have talks like this with anybody else."

Elliot was uncertain of the sort of talks she meant.

"For example . . . ," he said.

"Like that talk we had about fish. Why we have empathy for mammals but not fish. Nobody I know talks about life like that. I talk to my friend Viv. More than just small talk. We talk about stuff like kids and marriages. We talk about how it feels trying to get by and do a decent job on life every day. But nothing too philosophical. We never talked about anything like why nobody feels sorry for fish. Stan sure as hell doesn't talk like that. He's silent in the morning. Just drinks his coffee and goes to work. Then when he gets home, he'll talk about his day but not much else. Usually he complains. You know. Everybody is always unfair to him. Everybody always treats him bad. I meet all kinds of people who are good and kind, and I don't know why Stan doesn't, but I don't think it's any coincidence."

"No," Elliot said. "I don't think so either."

"Sometimes he'll talk about his day and he'll be happy. Well. Sort of happy. His version of happy. But his version of happy is always more like getting over on somebody else. Coming out on top, like he's the big man. I wonder if you know what I mean. I always had this theory that people who want to be the big man are really the smallest men."

He seemed to think about that, but offered no reply.

They walked again, and he was aware of the ragged puffing of her breath. Maybe he was taking her too far and too high, especially in this heat. It might be beyond her current abilities, and she might be shy to say so. But at least she would have that wonderful endorphin high later that evening. That would be something.

But he couldn't make her late. He glanced at his watch and made mental notes regarding where and when to turn back. He didn't want to get her in trouble. But some small part of him wanted to make her *think* she might be late. To see how she felt and acted when she *thought* she might be in trouble. Then he could see how afraid she really was of her husband. And maybe, just maybe, he could make *her* see it, too.

They crossed a little stream, narrow but surprisingly deep and fast, by hopping from one round, polished stone to the next.

"Do you still love him?" he asked. "After all these years? Never mind," he added quickly. "You don't have to answer that if you don't want. It was probably rude of me to ask. It's really none of my business."

They climbed in silence for a minute or two, Elliot watching the way his wet boots left dark footprints on the loose dirt of the trail.

He could hear scrub jays and Steller's jays chirping and shrieking in the treetops, and he craned his neck to see which birds were speaking. They sounded excited. As if they were telling one another that great danger was coming. For a moment, Elliot feared what they feared. Was there a bear or a mountain lion nearby? Then it struck him that *they* were the danger. He and Mary were the cause of all that panic.

"No," she said. "I've been thinking about it. And I don't believe I still do."

He waited a moment to see if she would say more. If she was just on the edge of baring her soul, he didn't want to bump her out of her thoughts. But she offered nothing more.

"When people abuse us," he said, "we can fall out of love with them."

"He doesn't abuse me." She fell into silence for a beat or two. Then she added, "Maybe I shouldn't say that, though. I'm categorizing abuse as only physical abuse. There's also emotional abuse and verbal abuse, and they call it abuse for a reason, right? Years ago I had a friend, somebody I don't see anymore, and she told me something I'll never forget. She said we'll let people abuse us as much as we're willing to abuse ourselves. But once they start treating us worse than we treat ourselves, then we know they have to go."

"So . . . are you worried that when you start to be better to yourself, there might be no room left for Stan?"

She didn't answer.

They walked in silence for several minutes, save the crunching of gravel under their feet, the wind against Elliot's ears, and the puffing of their breathing. Elliot was thinking he had probably offended her and gone too far. He wasn't sure how to make it right. Or even if he wanted to and thought he should.

"See?" she said after a time, her voice even and sure. A bit . . . curious, maybe. "I never have talks like this with anybody else."

———

They turned for home only ten minutes or so after the stream crossing. Elliot was beginning to fear that his chance to reach her was slipping away. It seemed wrong to purposely throw a scare into her. Then again, was anything worse than sending her back into a terrible marriage with her view of her options unchanged?

They crested a rise and Elliot saw the deep stream again, flowing through a cut in the foothills two or three hundred feet below where they stood.

He stopped suddenly. She noticed, and stopped with him. They stood staring at the stream below them without speaking. Then she shot him a questioning glance.

He swallowed hard and began, knowing he might lose her trust over this. But somehow it felt as though any effort would be better than nothing. Sometimes in life, he'd noticed, it's better to do nothing if you're unsure. In other situations, almost anything you did would be better than doing nothing at all. He'd had a boss once who had used to tell him, "Do something, even if it's wrong." Occasionally it was bad advice, but all too often it was right on point.

"What if I told you it wasn't safe to go back for hours?" he asked her.

He watched her face and saw the predictable shot of alarm in her eyes. He sank into a sitting position on the trail, cross-legged. She continued to stand for a few beats, frozen into place.

"Why wouldn't it be safe?"

"You know about flash floods, right?"

She sat in the dirt of the trail beside him, her legs outstretched. "I've heard of them," she said. "But it's summer. And it almost never rains here in the summer. Doesn't it have to be raining somewhere to make a flash flood?" Her voice sounded pleading. As if bargaining with reality to get her out of trouble.

He glanced over at her face before answering. She was scanning the skies, a look of abject alarm on her face and in her eyes.

"Yes, somewhere. But it can be somewhere very far away."

"Well, couldn't we just go down and run quick across it? There's no flooding now."

"But if a flash flood did come through, it would fill up that whole cut through the foothills. We'd need to be on much higher ground, the way we are now. It would take us at least fifteen minutes to walk down there and then climb up to higher ground again."

"Dear God," she said. "Stan will kill me." They sat in silence for a moment. Then he could feel something very different rise up in her, and when she opened her mouth to speak, he could hear it. It was a growing sense of confidence in her own observations. "Now wait just a minute," she said. "If you knew there was heavy rain somewhere and a flash flood was a possibility, then why did you even take us up here and across that stream in the first place? *Is* there a flash flood warning?"

"No," he said. "Not that I know of."

While she wasn't answering, he glanced at her face in his peripheral vision. He expected her to look angry. Instead she only looked more confused.

"Then why did you say there was?"

"I didn't say there was. Exactly. I was pretty much speaking hypothetically about flash floods the whole time. But, I know. I gave the impression that it was real. And I let you keep that impression for a minute. And I know that wasn't very fair."

She was looking at the side of his face now, but he didn't look back.

"Then why did you do it?"

"I wanted to know how much trouble you'd be in if you weren't there when he got home from work. I didn't want to get you into that trouble, because I don't wish anything bad on you, and I wouldn't hurt you if I could help it. I just wanted to know how much of a fear it really is."

"Well, that doesn't prove anything," she said, sounding a bit grumpier now.

"Doesn't it? You said he would kill you."

"Not *literally*."

"Then in what way?"

"What do you mean?"

"How would he figuratively kill you?"

"I don't know. He'd just be terrible about it, I guess."

"But your fear is an indication of how bad it would be. How much he'd make you suffer just for not being home when he expects you to be."

"But just because I'm afraid of a thing doesn't mean I'm right to be. People are afraid of all kinds of things, and sometimes their fear is too much. Overblown. You know?"

He turned his head and looked right into her eyes, and she predictably averted her gaze.

"Is your fear of Stan overblown?"

For a few moments they only stared down at the flowing water. The sound of it tumbling over the rocks felt peaceful to him, but it was the only thing that did.

"No," she said. "Probably not."

"One of the problems you have to deal with, living with someone like that, is that they tend to gaslight you. Always making it your fault when they do something mean. Always making you feel like you don't really see what you see. And like you're wrong to feel what you feel. Feelings aren't really right or wrong. They just are what they are. You've been living with him so long. You know him better than anybody. If you think you have reason to be scared of him, you probably do. I would say you'd be better off believing your fear. Stop trying to argue with it."

"Speaking of mean," she said, her voice solid and strong, "that wasn't very nice. Making me think I'd be home late."

"I know. I'm sorry. It might have been the wrong thing to do. If I hurt you, I'm sorry. I guess I just wanted you to open your eyes and really see how bad you've got it. If it was a mistake, it was a well-intentioned one. I'm not excusing myself. I'm just saying it was not my intention to be mean."

They sat for a time, and she said nothing in reply. He felt as though he could almost hear her brain at work. Thinking. But she never shared those thoughts with him. And, really, why should she? They didn't know each other well, and he had just played a trick to scare her.

"Let's go back now," he said. "I don't want you to be in trouble for real."

They rose and descended the steep trail together, and picked their way across the stream, jumping stone to stone.

He noticed she glanced quickly upstream as they crossed, wincingly, as though expecting to see a wall of water. Of course, there was nothing there.

As they climbed the steep bank of trail on the other side, she volunteered a few words.

"I don't know what I'm supposed to do about it."

"I offered you an option for a place to stay," he said. "And there are almost always entry-level jobs where I work."

"You're saying you could get me a job?"

"I think I could. Within a few months, anyway, something would open up."

"But I don't know how to do anything."

"That's what 'entry level' means."

"Oh."

They walked in silence for what felt like a long time. Until the town appeared, sprawled out below them. They both stopped and took it in, as if seeing it with new eyes. Or, at least, it looked different to Elliot. As if it was something he'd never so much as imagined.

"Will you at least consider it?"

"I think so," she said. To his surprise. "I think I *will* consider it. In fact . . . I think I might be starting to consider it now."

# Chapter Nineteen

*Bounce, Bounce, Crash*

**Abby**

It was the puppies who noticed the hikers first.

Abby had trudged uphill to the cabin and let them out of the shed to play. Elliot was gone and Abby had no idea where he was. Her mom was gone and Abby had no ideas about that, either. So she more or less emptied her mind and watched the puppies play.

While she was watching them, a couple of them began looking uphill—the more alert ones, like Tippy and Queen. Abby looked where they were looking and saw the shapes of two people—two hikers—coming down the trail.

They were too far away to see them in any detail.

It was the first time Abby had ever seen anybody walking up here.

Queen tipped her head back and let loose a stream of barking that turned into something like a coyote howl. Tippy ran around behind Abby's heels and hid there. The rest of the puppies never stopped playing.

Then Queen dropped her head and fell silent. As though she was now satisfied by knowing who was there.

It was maybe two minutes later before Abby thought she knew who was there. And, even then, she wasn't sure. At least, not sure enough. And she decided she didn't dare hope. But she kept watching the two distant figures, and they kept looking more and more like Elliot and her mom.

Abby felt herself bouncing up and down on the toes of her sneakers as she watched. A minute later, when she recognized the blouse her mother had worn that day, the bouncing turned into little jumps. She was literally jumping up and down while watching them walk back down to the cabin. Otherwise it would simply have been more energy than her body and brain could contain.

"It worked!" she said out loud.

A few of the puppies turned their heads to see if she was talking to them. So she said it again, a few times, directly to the pups.

"It worked, it worked, it worked! I knew it would work! I knew they would like each other and now they do and it worked!"

Still the soles of her sneakers cleared the ground on about every other word.

———

When they had arrived in the yard of the cabin, as their ankles were swarmed by enthusiastic puppies, Abby noticed Elliot giving her a searching look.

"Why were you jumping up and down?" he asked.

"Because I'm happy."

Needless to say, she did not go on to explain what she was happy about.

"Well, that's nice," he said.

Abby looked at her mom's face, but her mom didn't look back. She didn't seem to notice. She seemed entirely lost in her own head, as though anything or anyone outside her own thoughts failed to register at all.

Abby struggled briefly with the idea that her mom looked a bit . . . troubled.

But, in her elation, Abby decided not that her mom didn't like Elliot but that she *did* like him and felt guilty about the fact that she did. So in that way she avoided letting it dampen her high spirits.

"I should give you a ride home," Elliot said. He was speaking to Abby's mom. Not to Abby. His voice sounded different. The way he spoke to her had changed. Now he spoke as though she were someone he knew well, or had known for a long time. Someone who shared confidences with him. It was not the voice one used to talk to a stranger. "You know. So you won't be late."

Abby's mom did not respond. She did not appear to have heard. He reached out and touched her shoulder, and she jumped a little.

Then he said it again.

"I should give you a ride home. So you won't be late."

"I'm not sure that's such a good idea," she said.

Abby knew why she said it, too. Her father would be home from work soon. It would not do to have the two men cross paths. Even thirteen-year-old Abby knew what was what on that score. She knew enough to understand.

"I'll just take you most of the way. I'll drop you on a part of the road where nobody's likely to see."

"Yeah," Abby's mom said, still seeming a little lost. "I guess that would be good."

"Can I get a ride back, too?" Abby asked. "I sure am tired of walking up and down that steep hill."

It was true and it wasn't true, all at the same time. Yes, she was tired of the long walk. Sure, a ride in Elliot's truck sounded like a nice luxury. But she hadn't spent much time with the puppies on this visit. Not as much as she would have liked. And she would have stayed longer, but for one factor: She wanted to talk to her mom alone, and as soon as possible. She couldn't wait to know if what she thought she saw with her eyes was real.

—

Elliot dropped them on the paved part of the road, about a tenth of a mile above their house. They trudged downhill together on the shoulder, walking on the left to face traffic. Just out of habit, apparently. There was no traffic.

Abby was plotting in her head how to ask. How to phrase a question so important and so big. She wanted desperately to know, but had a resistance to asking. Maybe because she wasn't sure how to ask correctly, but more likely because she was afraid of the answer. Afraid to have her bubble of elation violently burst if she was wrong.

"He's nice," Abby said. "Isn't he?"

They walked for a few beats. Abby began to question whether her mother had even heard.

She opened her mouth to say more, but her mother spoke just in that moment.

"Would you really be happier if we didn't live with your dad?"

"Much happier," Abby said. Without hesitation.

Her mom stopped on the shoulder of the road, so Abby stopped. They looked into each other's faces.

"You never told me that."

"No."

"Seems strange to be so sure of a thing like that—so sure that you answered without even thinking—when you never said it to me out loud before."

"Kind of a weird thing to say to your mom."

"I guess. We wouldn't have nearly as much money."

"You act like we have a lot now. But we don't."

"We have a lot now compared to how it might be for a while if we left. Are you up for living on not much at all? Is it worth it to you?"

"Yes," Abby said.

They walked again. Abby could see a furrow in her mom's brow, as if she were thinking so hard it hurt.

Abby took a deep breath and asked the big question.

"Are we *going* to live someplace without Dad?"

But her mother didn't answer. Not as they crossed the first intersection of a town street. Not when they reached their corner, and turned onto their own road.

Abby looked quickly to see if her father's truck was parked in the driveway. Then she breathed more freely when she saw that it wasn't.

While she was looking, her mom stopped again.

"Elliot offered us his guest room," her mom said.

"What guest room? He doesn't have a guest room. It's all one room."

"Not in the cabin. In his real house. In the city. You know. Until we could get on our feet and get our own place."

"Could I take my puppies?"

"Oh," her mom said. "That's a big question. Isn't it?"

"Yeah. I guess. So what's the answer?"

"I'm not sure. I'm guessing we could take them to Elliot's house, because he seems to like them. After that, I don't know. I'm not sure how you rent a place with seven dogs. Or . . . five, I guess. I guess he wants to adopt two. You might need to find homes for some of them. I don't really know how this would go, Abby. There are a lot of wild cards here. We'd be stepping into something entirely new. We'd be making it up as we go along."

Abby was aware of a great deal of action in her own belly and chest. Tightness and tingling. Butterflies. She ignored it all as best she could, and spoke.

"So . . . ," she began.

She was hoping her mom would answer without Abby having to ask more. But her mom seemed lost in her own head again. So they just stood there on their own street, not a hundred yards from their own house, saying and doing nothing.

"You going to take him up on it?" Abby asked.

To her surprise, her mom looked directly into her eyes. Abby looked back but found it impossible to read what she saw there on her mom's face. It looked like . . . everything. Like every thought and emotion at once.

"It's a very complicated proposition," her mom said at last. "And I really need to think it out. I think it would be best if we didn't talk about it again until I've had time to. Think it out, I mean. And another thing. I don't want to take any more chances like we just did. Talking in the house about things your father mustn't hear, and then looking up to see him standing right there listening in. So I think it's best if we just don't talk about it for a while."

"Okay," Abby said.

They walked on toward home.

Every other step or so, Abby had to work hard to stop that little bounce from coming into her step.

—

They came into the house through the back door, the kitchen door. It hadn't been locked.

"Stan?" her mom shouted. Loudly enough and suddenly enough that it made Abby jump.

"He's not home," Abby said. "His truck's not in the driveway."

Her mother paid Abby's comment no mind. Maybe she never even heard it. Or maybe she heard it without registering it.

Or maybe . . . just maybe, Abby thought, her mother knew damn well that his truck was not in the driveway and was worried that it was a trick. Maybe her mom didn't trust simple facts anymore when it came to Abby's father. Maybe the house had become a minefield even by the old normal standard that was Abby's family.

Abby watched her mom move off into the living room, still calling for Abby's dad.

"Stan?"

Then, curiously, Abby heard another call, but it was cut off in the middle of that one simple syllable.

"Sta—"

Abby wanted to follow her mom into the living room. See what her mom had seen that had stopped her in her tracks. Stopped a one-syllable word before it could even come out of her mouth.

Abby meant to do that. She was just about to do it.

Before she could, something caught her eye.

It was her father's cell phone, sitting on the kitchen table. It was lit up, its face showing what looked like a photo. It had not put itself into a sleep mode.

Abby walked a step closer. Cautiously. As if the kitchen linoleum might be mined.

Abby's dad was the only one in the family who had a cell phone, because he got some reception at his work, which was downhill from town. Barely enough to make a call that wouldn't drop, but he prided himself on owning it. He kept it close to him, in a shirt pocket, as though he wanted it near his heart.

He did not forget and leave it on the kitchen table.

She moved another step closer, watching the face of the phone, expecting it to suddenly lock itself. Either her father had been here just a minute or two ago, or he had changed the settings so it would never go to sleep. Either way, he had just left it there on the kitchen table, face up, displaying a photo.

Abby leaned in to look, and immediately felt a hot tingling all around her ears.

It was a photo of Elliot and Abby's mom. They were sitting outside Elliot's cabin in two white plastic chairs. Which meant the photo could only have been taken that day, because the chairs were new. Abby's mom was leaning slightly in Elliot's direction, her face hovering about halfway between their two chairs. They weren't touching each other in any way, and yet Abby almost felt as though they were. Somehow it was a photo of two people who trusted each other. Knew each other. Abby couldn't find the word she wanted in her head, but it was some kind of familiarity.

One of the puppies had been captured in the photo, too. It was Kite. Kite had untied the laces of her mom's shoe and was tugging on them. But Abby's mom didn't seem to notice. All of her attention was focused on Elliot.

And it had been captured, all of it, for all to see. On her father's phone.

"Uh-oh," Abby said. Out loud, but quietly. Then she turned her head toward the living room and called for her mom. "Mom?" No answer. She called louder. "Mom?" Still nothing. "*Mom!* Seriously! I think you need to come in here and see this!"

Silence. Stillness.

Abby broke her statue pose and hurried into the living room.

Her mom was standing in the middle of the room, just staring at the chaos all around her.

All the books had been taken out of the bookcases. Most lay scattered on the hardwood floor, which Abby had never seen, except at its very edges. It had always been covered with a nearly wall-to-wall Persian carpet, which was now inexplicably gone. Some books lay in tilted piles, some had seemingly been thrown down at random. Some had been arranged in cardboard cartons. The lamps were gone. All of them. The antique quilt that had belonged to her paternal grandmother was missing from the back of the couch. There were no pictures on the walls.

"Did we get robbed?" Abby asked her mom. "See? We leave the back door open. I know it's a small town but I'm always saying we shouldn't leave the back door open."

"I don't think we were robbed. Robbers don't usually bring packing cartons and take books."

"Well . . . what's happening, then?"

"I have no idea," her mom said.

"There's something in the kitchen I think you need to see."

Abby walked back toward the kitchen, thinking her mom would follow. But when she looked back over her shoulder, she saw that her mother hadn't moved. It struck Abby that they were probably both in a mild state of shock.

"Seriously, Mom. You need to see this."

Her mother glanced over her shoulder at Abby. As if Abby had wakened her out of a sound sleep. Then she turned and followed Abby into the kitchen.

Abby stayed back, hovering near the fridge, and let her mom approach the dangerous phone alone.

For the longest time, her mom just stared at it. Just watched it sit there on the table, as though expecting it to make a sudden move. It still hadn't put itself to sleep, so Abby assumed it never would. That her father had purposely instructed it never to sleep.

"Is this, like . . . ," Abby began. Then she wasn't sure if it was safe to go on. But in time she did. Because she felt as though she had to. Somebody had to say something. Somebody had to at least *try* to clarify what this was, this sudden moment swirling all around them. Abby decided she could be brave enough to try. ". . . a big problem?"

"Oh yeah," Abby's mom said. "Definitely a problem. Definitely big."

A thought poured into Abby's brain. A sort of sudden knowing.

"He's packing us up?" she asked her mom. "He's packing all our stuff because . . . you think he's going to make us *move* over this?"

Her mother never answered.

They both looked toward the living room in response to a series of sounds. First it was the turning of the lock on the front door—the dead bolt sliding open. Then it was the click of the latch on the door handle. Then the creak of the hinges as the front door opened and someone stepped inside.

There was only one someone it could have been.

The only thing Abby could remember thinking is that she had cut short her visit with the puppies. It had never occurred to her that it might be the last visit. But she had ducked out on spending time with them. And now she might never see them again.

# Chapter Twenty

*Unfaithful*

**Mary**

Mary held perfectly still and listened to the thump of his hard boot soles on the hardwood of the living room floor. The room seemed to echo in its emptiness.

She glanced nervously at her daughter, who glanced back. Neither said a word. Mary wondered first if Abby was breathing. Then next she wondered if *she* was.

It was a bizarrely disconnected thought, but an airline flight attendant in her head seemed to be saying, "Secure your own mask first, before helping others."

She gasped a huge breath.

Stan walked into the kitchen. He did not look at either Mary or his daughter. He did not seem upset. No, obviously he was upset, Mary thought. That went without saying, and it showed. What he didn't seem was explosive. Instead he looked weirdly calm. Eerily calm, as if disconnected from his family, or even from his life.

He held four cardboard packing cartons, two in each hand, his tightly gripping fingers white on their flaps.

He held the cartons out to each of them, Mary and Abby. But he never looked at either one of them. He kept his eyes trained down to the kitchen linoleum.

"When's the last time you waxed this floor?" he asked, apparently of Mary.

It struck her as so odd and out of place as to be unbalanced. As if he had literally lost his mind.

She opened her mouth to answer, but he cut her off.

"Never mind. Not important now. Somebody else's problem. Go fill up these boxes with anything you want to take. If it doesn't fit in the boxes, it doesn't go."

Mary could feel her heart pounding. She could hear it, too. It was so strong in her ears that it made it nearly impossible to listen to anything else.

She glanced over at her daughter again, who was attempting to catch her eye. Mary tried to read the message there in Abby's eyes. But she might not have read it correctly.

"I'm not moving," Mary said.

It felt and sounded as though someone else had said it. It sounded like words spoken by a real person, and Mary felt imaginary.

For one weirdly long beat, the world seemed to hold still.

Then Stan dropped the boxes and lunged at her. It was so sudden and violent that Mary heard a little sound escape her own throat. A miniature scream. He had his hands out, headed for her neck. She thought he was going to strangle her. Instead he grabbed her by the shirt and brought his face close to hers.

She could smell the stale odor of beer on his breath.

"We'll go!" Abby shouted.

The world stood still again.

"She didn't mean it," Abby said. "She doesn't know what she's saying. I'll talk to her. We'll go. Of course we'll go."

Stan dropped his hands to his sides and took one step backward. Mary breathed again. Too much, and too suddenly. It made her feel as though she might pass out.

"Your daughter's smarter than you are," he said.

Then he walked out of the room.

Mary and her daughter stood perfectly still and listened to his boots clattering on the living room hardwood again. Then they heard the front door slam behind him.

"What was that?" Mary said, a hiss under her breath. "Why did you say that?"

"This is not the time to stand up to him. I'll go get a neighbor. Or I'll call the sheriff. And we can tell him *in front* of somebody. It'll be safer that way."

For a moment Mary only stood there blinking, trying to settle her heartbeat.

"He's right," she said to her daughter.

"About what?"

"You *are* smarter than I am."

"Nah," Abby said. "You just freeze when you're scared. You go pack some stuff. I'll go over to one of the neighbors and call the sheriff."

"Not Effie Winger. Go to the Blakes on the other side."

Abby didn't ask why.

After her daughter left the house, Mary stood a moment, wondering why Abby so clearly knew something about Mary that Mary had barely acknowledged herself.

Then she made herself move.

She began plowing through the books scattered all over the living room floor, looking for the Emily Dickinson poetry book. She would have to hide it among the few books Stan had chosen to pack. She didn't dare keep it in her own boxes with her own things, because she knew Stan would now be searching all of her belongings regularly.

When she found it, in what appeared to be a discard pile near the door, she chose two other books of poetry to take along. She was afraid that rescuing only one book would draw too much attention to the book she had chosen.

She placed them at the very bottom of a carton that she figured Stan had meant to go along. It was all full of his World War II dramas.

Then she ran upstairs and checked for her stash in the sock at the back of her dresser drawer. The sock was there, but it was empty.

Mary was not surprised. In fact, she had assumed for several days that Stan's having found her stash made it fundamentally unsafe. So she had divided the money and hid the lion's share of it under the corner of her side of the mattress, hoping that if Stan ever found out, he would assume she had spent it on a gift for him. Or, at least, she figured she could claim that's where it went, and she hoped that claiming so might buy her a little time.

She retrieved the money and placed it in her shoe.

Then she set about packing, though she wasn't sure why. Maybe so they could keep up the charade until the sheriff arrived.

———

"I . . . ," Abby said, and then paused, ". . . just remembered something I forgot."

They had been sitting on the front porch swing, watching Stan load the back of his truck. Also waiting for the sheriff, but hopefully Stan had no idea they were doing that.

Unfortunately, now he seemed to be done loading and tying down all their belongings. Or, at least, everything they would own going forward.

He had been leaning on the truck, arms crossed. Tapping one booted foot and waiting.

Mary and Abby had run back into the house for tasks or items they pretended to have forgotten—twice each.

"What, *again*?" Stan bellowed.

It was too late. Abby had already jumped up and disappeared inside.

Stan crossed the dirt of the front yard and stepped up onto the porch. It made Mary's heart pound. It made the blood her heart was frantically circulating feel colder.

He leaned down until his face was level with hers, and very close. He seemed calm. His calmness did nothing to ease her fear.

"I never cheated on you," he said, his voice soft. It struck her that, at least in that moment, he was more wounded than angry. "I know you think I'm a bad husband and a bad person because I'm not what you might call a ray of sunshine around the house, but I put food on the table every day and I was faithful. I never so much as looked at another woman in a way that meant anything much."

She of course did not ask him to define "anything much."

He paused, and Mary had no idea which would be safer—to talk or to remain silent. And, in the process of deciding, she managed no words for an awkward length of time.

"You got nothing to say about that?"

"I never cheated on you, either," she said.

"Oh, but you did, Mary. You did and you know it. I know you're gonna say you didn't do anything physical with that man and I have no idea if that's the truth or not. Maybe it is. Let's just say it is, for the sake of conversation. But you were off spending time with him and keeping it secret from me, and you had feelings for him. Don't tell me you didn't, because I know. I saw it with my own eyes. I saw you looking at him the way you used to look at me, all those years ago when we were young—back when I was so young and stupid I thought you always would. But you haven't looked at me that way in as long as I can remember, and now I see that look in your eyes, but it's for some other guy. So that's not faithful, now, is it?"

Mary opened her mouth and tried to speak, but no sound came out. She had no idea what words to offer him anyway. Everything he had just said to her was true.

"Go ahead and tell me what you got on your mind about that," he said when he had clearly grown impatient with the waiting. He leaned in even closer, until their noses almost touched. She could smell cigarettes on his breath, even though he'd quit them twenty years before and she hadn't noticed him falling off the wagon before this. "I hope all this stalling around isn't about waiting for the sheriff," he said. "Because he's not coming."

At the corner of her eye, Mary saw Effie Winger step out into her front yard. Watched the older woman pretend to stare closely at her own roses. Mary knew Effie must have wanted to know what was going on, because who goes outside just to stare at their flowers?

She wondered if Effie had ratted her out to Stan. Or maybe Stan just kept closer tabs on her than she had realized.

Meanwhile Stan was still talking.

"Deputy saw my truck and stopped me while I was down in town getting gas and some more rope to tie everything down. Asked if everything was okay. I assured him it was. You don't know Eddie like I do. I used to go fishing with him."

Mary knew, of course, that Stan had used to fish with a local sheriff's deputy. She just hadn't realized that simple good fortune would run so deeply against her and her daughter that day. She assumed that the chances were awfully good someone else at the sheriff's office would catch the call.

"He doesn't like to get between a man and his wife," Stan said. "He figures these things are best worked out at home. Now come along and get in the truck so's we can go."

Mary glanced sideways at Effie Winger, and caught Effie sneaking a glance back. An older woman neighbor wasn't much in the way of safety, Mary thought, but it would simply have to do.

"I'm not going," she said.

Then she winced, waiting to see what he would do. Or, more likely, waiting to feel it.

Just in that moment Abby burst out the front door and onto the porch.

Much to Mary's surprise, when Stan's hand lashed out, it wasn't Mary he was looking to grab. He took hold of Abby by the back of her shirt and marched her along to the truck.

Mary watched helplessly as he lifted up on the back of her daughter's shirt just below the collar, causing her to have to walk on her tiptoes, her upper arms raised like a marionette, forearms dangling in a way that might have seemed comical in less dire circumstances.

He opened the little half door to the extra-cab truck's back seat. Then he pushed Abby inside.

Abby tried to slither right back out the other side, but Stan grabbed her again, this time by the waistband of her jeans, and thumped her back down onto the seat, where he buckled the seat belt across her.

Still holding one of her upper arms, he turned back to Mary.

"Your daughter's going," he called up onto the porch. "And I'm just assuming you want to see her again, like . . . you know . . . ever."

Mary turned her head to Effie Winger's yard, but her neighbor had gone back inside.

She rose to her feet and walked to the truck.

She got in with no more resistance and no further words spoken.

———

They drove for thirty or forty miles in absolute silence. It was heavy dusk now, and Mary had no idea where they were being taken.

Now and then she caught Abby's eyes in the rearview mirror. Every time she looked, it seemed her daughter was looking back.

When Stan spoke up without warning, it startled them both.

"Can't wait to see what you got me for my birthday," he said.

Mary sat frozen, watching the headlights of approaching cars, wondering if that had been a serious statement on his part.

She said nothing in reply.

Did he really believe that all of this would end with a nice birthday celebration for him? Did he think he could practically kidnap them against their will and then go back to being some kind of happy family?

It seemed nearly insane to think so.

Then again, it might have been a warning. It might have been his way of letting her know that he had noticed how much of the money was gone. That he would be watching her to see where she had hidden it and what she planned to do with it now.

She could feel the lump of it under her right heel.

She went back and forth about which way he might have meant it. She even tried to catch Abby's eye again in the mirror, but by then it was too dark to see much.

She never asked him to clarify the comment, and she never offered anything in the way of an answer.

———

"I have to go to the bathroom," Mary said suddenly.

They were on that long stretch of two-lane highway, headed into the city, and the gas stations were few and far between. But down the hill, in the dark, she could see the lights of that great big new station. It was a really nice one like the kind they have in good neighborhoods in the suburbs, and she wanted to stop.

She did not really need to use the restroom. It was more of a need to regroup. And if she was extra fortunate she might get a chance to talk to her daughter alone. Away from Stan's prying attention.

"Wasn't that one of your *many* last-minute trips back into the house just a few minutes ago?"

Mary thought they had been driving for more like an hour. Also it was Abby who had gone back inside to use the bathroom. Mary didn't say so. She didn't correct him on either mistake.

"I drank a lot of soda today," she said.

She glanced over at his face, lit up by the headlights of an oncoming car, and realized she had made a mistake. She watched his forehead furrow. Enough to be troubling.

Stan didn't buy soda for the house, or allow Mary to buy it. He thought soda was only a waste of his hard-earned money. He always said you could just drink water, because water was close enough to free. Every now and then Mary drank instant iced tea with a little bit of sugar as a ridiculous luxury.

"Soda? Where the hell would you be getting—"

But he stopped himself and did not finish.

The gas station came up on their right, and Stan swung the steering wheel too hard, veering wildly into its parking lot.

"Never mind," he said. "I don't even want to know."

He screeched to a halt in one of the parking spots in front of the convenience store. Other than a barely grown-looking boy inside, behind the cash register, the place appeared deserted.

"Make it quick," Stan said.

Mary unbuckled her seat belt and turned around to look into her daughter's face. The convenience store was lit up like daylight, and the lights shone through its big glass windows and illuminated her daughter's face. Abby looked maybe a little scared but mostly sad.

"Come with me and use the bathroom," Mary said. "Because your father won't want to stop again."

"Now how're both of you supposed to use the ladies' room at the same time?" Stan bellowed.

"This is one of those big new ones. Two stalls inside an outer door."

Mary had never been in this gas station restroom before, and she had no idea if that would turn out to be the case.

"Whatever," Stan said. "Just remember I'm sitting right here watching."

Mary stepped out into the barely cool night. She slipped her arm around her daughter, and they swung the door of the store wide, setting off an electronic bell. Mary expected the young employee to tell them the restroom was for customers only, in which case she would need to buy a pack of gum or something. But he never bothered to look up.

Abby pulled open the door of the ladies' room. It had three separate stalls, none in use.

"Did you know that?" Abby asked quietly.

"Nope. Just trying to get where we can talk."

They stepped into separate stalls, and Mary really did take the opportunity to relieve herself. Because it was true that Stan might not stop again if she asked.

"I'm worried about my puppies," Abby said through the partition.

"I know you are, honey."

"What'll Elliot think when I don't come back to tend 'em?"

Mary wasn't sure how to answer that question, so a silence fell.

"You know . . . ," Abby began, ". . . we don't have to get back in that truck. We could just ask that clerk guy to call the cops for us. We could just stand with him till they come."

"A couple of problems with that," Mary said. "First off, he'll drive away with everything we own. We won't even have a change of clothes or a toothbrush. But there's one thing on the back of that truck that's more important even than that. It's Elliot's business card, with his address and phone number in the city. Unless you know where to reach him."

"Not in the city," Abby said.

They both just sat, even though they had no further need of the toilet. Neither got up, or flushed, or put their clothes back together, or stepped out to wash their hands.

"Do you know his last name?" Mary asked.

"No. I don't think he ever told me. Or if he did it was way back at the beginning when I first met him and I didn't even know how much it mattered. And if it happened like that, well, I don't remember it now. Why didn't you put that card in your pocket or in your purse or something?"

"Because I figure your dad will be going through my pockets and my purse from now on. I have it hidden in a book he'd never want to open. And it's a book from the thrift store, so I figured if he ever did find it I could just say the old owner of the book had it in there as a bookmark."

"Oh," Abby said. "That's smart."

"It was Viv's idea," Mary said, feeling shame over having to admit she hadn't thought of it herself. "I wanted to open the book and memorize the address and phone number before we left, but I kept thinking your father was just about to walk through the door. I wanted to get it into the box with his books as fast as possible because I knew if he saw me he wouldn't let me take it. Now I'm wondering why I didn't memorize it days ago."

"You didn't know," Abby said.

Mary felt a flood of gratitude for that simple statement. Here she was kicking herself for doing everything wrong, and Abby was being gentle and making it clear she held nothing against her mother. It almost made Mary want to cry, but probably the tears had been hovering close to the surface anyway.

She heard Abby stand up and flush, so she did the same. They stepped out of the stalls and looked at each other in the bright fluorescent light.

There was only one sink.

"You go first," Mary said.

"You know," Abby said as she soaped up her wet hands, "I don't know why we even need his address and phone number in the city. We know where he is right now. He's at the cabin."

The water turned itself off, and Abby reached for a paper towel, but the dispenser was empty. So she just stood there, hands dripping awkwardly at her sides, while Mary stepped up to the sink.

"I don't want to go find him at the cabin," Mary said, "because your father would know exactly where we'd gone, and he'd come after us. And it would be putting Elliot in danger. And I don't want to do that. I'd never forgive myself if something violent happened. And I know you don't want that, either."

"No," Abby said, seeming even more down now. "Of course not."

"If we wait and leave while your dad is out of the house in the next couple of days . . ." Mary instinctively lowered her voice to a whisper. In case Stan was standing right outside the door trying to guard. Or listen: "If we can catch up with Elliot in the city, there's no way your dad will know where we are. It'll be safer that way."

"But my puppies. What'll Elliot think if I don't come back for 'em?"

"Tell you what. As soon as I can make a phone call without your dad hearing, I'll call Viv and ask her to go up there and tell him what's what. Explain to him what happened."

She heard her daughter breathe more deeply. It was a welcome sound.

"Now come on," Mary said. "Let's get back out to the truck before he gets upset."

# Chapter Twenty-One

*Perfect Things*

**Abby**

Abby opened her eyes and blinked into the light. She stretched her lower back as best she could. It was stiff from trying to sleep sitting up. She looked up and found herself staring at the back of her father's head.

It was morning, and they were still driving.

Her mom was asleep in the passenger seat of the truck, her head dropped back. Mouth wide open, snoring lightly. It comforted Abby, hearing that steady presence of her mother. Just being able to hear that her mom was there. Not that she couldn't see her mom, sitting right there. But somehow the comforting sound of her meant more in that difficult moment.

She saw her father raise and angle his head to look at Abby in the rearview mirror. They briefly caught each other's eyes. Then he looked away. *He* looked away. Abby thought that was interesting. She was prepared to challenge him by holding his gaze, but he backed down.

"Where're we going?" she asked quietly.

But she figured she knew.

An image of her gang of puppies filled her mind, and she was stunned by how much she missed them. She felt bowled down and absolutely overwhelmed by the profound loss of the opportunity to simply trot up the hill and say good morning to the litter.

"We'll stay with your uncle Merle for a bit," he said.

It was just what Abby had expected him to say.

Meanwhile her father seemed to be waiting for something from her. Abby had no idea what. But whatever it was, he clearly wasn't getting it.

"You like your uncle Merle," he said. Another pause. "Don't you?"

"No."

"You never told me that before."

"You never asked me."

They drove in silence for a time.

Abby knew they were already in Oregon, because she had been to Uncle Merle and Aunt Judy's before. She recognized that they were near Klamath Falls, on the section of highway with that big, long lake on the left side of the truck. On the left, that is, if you were unlucky enough to be driving north. *Toward* Merle and Judy, not away from them and on your way home.

Then Abby looked up to see him watching her again in the rearview mirror. He was examining her more closely now, as if trying to decide something about her. His forehead was furrowed down.

"You gonna grow up to be like your mother?" he asked her.

His voice was full of that signature scorn. Though it wasn't a word she would have used herself—she struggled for the right word, but all she could come up with was "disrespect"—she recognized that everything he saw seemed to deserve that scorn in his eyes. He poured it over everything like dessert topping. At least, that was the image that came into her head.

Abby didn't feel afraid of him in that moment, because she was seeing him more clearly now, and he only seemed sad to her.

"I hope so," she said.

"I didn't mean it like a good thing."

"I know exactly how you meant it," she said, feeling stronger by the word. "And I still hope I do. You shouldn't blame what happened on her at all. You should blame it on me. I'm the one who introduced her to him anyway."

As she spoke, Abby thought about the birds in the foothills who nested in the earth. If the momma bird saw or heard you coming, she'd dart out into the open, fly right at you, then try to draw you away. Anything to protect her babies. Except Abby was an offspring protecting her mother. She knew her father always wanted to take everything out on her mother and never bothered to take anything out on Abby. It was as though he didn't even care enough about his daughter to get mad.

Also, if he lashed out at her now, even physically, she didn't care.

"Why would you do a thing like that?" he asked, still holding her eyes in the mirror.

Abby thought it was high time he looked back at the road.

"Because she's not happy. And neither am I."

For a time Abby watched him moving his jaw on one side—the only side of him she could see. She thought maybe he was grinding his molars with tension. But it turned out he was chewing on a toothpick. She saw him shift it over to a spot where she could see it bouncing with every chew.

"You saying you'd be better off if I wasn't your father?"

"I'm not even going to say what I think about that, because you don't really want to know. It's not like you're asking because you really want to change. Like, if you wanted to be a better person, so you wanted to know what I thought about you, I would tell you. But you don't."

"You got no idea what I want," he said. Once again, he let her down by not even caring enough to raise his voice at her. "You think you can see what somebody wants just by seeing what they do?"

"Pretty much, yeah."

"Well, that's a very immature viewpoint, little girl. The world is not a place where everybody gets to run around doing only what they want."

"Maybe not," she said. "But if somebody says they want to do something, but then they never do? I'm going to figure they don't want it bad enough. Know what I mean?"

Abby heard her father sigh. He returned his eyes fully to the road at last.

"You *are* gonna grow up to be like your mom."

"Thank you," Abby said.

He didn't reply. In fact, he didn't say another word to her for many miles, which felt like a blessing.

Then, just out of nowhere, he did.

"Know what your problem is?" he asked.

Abby noticed that her mom was no longer snoring lightly, and wondered if that meant she was awake and listening. If so, she did nothing to let on. *Probably smart,* Abby thought.

"No," Abby said. "I *don't* know. What's my problem?"

"You're too young to know that nothing's ever perfect, and that you're better off not even expecting it to be. You can't see how you just take your best shot when you choose what you want in this life, but then later you get a better look at what you got and it's never quite what you thought it would be. You want this perfect family, but it doesn't exist. In fact, I dare you to name one thing in this life that's perfect."

Abby's brain filled with an image. She could see it so clearly behind her eyes, even though they were open. For a moment she closed her eyes to see it more clearly.

It was a memory from the time she took the puppies into the county shelter. They were sitting in a box on the counter, and Abby was railing at the shelter lady about the unfairness of anybody wanting to kill them. The man who threw them into the river, sure, but also the county. Because they were perfect. "These perfect little living things," she remembered saying. She could see their round, shiny, miniature eyes. Watching. Seeming to know somehow that their fate hung in the balance. She could see their pudgy sides puff in and out with their breath. Their floppy ears bounce with the slightest movement.

"I could name you seven," she said, out loud. She said it loudly enough for her dad to hear it, but in a very real way she was only talking to herself.

"Go right ahead," he said.

"Nah. You wouldn't understand."

Even if she could have trusted him with the information about the puppies, he would only point to the fact that they made messes, and chewed things. And needed to be trained. And got hurt and required vet bills. And yes, there was that side of the thing, and Abby knew it. Life with them was not always perfect. But *they* were. The pure essence of their existence in the world was perfect. But her father only saw messes. He had no eyes for the pure essence of anything. Without being able to put it into words, and certainly not those words, Abby had always known this about him.

She wondered for at least the twentieth time what would happen to the puppies while she was gone. How long Elliot would take care of them without knowing where she was or whether she would ever make it back to claim them.

Her father did not speak again on the drive, which was just as well.

———

Aunt Judy showed Abby to her room, which was, unfortunately, the basement. There was only one guest room upstairs, and it would be for her parents.

"There's no bed," Abby said.

Technically there was no anything. It was, after all, a basement. There was an old furnace, and a washer and dryer. A clothesline that

Aunt Judy must've used to hang laundry. Why anybody would hang laundry in a dank basement when they could hang it outside in the sun and the breeze, Abby had no idea.

In the past, when they had visited, there had been a second guest room. Small, but Abby had liked it. It had been the only thing about the visits she did like. But Uncle Merle had made it into a weight room, and he wasn't about to change it back on Abby's account.

"We got a cot," Aunt Judy said. In that loud, terrible voice. It had a discordant twang to it, Judy's voice. It didn't actually sound like fingernails on a blackboard. You wouldn't mistake the two, Abby thought. But it affected her much the same way. "Soon as the football game's over he'll haul it down. Now go on out to your dad's truck and get your belongings. Bring it all down here."

"And put it where?" Abby asked.

There was plenty of space. That wasn't the problem. The point of the question was to draw attention to the fact that there was no dresser. Nothing with drawers. No place to hang anything up. Not even a hook for a jacket.

"Anyplace you like," Aunt Judy said. She was already halfway back up the stairs to the kitchen when she said it.

Abby winced when her aunt slammed the kitchen door. Not slammed it in anger, as far as Abby could tell. Aunt Judy just did everything at maximum volume and with the most drama possible.

Abby sighed and trudged up the stairs. Uncle Merle's football game was blaring at easily twice the volume she figured anyone needed to hear it.

She was halfway through the living room, on her way to her dad's truck, when Uncle Merle spoke to her. Which, as an event, was blessedly rare.

"Be a good girl," he said, shouting to be heard over the game. "Go fetch me another beer."

Abby stopped and stood a moment, watching her uncle watch the game. He had never once looked at her. That is, not this visit. Not when she came in the door. Not when he asked her to put her own tasks on hold to wait on him.

"Yeah," she muttered under her breath. "Sure. It's not like I have anything better to do, like try to make a room I can live in out of your old smelly basement. Sure, I can take a break from unpacking the two boxes of stuff that's everything I own now. No. Problem. At. All."

Her uncle never seemed to hear or notice.

Abby sighed and walked back into the kitchen.

Aunt Judy was nowhere around, and Abby had no idea where her mother had gone. But her father was sitting at the kitchen table staring out the window as if he had heavy and important thoughts to consider. He seemed to be watching a squirrel running up and down the trunk of the neighbor's tree. He was definitely staring in its direction.

"Don't you have some unpacking to do?" she asked him.

He didn't answer, or look in her direction. If he even knew she was in the room and speaking, he didn't let on.

Abby sighed again and pulled a beer out of the fridge.

As she crossed the kitchen with the cold bottle in her hand, he seemed to awaken.

"Ho, ho, whoa," he said, and grabbed her by the wrist. "You don't get to take a beer."

"I'm not *taking* it. I'm taking it to Uncle Merle. He *asked* me for it."

"So you say."

Something snapped in Abby at that moment.

"Fine," she said, "*you* give it to him. I'm not his waitress anyway."

She slid the bottle hard across the table. Too hard. It slid right off the other side and fell to the kitchen linoleum, where it shattered. Beer foamed across the floor, floating shards of brown glass as it spread. And Abby was not done being mad.

"Why do we have to be here, anyway? Why do we have to go where *you* say we have to go? Who would want to be *here*? We had a whole *life* back at home. This totally sucks and it's so unfair and I hate it!"

He let go of her wrist, but offered no other reaction. She expected him to counter her anger. To see her outburst and raise it with his own unparalleled rage. But once again she failed to evoke any caring in him, positive or otherwise.

They both looked up to see Abby's mother standing in the kitchen doorway. Abby thought her mom's face looked white and drained, as though she'd just witnessed an act of violence or experienced some sort of fright.

"You hear the way your daughter talks to me?" her father asked.

"*Our* daughter," she said. She clearly had something on her mind and resented the distraction.

"No, when she's running her mouth like this, she's all yours. Especially since it's your fault how she does this. You been too permissive with her. You know what would've happened to me if I'd talked to my daddy that way?"

*Of course we know,* Abby thought. And almost said. *You've only told us, like, a zillion times.*

"That's not important now," Abby's mom said.

"It is to me."

"Listen to me!" Mary screamed. Screamed. Abby had never seen her lose her temper that way.

Her father raised his eyebrows but nothing more.

"Where are my poetry books? I put them in the box with your books."

"And I took 'em out again. I told you. Two cartons each. Anything that doesn't fit doesn't go."

"But there was room in those boxes. I loved those poetry books. Why did you do that, Stan? Why?"

Abby stood very still and stared at her mother's face. It looked as though she might be about to cry. At the very least, as though it would be a relief to let some tears out. But Abby figured she wouldn't want to give Stan the satisfaction.

"Because all our stuff has to fit into less room here," he said, "in case you hadn't noticed. So we're only keeping what we need. And nobody needs poetry books."

"Wrong," Abby's mother said, and in that moment she lost her battle with the tears. "I needed them."

She swiped a tear away with the back of her hand, as if angry at it. Then she stormed upstairs.

Abby stood a minute, staring after her. In her mind and heart she was trying to understand her mother's upset. Of course she understood why her mom would be unhappy. Who wouldn't be, in the middle of this miserable turn of events? Abby just wasn't sure how it had all gotten to be about a couple of books.

Maybe they had sentimental value, Abby thought. Or maybe just losing one or two things she really liked had somehow served as a lit fuse into all the other losses. It must have just hit her at a time when she was feeling vulnerable and emotional.

And then Abby remembered.

*I have it hidden in a book he'd never want to open.*

That's what her mother had said to her in that gas station restroom. They didn't know Elliot's last name. Her mother hadn't memorized the card. She had told Abby she'd hidden it in a book her father would never want to open. But now that book had been left behind.

"Oh no," Abby said out loud.

"Oh no what?" her father asked.

"Nothing," Abby said, and ran after her mother.

"Hey! You get back here and clean up that spilt beer, little girl!"

"No!" Abby called over her shoulder.

She brushed past her uncle leaning in the kitchen doorway. His football game had gone to commercial. Abby could hear it blaring.

"You let her talk to you like that?" he asked Abby's father.

Abby didn't wait around to hear the answer. She ran up the stairs two at a time and found her mother in the guest bedroom, facedown on the bed and crying.

Abby sat on the edge of the bed and put her hand on her mom's shoulder. But she didn't say anything for a few beats. Then she decided she'd better hurry up and say what she wanted to say in case her father was coming up to finish their conversation.

"It's okay," Abby whispered. "You can just call Viv. And when she goes up there to tell him what's going on, she can tell him we don't have his address anymore. And he can write it down for her or something."

As she spoke, she watched the top of the stairs through the open bedroom door, so she would know if her father was coming.

"I've been trying to get near the phone ever since we got here," Abby's mom said. "And Judy's always right there. I think Stan told her to keep an eye on me."

"Oh, I don't know," Abby said. "You don't really need to *tell* Aunt Judy to be terrible. She just kind of does it on her own."

To Abby's surprise, her mom laughed out loud. It made Abby smile to hear it.

"It's going to be okay," Abby said. "Just write Viv's number down for me. I'll figure something out."

———

When Abby moved to the living room door, Viv's phone number and a five-dollar bill in her pocket, she expected to leave the house unnoticed.

It didn't pan out that way at all.

"And where are *you* going?" her uncle asked, muting the volume on the TV. The silence felt absolutely stunning.

"Just out for a walk," Abby said.

"Nope."

"What do you mean, nope?"

"You don't know what the word 'nope' means?"

"I don't even get to take a walk?"

"Your daddy told me to keep an eye on you."

Abby had no idea where her father was. And she didn't care to ask.

Without thinking it out too clearly, Abby opened the front door and made a run for it, leaving the door yawning open behind her. Maybe Merle would consider it too much trouble to try to outrun her. Maybe he wouldn't want to miss his stupid game.

Or maybe, just maybe, she was faster.

She dashed across the street at an angle and scrambled over a neighbor's chain-link fence. She looked over her shoulder before crossing their yard. Uncle Merle was standing in the open doorway, looking to see which way she had gone. But he wasn't running after her.

Abby cut across the yard and climbed the fence on the rear side.

She heard somebody yell "Hey!" but she didn't stop.

She came out on the avenue side and sprinted down to the convenience store where she had used to buy ice cream sandwiches on previous visits.

There was still a pay phone out front.

Abby ran inside and up to the counter, where an older man sat on a stool looking bored.

"I need change," she said, and pushed the five-dollar bill across the counter to him.

"Then buy something," he said.

Abby sighed and grabbed the first candy bar her hand touched. She set it on the counter next to the money.

"All coins," she said. "No bills."

She waited. But the old man moved with infuriating slowness, counting out quarters onto the counter.

She grabbed them up, stuck the candy bar in her jeans pocket, and ran outside to the phone. She dialed Viv's number and then pumped in the amount of money the robotic voice told her to insert.

She heard the line ringing. And ringing. And ringing.

Finally Abby heard the click of the call being picked up.

"You have reached the voice mailbox for . . ." Abby's heart fell. A pause. Then Viv's voice, a contrast to the generic recorded message. "Vivian Sprague." Then another pause.

Abby waited through a silence that seemed to last forever. She thought she was waiting to be told it was time to leave a message. But how often did Viv pick up her messages? Abby knew it would kill her to wait and not know. Viv wouldn't even be able to call Abby back so Abby would know she'd gotten the message.

The recorded robotic voice came back, startling Abby out of her thoughts.

"We're sorry. Your party's voice message mailbox is full. Please try your call again later."

Another click.

Abby stood, just waiting. For what, she had no idea. But there was only silence on the line. The call had ended.

She hung up the receiver, hoping her money would come rolling back down into the slot. But apparently that had been Abby's call, and she had paid for it. Voicemail had picked up, and she would receive no refund. Abby dug the last of the change out of her pocket, already knowing it wasn't enough. If it had been enough, she could have hidden behind the store for a while, then called again to try to catch Viv at home. She knew she had spent too much of her money on the first call, but she counted it anyway. As if expecting a miracle.

No miracle occurred.

Abby sighed, and began the walk back to her aunt and uncle's house.

She briefly considered trying to panhandle for more money, but there was no one on the street. People drove in this neighborhood. No one much walked it.

Besides, it would be less of a waste of money to call *much* later. After everybody had gone to bed. Surely Viv would be home by a normal bedtime. And her mom would have more money to give her. Or, even if she didn't, Abby could dip into her own stash.

She turned a corner and immediately saw her father, driving slowly in his truck, clearly out looking for her. She briefly thought about vaulting another fence, but she couldn't imagine what she would gain by it. She was going back to the house anyway. She would see him there soon enough. She might as well take the ride.

He swung a U-turn, pulled level with her, and leaned across the seat, throwing his passenger-side door open.

"Get in," he said.

Abby got in.

"What the hell was that all about?" he asked as he gunned the engine in the direction of "home."

It pained Abby to use that word for it, even in the silence of her own head.

"I just wanted to go out for a walk. Get a candy bar." She pulled the candy bar out of her pocket and held it up where he could see it if he cared enough to turn his head. He never turned his head. "Why can't I do that? What's so bad about it? What am I, a prisoner?"

"I don't trust either one of you," he said.

Abby lost her temper again.

"Well, why didn't you just go away and leave us, then?" she shouted. "Why did you have to haul us with you if you don't even trust us? Why don't you just move away without us and leave us alone?"

As she listened to herself shouting, Abby was vaguely aware that she was purposely trying to draw a reaction from him. It infuriated her that he didn't even care about her enough to get mad.

"You'd like that," he said. "Wouldn't you?"

*So that's the real answer?* Abby thought. *We have to go with you just because you know we don't want to? Because you couldn't bear to do anything you thought we might like?*

She almost expressed those thoughts out loud. But she was tired and discouraged and nothing seemed to do any good, so she remained silent for the rest of the short ride back.

———

At a little after 11:00 p.m., Abby slipped out of her cot in the basement. She had been under the covers fully dressed. She had Viv's phone number in her pocket, along with all the change her mom had gathered.

But maybe she wouldn't even need the money, Abby thought. Maybe everybody would be asleep and she could use her aunt and uncle's phone, and they would never know. Until the bill came in. But Abby and her mother would be gone by then—with any luck, at least.

She crept up the stairs and turned the knob on the door to the kitchen.

It was locked.

"What the . . . ," Abby said out loud. "What if I had to go to the bathroom?"

And then, realizing she could not go to the bathroom if she needed to, she began to feel that she needed to.

She pounded on the door as hard and as loudly as she could.

"Hey!" she shouted at the top of her lungs.

She waited. Pounded. Shouted.

Waited. Pounded. Shouted.

Finally she heard her aunt's terrible voice.

"What?" it said on the other side of the door. "People are trying to sleep!"

"Why am I locked in here? I have to go to the bathroom."

Silence. No reply.

Abby stood in silence for a moment, not knowing if her aunt was even on the other side of the door. A minute might have passed. Or, if not that long, something close to it.

Then the door opened about a third of the way and her aunt thrust a pot into Abby's arms. An old cooking pot like the kind you might use to make a big batch of soup.

Before Abby could even react, the door slammed shut again. Abby heard the dead bolt click into place.

She sighed deeply, feeling her hopes and plans sink out of her, leaving . . . well, she wasn't even sure what. Not much, from the feel of it.

"Remind me never to eat the soup in this house," she said out loud to herself as she tramped back down the stairs.

She did not use the pot. She decided to hold her bladder all night if possible.

She went to bed in the uncomfortable cot, but did not sleep much.

# Chapter Twenty-Two

## Seven Complications

### Elliot

Elliot woke in the morning, laced his fingers behind his head, and remembered that Pat was gone. He stared up at the ceiling for a time. It was light, but probably early, and he felt no strong motivation to get out of bed.

Then he remembered that Abby hadn't shown up even once the previous day.

He jumped up, pulling on jeans over his boxer shorts. Grabbing a sweater out of the tiny closet.

He threw the door open wide, still barefoot, and looked out. He fully expected to see her. He'd had no doubt she would show up that morning, full of apologies and sheepish excuses for what had kept her away the day before.

There was no one there.

He stood in the doorway for a time, enjoying the coolness of the mountain air. Experiencing the feel of a very early summer morning. But behind and underneath that pleasant sensation, he was troubled by this turn of events. Perhaps most troubling was the sense that he didn't know whether to be angry or worried.

He thought of coffee, but decided to let the puppies out first.

He walked to the shed, still barefoot, and they began to yip and whimper at the sound of his approach.

Elliot threw the door wide and they came rolling out, jumping on him and each other. Only Tippy stayed back, sitting crookedly in a corner of the shed as if happy to spend a little time on her own.

The smell of their urine and feces was nearly overwhelming. And they had shredded the papers, which would make the shed harder to clean. Also Elliot noticed that Patches had managed to shred the little rubber cover for his bandage. Either that or one of the other pups had shredded it for him. The bandage was half off, a flag of it trailing as he ran. Patches would need to go to the vet today and get his paw rebandaged.

And none of this was supposed to be Elliot's job.

Tippy came to the door, swinging her tail at him. Elliot picked her up and held her. Then he lay down on his back in the cool dirt, and set her on his chest. She curled up as though to go back to sleep, but she kept her eyes open and watched his face.

"Which should I do first?" he asked her. "Coffee? Or that terrible cleaning job? Never mind. I already know. I should have coffee and leave the shed just the way it is because Abby might come trotting up the hill at any minute, and then *she* can do the shed. Until I have to put you back in there, it's not a problem. But if she's not back by then . . ."

Elliot frowned. Amazingly, Tippy noticed, and lifted her head as if deciding whether to leave. To get out of the way of his bad mood.

"No, stay," he said, and stroked her ears. "It's okay."

The pup settled again.

"I'm just trying to decide if Abby would do a thing like this out of carelessness. She didn't seem like the type. She seemed so devoted to you. Then again, parents are always getting puppies for kids after the kids swear on a stack of Bibles that they'll be the ones to take care of them. And then the parents end up taking care of them. I mean, that's been playing out since the beginning of time, right?"

Tippy lifted her head and tilted it slightly. As if paying attention to the question in case Elliot really demanded an answer.

"Then there's the even worse idea," Elliot said, and the puppy's ears fell more closely against her head. "What if she's not coming because she can't come? What if her mother really did go home and tell her father they were leaving him? And then . . . well, I don't even know what. I don't even know what to picture, but they could be in too much trouble for either one of them to get away. They could even . . ."

They both lay still for a moment. Elliot turned his head to watch the six puppies playing. Tippy seemed to be watching, too, but she did not seem inclined to join them.

"You're different from the rest of them," he said, "aren't you? You don't seem very happy as part of a thundering herd."

They watched in silence for a few moments longer.

"Well," he said. "I'll drink some coffee and have some breakfast. And then if she's still not here, I might have to go down there and see if I can see what's going on."

———

He almost left the puppies in the shed, but to do so in good conscience he would have had to clean it. And he still very much wanted Abby to be the one to clean it.

Besides, he had to stop by the vet with Patches.

So he loaded all seven of them into the bed of his pickup. Then he purposely stepped into the cabin for several minutes to make sure they couldn't jump out, even if highly motivated to do so.

Once he was satisfied that they were still too small to scramble out, he drove carefully down the hill.

He parked a hundred yards or so above Mary and Abby's street, purposely choosing a spot in the shade. Then he walked downhill and turned the corner toward their house, his head roiling with thoughts.

He should have waited till later, Elliot thought, when Mary's husband would be at work. So he didn't get them in trouble. But would he even know who Elliot was on sight? And besides, maybe the time of avoiding trouble was over.

Mary's very yellow car sat parked in the driveway, which Elliot found irritating. If she was home, and everything was normal, why was he on his own with seven puppies, and why was nobody telling him what was going on?

As he walked closer to the car, Elliot saw that a handmade **FOR SALE** sign had been taped to the back window, facing the street. It had no phone number on it, which seemed odd. Was someone supposed to just knock on the door if they wanted to buy it?

It struck Elliot as a good break. He could walk right up onto the porch and knock, and if the dreaded husband answered, he could inquire about the car.

He stepped up onto the porch, which sagged slightly under his weight.

Through the front window he could see disarray in the living room. The bookshelves lay completely empty. Surely they hadn't always been. But Elliot had never looked into the house before, so it was hard to know. The matching throw pillows that seemed to go with the couch lay scattered on the floor, and the couch cushions themselves were piled at a wild angle, as though someone had been searching for something underneath them.

And there were cardboard cartons stacked in the corner. As though someone had been packing to move.

Elliot rapped hard on the door.

He waited, but saw and heard no movement inside.

A big voice startled him, but it didn't come from inside the house. Someone was standing behind him. An older woman, from the sound of it.

"They're gone," the voice said.

Elliot turned to stare at the woman. She was wearing a bathrobe and pink fuzzy slippers, and her hair had been put up in huge wide curlers. Elliot figured she must be a neighbor, because he couldn't imagine that anyone would go very far from home dressed like that.

"Where did they go?" he asked her.

"I wouldn't know."

Her voice sounded tight, and almost . . . Elliot couldn't quite put his finger on it. But it felt as though she disapproved of him, or had already decided she didn't like him. Which seemed odd. *Based on what?* he wondered. He couldn't imagine.

"They just left all at once like that? Yesterday? Or day before yesterday afternoon?"

"Well, you seem to know a good bit about it," she said. Almost . . . suspiciously.

"I know nothing about it." Only that he had seen them the day before yesterday afternoon. "Why would they leave so fast?"

Elliot had other questions on his mind. How long had they lived in this house? How many years of their life here had they just abandoned? Was it really because of Elliot? And why did they go with that terrible man? Did they just consent: "Yes, we'll drop everything and accompany you"? Which for Abby meant dumping her seven puppies on Elliot? Or had they somehow been given no real choice in the matter?

"*You* tell *me*," the neighbor said.

So it wasn't Elliot's imagination. She really didn't like him.

"I know nothing about it," he said for the second time.

She raised her eyebrows at him. "I'm just saying . . . ," she began. But then, for a strange length of time, she didn't go on to share what she was "just saying."

"What?" he asked when he grew tired of waiting.

"When you get between a man and his wife . . ."

Elliot felt his own eyebrows go up slightly. "Who got between a man and his wife?"

No reply from her. But she did roll her eyes.

"*Me?* Why would you say that about *me?* I didn't get between . . ." But he trailed off and did not finish the thought. Because he had, actually. He had encouraged her to leave him. He had even offered his home as a refuge. "And you have no idea where they went?" he asked her.

"They don't talk to me. I do know they have family in Oregon. But they didn't tell me their plans."

She turned on the heel of one of her fuzzy slippers and walked to the house next door, where she stepped in, slamming the door behind her.

Elliot just stood a moment, trying to organize his thoughts.

Now he knew that Abby and Mary were not in the immediate area. They might not even be in the state of California. Obviously nobody was going to walk up the hill to his cabin. Nobody was going to clean the shed for him, or tell him what to expect next. If anyone was going to make contact with him, it would likely be by phone. And there was no phone in the cabin.

But Mary had his number in the city. He had given her his card, and encouraged her to hold on to it whether she thought she would use it or not. So she could call him. But only if he got home to the city.

Yes. That was it. He would have to get home as soon as he could.

He walked back around the corner and uphill to his truck.

When he got there, he heard the commotion of them in the truck bed. The whimpering and yipping. The scratching of their little nails on the corrugated metal of his truck bed.

He stood over the bed and looked in at them. And they looked back. For a moment he only watched their tails swing.

"Right," he said. "That's a bit of a complication, isn't it? For a second I forgot about all of you."

—

The veterinary technician, a girl who looked barely beyond her teens, brought Patches back out into the waiting room.

"The vet says it doesn't need to be bandaged again," she said. "It's doing really well. It's clean and dry, and the cut is closed. But leave the collar on him so he doesn't chew the stiches. And bring him back in about four or five days to get them taken out."

Elliot took the puppy into his arms. Patches felt warm and plump, and seemed vastly relieved to be back with Elliot.

"We won't be here in four or five days," he said. "But I'll get his stitches taken out. Just not here." He took a few steps toward the door, then stopped and turned back to her. "I'm sorry. Do I owe you for that?"

She waved his question away. "No charge."

"Thank you."

Elliot stepped outside. The morning had grown hotter, with the sun more directly overhead. Elliot carried Patches to his truck, still held closely to his side.

"You guys are a lot of responsibility," he said. "You know that?"

He set the pup in the truck bed with his brothers and sisters.

He would have to go up the hill and feed them, and clean the shed for the last time. And pack all of his own belongings. And he would have to get his hands on some kind of box or carrier. A big packing carton from outside the supermarket, maybe. Because there was no way he would ask them to ride all that way in the back of his truck.

And he was tired. The grief made him so tired, and already the day had become more trying than he could muster the energy to bear.

He wondered over the whole situation, once again, as he started his truck. How had he been saddled with this? How had the care of seven pups—*seven*—suddenly become his responsibility? But the answer eluded him, and besides, the *how* of it hardly seemed to matter. Their care had fallen to him, and there wasn't much he could do about it now.

He could give them away if Abby never came back. But in the meantime somebody had to take care of them, and Elliot was the only somebody they had.

———

He arrived at his home in the city at about 1:00 in the afternoon, hungry and more than a little perturbed.

He entered the yard through the side gate and set the box of puppies down in his backyard, casting a wistful glance at Pat's lovely garden. Not that it had really been Pat's anytime recently. She had created the lines of rosebushes on the fence, and the carefully tilled flower beds, but Elliot had been maintaining them for years.

He figured it would take the gang of pups less than a day to destroy everything. Maybe less than an hour.

He left them in their box in the yard for the time being. He had made a decision that he would go to the hardware store and buy some kind of fencing, and build an area of the yard that was especially for puppies. A space where there was nothing much to shred.

And maybe a doghouse. Depending on how long they were with him. They couldn't just live out in the elements. Elliot figured he could puppy-proof the laundry room and bring them in at night, in the short run.

He ran inside and straight to his answering machine, his heart hammering.

No one had called to tell him what was going on.

# Chapter Twenty-Three

## Open the Cage

**Mary**

There was one thing to be said for Stan, Mary thought as she watched and listened to him snoring. He slept like the dead. Sometimes she couldn't wake him even when she was trying.

On this night she would not be trying.

She slid out of bed and stepped into her bedroom slippers.

There was no bathroom off Merle and Judy's guest room. To use the bathroom one had to walk a good way down the upstairs hall. Mary did that first, even though she was in no need of a restroom, just on the off chance that he noticed her leaving.

She flushed the toilet without having used it, and washed her hands for no reason.

She peeked in through the open bedroom door as she walked past it. Stan seemed to be deeply asleep.

She crept down the stairs to the kitchen, and the phone.

Looking again over her shoulder, she punched in Viv's number by heart.

Viv picked up on the second ring, her voice muddy with sleep.

"Mary?" she asked first thing.

"Yeah, it's me," Mary said in a whisper.

"I figured nobody else would be calling me at this hour."

Mary glanced at the time readout on the microwave. It was nearly 2:00 a.m. She opened her mouth to apologize, but Viv spoke first.

"Where are you?"

"Oregon."

"*Oregon.* Why did you go to *Oregon?*"

"Didn't have much choice," Mary whispered.

She sat down at the kitchen table, where she had a good, unobstructed view of the bottom of the stairs and the hallway into the kitchen.

No one was coming.

A nearly full moon hung over the neighbors' garage. It lit up the world so fully and so brightly that Mary could see individual leaves shuddering in the breeze on the tree in the corner of the yard. It made her think of Elliot and the things she had told him that day. That last day.

She looked back to the hallway, but she was still alone.

"So you're just going to stay there with him?" Viv asked in her ear.

"No," Mary said. It came out louder than a whisper, but it didn't matter. There was no one there to hear. "So listen." She cupped her hand around the mouthpiece to direct the sound of her voice. Keep it out of that room and that house as much as possible. "I need you to do me a favor, and I'm going to talk fast in case he wakes up and I have to hang up suddenly. I lost that card."

A pause on the line.

Then, "What card?"

"The card. The one I was so upset about. You told me to keep it. You even told me *where* to keep it."

"Oh, the card. Right. Well, what can *I* do about it?"

"You can go up there and get his address and phone number again. I know it's a lot to ask, because your little car probably won't make it up that four-wheel-drive road . . ."

"I'll bet my neighbor would let me borrow his truck."

"Good. You think you can find his cabin from what I told you about it?"

"I think so. It'll have to wait till I get the kids off to school."

"That's fine. Just . . . it's so important to catch him before he goes home. We don't even remember his last name, so once he goes home he's pretty much lost to us forever. Oh, I suppose we could leave a note on his cabin door or something. But who knows when he'll go up there again? Could be months. Could be years."

"I'll do what I can. Look, are you okay there?"

"For the time being. I'm going to hang up now so I don't get caught on the phone. But listen . . . I'm sorry to call you on Merle's phone, but it was an emergency."

A brief silence.

Then Viv said, "What do I care what phone you call me on?"

"It'll come up on their phone bill at the end of the month. We'll be long gone by then, but Stan might think it's the number of . . . you know . . ."

"The other man."

"Right. He might call. He might have some choice words for you."

"I hope he does call," Viv said, her voice big and firm. "I have some choice words for him, too. That man has met his match in me, honey."

Mary could feel herself smile. It felt unfamiliar but welcome.

"You're a good friend," Mary said. "I'd better get off the phone while I'm ahead."

—

Mary checked on Stan again, then stole downstairs to the basement.

When she tried the door, she was surprised to find that it was locked. She had to turn a dead bolt to open it.

She padded carefully down the stairs in the dark and sat on the edge of her daughter's cot. Abby did not wake up. She had apparently inherited the tendency to sleep heavily from her father.

Mary stroked Abby's hair back off her forehead until she began to stir.

"Mmmmph?" Abby said. It was a sound more than a word.

"It's Mom."

Abby opened her eyes. Mary and her daughter just hung motionless that way for several beats in the mostly dark basement, looking at each other. There were two high, narrow windows onto the driveway, and light from the moon spilled in and helped Mary to see her daughter's face fairly clearly.

"I called Viv," Mary said.

Abby yawned expansively. "Oh. Good."

"You want to leave right now?"

Abby's eyes grew wider. "You would do that? Just . . . leave him? Right now?"

"I would do that."

The words caused a jangling in Mary's belly, but she said them. And she meant them. Her eyes obsessively darted to the top of the basement stairs, but they were still alone.

They sat in silence for a couple moments more.

"I think we should wait a few days," Abby said.

"You do? Why?"

"The plan is to go to Elliot's house in the city. Right?"

"Right."

"Well, he's not *at* his house in the city. He's at the cabin. And there's no room for us there. Plus Dad would find us there in a heartbeat. And if we tried to stay in our house, he would find us *there*. I think we should wait until we know Elliot's at his house and then go straight there. And then Dad'll never find us."

Mary felt herself smiling for the second time in just a handful of minutes. And after how long? She couldn't even remember. Maybe she had smiled at Elliot's cabin, or maybe she had been too nervous in his presence. That time was all a blur to her now.

"You're a very thoughtful girl," Mary said. "Very careful and smart. I'm lucky to have you." She kissed Abby on the forehead. And then Abby smiled, too. Mary could see it in the soft moonlight. "Why do they have you locked in down here?"

"I have no idea."

"What if you have to go to the bathroom?"

Abby indicated a spot on the floor with a flip of her head. Mary looked to see a pot, like a big soup pot, sitting on the concrete of the basement floor in a stream of moonlight.

"Oh dear," Mary said. "Remind me never to have any of Judy's soup."

Abby laughed out loud, which was delightful. Such a welcome sound. "That's exactly what *I* thought!" she squealed.

Mary put a finger to her lips to remind her daughter to be quiet. Then she leaned down and kissed Abby on the forehead again. "Well, I'm sorry," she said. "You don't deserve to live like this."

"Neither one of us does," Abby said. "Neither one of us ever did."

"But we'll be gone soon."

"Good."

Mary stood and quietly climbed the stairs back to the kitchen.

"Hey," Abby said as Mary reached the landing. "Thanks."

"For what?"

"For giving me the choice. For saying you would, if I thought now was the right time."

Mary felt another smile rise up, but sadder this time. Because she knew it was something she should have offered her daughter a long time ago.

"Try to get back to sleep," she said. "I'm sorry I woke you."

"It was worth it," Abby said.

Mary left the door to the basement unlocked. After all, her daughter was not an animal. Then she corrected the words in her head to match what she knew Abby would say. *She and* her daughter were not animals. They could not be forced to live like animals, locked into the equivalent of cages. At least, not for long.

*We'll be gone soon,* Mary thought to herself.

Then she climbed the stairs and quietly slipped into bed beside the still-snoring Stan.

—

In the morning she found Stan at the kitchen table, scowling into a cup of coffee. Neither Merle nor Judy seemed to be around.

Mary checked the coffeepot, but Stan had drunk it all. Or somebody had.

"There's no coffee," she said.

"So make some. Your hands aren't broken. I'm going out to look for a job today. And I want both of you right here. I don't want to get a call from Merle or Judy saying you're out of the house. I don't want to have to drop what I'm doing and come find you to see what you're up to. Got that?"

Mary sat down across from him without starting another pot of coffee.

"You're getting a job . . . here? So you're staying here?"

The minute it was out of her mouth, Mary heard her mistake.

"*We're* staying here," Stan said.

"I didn't mean . . . I just meant . . . so that's what *you* decided."

Stan never answered. He slugged down the last of his coffee and rose, walking to the sink, where he left the mug without rinsing it.

"What am I supposed to do all day while you're out looking for work?"

"What do you usually do?"

"Cook. But it's not my kitchen. Or read, but you dumped all my books at home."

"So read *my* books. Read Merle's books. I don't care what you do. Just make sure you do it *here*."

———

"I can get out of here and make a phone call," Abby said, her voice a tiny whisper. "That way we won't have to wait till tonight. You know. To see what Viv found out. I would hate to wait that long. Wouldn't you? That would drive me crazy. But I can get out of here."

They were sitting in the grass at the far corner of the yard, their backs up against the fence. Because it seemed the best place not to be overheard.

It was well after noon, and they had been doing quite a bit of waiting already.

"How?"

"Leave it to me."

"You have change for a pay phone?"

"Yeah, I have it left over from that second time I tried. Remember?"

Mary did not remember. She couldn't even remember if they had been here one full day or two or three, and the day Abby had run out of the house to use the phone felt like a month ago in Mary's memory.

"I forgot to ask her something. So ask her for me, please. I should have had her ask when he thinks he'll go back to the city. She may have to go up there again to find out, but we really need to know. Tell her I'm sorry about that."

"Okay. Come inside with me."

They walked together into the kitchen, where Judy was making sandwiches. Merle was sitting at the table, apparently waiting for one. Mary noted, without thinking too much about it, that Judy was making only two. Just one for her and one for her husband. Nothing for the extended family. It was as if she and her daughter didn't exist, except in the negative. Things had to be done against them, but nothing seemed to be done for them.

"I'm going to take a nap," Abby said, to no one in particular.

Only Merle seemed to be listening.

"You just got up a few hours ago."

"I didn't sleep much last night."

Abby hung there for a moment, as though waiting for some comment from her uncle. But Merle seemed to have gone somewhere else in his head. Once again, he was there to criticize a plan. To speak against it. When the time came to say it sounded reasonable enough, his attention was nowhere to be found.

Abby finally shrugged and let herself into the basement. Mary could hear the sound of her footsteps trotting down the stairs.

"I'm going to go look and see if you have any books I can read," Mary said.

She waited, but nobody was paying the slightest bit of attention to her.

Mary walked into the living room, glanced once across her shoulder to be sure no one was watching, then drew back the curtain. Abby was sprinting down the street. She had nearly reached the end of the block already.

"Well, I'll be damned," she said under her breath.

Her head and chest filled with an emotion Mary could only describe as admiration.

—

While Mary was waiting, she packed. But it was hard, because she had to pack in a way Stan wouldn't notice.

She pulled down two huge army-style duffel bags that Stan had left empty on a high closet shelf. Whether he would notice they were missing was hard to say, but it felt like a chance she would need to take.

She packed about half of her clothes. She trusted he had paid no attention to how much she'd brought. She packed a watch and a few pieces of not-too-expensive jewelry that had belonged to her late mother. She tucked the money into her bra, where it could live until it was time to go. Maybe she would even wear it under her nightgown in her sleep.

The last-minute items such as her hairbrush and toothbrush she simply gathered close together in a spot in the bathroom where they could be easily swept into her purse.

She checked around downstairs, but Judy seemed to have gone out. Her car was gone. And the unfortunately retired Merle was watching TV in the living room. Mary took a chance and carried the duffel bag—along with the second, empty one that Abby could use to pack her things—down to the basement, where her plan was to stash them under Abby's cot.

To her surprise, Abby was back. She was just sitting there on her cot, her back against the concrete wall, arms wrapped around her knees. She was staring at a spot on the basement floor, and did not look up as Mary came down the stairs. It was obvious to Mary that her daughter was not happy.

She tucked the duffel bags under the cot and sat down next to her daughter.

"How are you getting in and out?" she asked Abby.

It seemed a bit odd to Mary that she hadn't first asked why her daughter looked so down. It occurred to her that maybe she was postponing hearing that news because she didn't want to know.

Abby pointed up to the two narrow windows. One was sitting open. But they didn't even open all the way. They just tilted out at the top, on a sort of long metal hinge.

"No," Mary said, drawing out the word into several long syllables. "No way. Nobody could get through there. Not even you."

"Well, I just did," Abby said. "Twice."

Mary took a deep breath and addressed the obvious concern. "You don't look very happy. What's wrong? Wasn't Viv there?"

"She was there. But she said Elliot's gone."

"Maybe she had the wrong cabin," Mary said, talking around a sudden and severe discomfort in her low belly.

"No. It was the right place. She described it."

"Maybe he just went into town."

"But she drove up there twice. She borrowed her neighbor's truck and went up there once after she took her kids to school and then again a couple hours later. And he wasn't there."

"Were the dogs there?"

"I don't know. She didn't know. We didn't ask her to check on the dogs, so she didn't think to. But he wouldn't just go off and leave them . . . would he? I mean, who would do that? They'd starve. Nobody would do that to a bunch of puppies. Right?"

Mary sat still for a moment, trying to remember to breathe. She checked with her gut and found that she was utterly unwilling—or unable—to believe Elliot had gone back to the city.

"I don't think he would hurt them in any way, including neglectful ways."

"She'll try again at the end of the day," Abby said.

"Oh good," Mary said.

And, inside her, that seemed to settle everything. Viv would find him there on the third try. There was no other way it could go, as far as Mary was concerned. It would happen that way because it had to happen that way. There was no other outcome she was willing to believe.

—

Mary padded down the stairs to the kitchen at a little after 1:00 a.m. and called Viv on the phone.

"I'm sorry to wake you," she said, before Viv could even speak.

"You didn't."

"It's one in the morning."

"I was waiting up because I knew you would call."

A sickening sense of dread began to form in Mary's gut. Maybe because of the tone and timbre of her friend's voice. Her insides felt like the clammy walls of a cold and damp basement, but more sickening. She tried to speak to postpone the news, but no words came out.

"Honey, I'm sorry," Viv said. "He's gone."

"Oh."

The line went dead quiet for several beats. Mary looked up expecting to see Stan watching her, but she was blessedly alone. The whole house was asleep, minus her.

"I don't know what to do, then," Mary said.

Viv's voice came out hard and surprisingly strident. As if she were angry at what she was about to say. "I'll tell you what you *don't* do, Mary. You don't stay with him because of this."

"But there's nowhere else to go."

"There's my house."

"He could find me there."

"He doesn't know where I live."

"That's what we thought about Elliot."

"Look. Just get here. We'll work it out. I'll hide you in my basement. No one will know you're down there. You left before I could tell you, but I'm seeing a new guy. One of the sheriff's deputies. It's really new, but he takes care of me. And if I ask him, he'll take care of you, too."

"Not Eddie."

"No. He's new. His name is Gerald. Just get here, honey. People can be found."

"Not if you don't know their last name, they can't."

"Last names can be found out. Maybe Gerald can help. Go through the county records and see who's listed as the owner of that property or something. Or maybe he writes checks at the supermarket while he's here. But, please, honey. Please. Don't lose your nerve over this and stay. Just get out of there. We'll figure the rest out later."

Mary said nothing for a moment. Just stood and watched the bottom of the stairs and marveled at how well her friend knew her. Because she *was* losing her nerve. She could feel it go. Without the safe haven of a guest room in a home Stan knew nothing about, it just all felt too terrifying.

She opened her mouth to say so, but never did. Because she realized she could tell Viv she was afraid to go, but she couldn't break news like that to Abby. Abby had been so relieved and so proud when Mary had told her she would really do it. There was no way she could stand to see the look in her daughter's eyes if she took it all back again.

"I'll get there as soon as I can," Mary said.

She heard her friend let out a long and noisy breath on the other end of the line. A breath Viv must have been holding for a very long time.

# Chapter Twenty-Four

*Freedom, and Lack of Same*

*Abby*

Abby stood in the dark hallway with her back up against the wall, breathing quietly. She heard footsteps coming down the stairs, and just for a moment she thought they might belong to her father. She felt a sensation of fear like something trying to jump up through her throat. She swallowed it down as best she could.

A few seconds later the feet reached the bottom of the stairs and turned into the hallway, and Abby could see it was her mom. A long sigh flew out of her.

She waited until her mom was nearly level with her before speaking. Abby's eyes were adjusted to the dark, and she figured her mom's were, too. She just assumed that her mom saw her standing there.

"Hey," she whispered.

Her mom jumped as though Abby had fired off a gun. A little shriek came out of her throat.

They both stood perfectly still and waited. Waited to see if they had wakened anybody. Waited to see how much trouble they were in.

"If we hear him," Abby whispered, "I'll run back down to the basement. You can pretend you just got up for a glass of water or a cup of tea or something."

They held still a moment longer, in silence. Nothing seemed to stir.

"But if he comes down here while we're walking out with duffel bags . . ." Her mom seemed to barely breathe the words. ". . . oh, honey. That will be bad like we've never seen bad."

"Which is why I already snuck the duffel bags out and hid them behind those hedges at the end of the block."

For a moment, nothing. No sound. No movement. Then Abby felt her mother's hands on either side of her face, and lips pressed to her forehead.

"You're a brilliant girl. I'm lucky to have you."

A toilet flushed upstairs. Abby felt it like a cold knife of fear in her stomach.

They froze there for another few seconds.

"It's Judy," her mom whispered. "Judy gets up every night to go. Your father never does."

But they continued to hold still, just to be on the safe side.

"We'll go out the door separately," Abby's mom whispered. "That way he can only catch one of us leaving. When I'm sure you've made it, I'll follow. I'll meet you at the end of the block."

Abby took a deep breath. Then she slipped down the hall and out the door. She trotted down the cold, dark street, wondering what she would do if her mom never followed.

When she finally saw the dim figure of her, Abby breathed, feeling as though it was her first breath since leaving Merle's house. It couldn't possibly have been. But it felt like it.

———

Abby couldn't let go of the sensation that her feet were barely touching the ground. She could hear the soles of her sneakers slapping on the pavement as she ran, and she believed what she heard. Still it felt like flying. It was such a wonderful, freeing sensation that she felt hugely invested in keeping it with her as long as she could.

Even the heavy duffel bag on her shoulder seemed incapable of weighing her down.

"It feels so *free!*" she called over her shoulder.

Her mother was a step or two behind her on the dark sidewalk, and Abby could hear her panting. There was a raggedness to the breath she heard, so Abby figured her mom had run as far as she could, and it was time to slow down.

She hated to do it. But she did it for her mom.

"Want me to take your duffel bag?" Abby asked.

"That doesn't seem fair," her mom said, gasping the words out with her breath.

"I can take both. I don't mind."

Abby hoisted the second bag up onto her free shoulder, and they walked that way for several blocks in the pitch-dark. The moon had gone down, and there were very few streetlights. Only the fact that their eyes had adjusted allowed them to navigate through that blackness.

Abby still felt a spring in her step. As though nothing could slow her down or weigh her down.

"Do we know where the bus station is?" Abby asked.

"We took the bus up here twice. Don't you remember?"

"Yeah. I remember. When Dad was all paranoid about our old car and he wouldn't drive it over fifty and he was always sure it was going to break down. But that was so many years ago. What if they moved it?"

"Why would they move it?"

"I don't know. Sometimes cities build bigger, nicer bus stations."

"Let's just hope that's not the case," her mom said.

"It just feels so free," Abby said again. The words were so exciting and so true that she couldn't contain them. "Do you feel free?"

"I feel . . . ," her mom began. Then they walked a few steps without speaking. ". . . very different."

"Are you scared?"

"Yes."

"Oh. I'm sorry."

"You're not scared?"

"Nope. Never been happier in my life. Going to see my *puppies!* You have any idea how much I miss my puppies?"

They walked another block in silence, and Abby wasn't sure why. It felt almost as though there was something right there, something that her mother knew existed but that she didn't care to say out loud. But Abby wasn't sure how to go digging for it, or even if she should.

"You're not sorry you decided it, are you?" Abby asked.

"I don't think so."

They stepped out onto the big boulevard, and walked toward the distant bus station that Abby could already see was still there. She would have liked something a bit more enthusiastic and sure from her mom, but after a time she decided it would have to do. They were out, after all. And if it hadn't been a difficult thing to do, her mother would have done it years ago.

"So did you call Elliot and tell him we were coming?" Abby asked, hoping to steer the conversation in a more joyful direction.

"No."

"Just want to surprise him?"

"Yeah. I think I like that idea better. Oh, good. The bus station is still there. You scared me with that."

"Sorry," Abby said.

They walked the two blocks to it in silence. On the big boulevard there were streetlights. As they passed under each one, Abby glanced over at her mom's face. She looked more than just nervous. She looked deeply worried.

They passed storefront businesses—antique stores and markets and an art gallery—but everything was locked up for the night, silent and closed. Not a single car passed them.

The duffel bags began to feel heavy on Abby's shoulders for the first time.

"Here's the thing," Abby's mom said.

And Abby knew what was coming. Not the specifics of what the bad news would contain. But she knew she was about to understand her mother's silences, and the look of strain on her face.

"Okay," Abby said. "What's the thing?"

"We still don't have Elliot's address or phone number."

"Or last name?"

"Right. Or that either. He was really gone."

They stepped up three concrete stairs to the front door of the bus station. Abby's mom tried the door, but it was locked.

"Can you read that sign?" Abby's mom asked her. "The print is so small and it's dark."

Abby leaned in close, uncomfortably aware of the weight of all their belongings on her shoulders. "It says the lobby opens at five. What time is it?"

She watched her mom peer closely at her wristwatch in the dark.

"Not even three."

"Well, then . . . we need to get where Dad can't see us if he's out driving around looking."

The weight of the world was beginning to descend hard on Abby, in more than just the literal sense, and it was dropping fast. Suddenly there was no Elliot to go to. No puppies to reclaim. And her father might be about to find them and take them back.

They walked around to the parking lot side of the station, where the buses pulled in—when there were buses running. It was absolutely deserted. There were no buses idling, no parked cars. No other people milling about, waiting for the place to open.

"This is no good," Abby said. "He could drive right through here and shine his lights on us."

They kept walking. Abby felt no more spring in her step, and nothing felt like flying or freedom anymore. Now it was just a big, dangerous world that required careful navigating.

They turned the corner behind the building.

"This is perfect," Abby said.

It was nothing but a strip of ivy-covered dirt between the wall of the station and an ivy-covered fence. The only way to get to it was on foot. And there was no way for anybody to shine his car lights onto it.

Abby dropped the heavy bags and they sat cross-legged with their backs up against the wall. It was a cool summer night, but the coolness felt good. Abby could believe they would be safe here for a couple of hours.

She looked up to see a riot of stars.

"So what are we going to do?" she asked her mom, still staring at the night sky.

"We're going to go to Viv's and hide in her basement for a while. She has a new guy she's been dating, and he's a sheriff's deputy. She says he'll keep us safe, and maybe he can even find Elliot."

"How?"

"I don't know, but she said they have ways. Like maybe he can look into the county records of who owns that property."

"Oh," Abby said. "That would be good."

A long, long silence fell, and Abby allowed it.

Then she said, "Because if we don't find him, he'll probably give my puppies away."

"Except for two. He said he wanted two for himself."

"Still. Five out of seven."

"But that might not be the end of the world. Right? I mean, wasn't that what you wanted for them? Wouldn't you have left them at the pound if you thought they'd go to good homes?"

"Well. Yeah. But that was before I *knew* them. Before they were *mine*."

Abby heard a deep sigh from her mom. It seemed to cut through the darkness.

"Well, honey . . . there was always a chance that trying to save seven puppies by keeping all of them was going to end with a broken heart. But it's not over yet. We're doing the best we can. Can't we just hope for the best for now?"

"Yeah," Abby said. "Good idea. Let's hope for the best for now."

But their freedom was feeling more and more like a tightly confining prison with every breath she drew.

———

Abby woke to a hand shaking her shoulder, and it was a surprise to her, because she'd had no idea she had fallen asleep.

"It's five," her mom said, her lips close to Abby's ear. "We should go in and buy our tickets."

They rose and stretched. Abby's legs were half-asleep from having been crossed for so long, and they felt wobbly and strange. Her eyes felt grainy, as though someone had thrown sand in them, and her stomach was rocky. Still she picked up both duffel bags and they walked to the end of the building.

They stopped and looked before stepping out into the parking lot. Neither said a word about it, but Abby figured they both knew what they were looking for.

There was one car in the lot now. As though one employee had shown up to work. But otherwise the place still seemed deserted.

"I think it's okay," her mother said.

They walked through the parking lot together.

"Wait," Abby said.

"What?"

"Do we have enough money for bus tickets?"

Abby felt as though something were squeezing her stomach in a tight grip. But she wasn't giving much attention to what she thought it was.

"I think so. I hope so. I have almost all that money I saved, minus what I gave you for the puppies."

"You didn't give it to me for the puppies. You didn't even know about them yet."

Abby's mom shot Abby a look over her shoulder, and Abby knew her mom well enough to read it.

"Wait. You knew? How did you know?"

"Come on, honey. Moms aren't stupid. You come home and tell me you rescued a bunch of puppies and then all of a sudden you're gone almost all day, every day, and you come home with little scratches and bites on your arms and muddy paw prints on your clothes? It wasn't very hard."

"Oh," Abby said. "Well, I feel stupid now."

They walked up the three steps to the door of the station, and Abby's mom pushed hard on the door. It opened.

They stepped inside and up to the ticket counter. No one seemed to be manning it, but Abby could hear the sound of someone walking around in the back.

"What if we don't have enough money for the tickets?" Abby asked.

"Let's just hope until we know. If we get into a bind, I'm thinking Viv will help us out with a small loan."

Abby carried the heavy duffel bags over to the window, where she watched the street, hoping not to see her father's truck. But that way, she figured, if she did see it, they could get out of view before he saw them.

When she turned around again, her mom was counting out money onto the counter, and then pushing it across to a lady. Which seemed to suggest that it was enough.

It didn't stop the grip of whatever was crushing her belly.

She walked over to the counter.

"Why don't you set those heavy bags down, honey?" her mom said.

Abby let them thump onto the bus station linoleum. She thought she would feel lighter and freer without them. And in one sense, the purely physical one, she did. But that was when she learned that the heaviness, the sense of something weighing on her, was unrelated to baggage.

Meanwhile her mom was talking.

"We're taking the first bus out, even though it takes us a little out of our way. We'll change buses in San Francisco. I don't think I have to tell you why I want us out of here as soon as possible."

"No," Abby said. "You don't have to tell me why."

"Now we just have to manage until the bus leaves."

"How long?"

"An hour."

Abby frowned. She could feel the muscles in her face contracting with the expression.

She walked up to the woman behind the counter. Leaned over, as if to whisper to her. She was an older woman with a pleasant face and rosy cheeks, like Mrs. Santa Claus. She seemed to sense weighty information coming her way.

"My mom and I left home in the night," she said. "We left my dad. He'll be waking up any time now, and he'll try to find us. And that won't be a good thing, let me tell you."

The woman leaned in even closer and lowered her voice to a whisper. "You're telling me you two are in danger?"

"I'm telling you we *will* be if he finds us here."

"You should come back here with me, then."

The woman walked to a door separating the employee-only area from the waiting room. She unlocked it and swung it open.

"Mom," Abby said, and motioned with her head.

The woman led them into a room with coat hooks and a few abandoned pieces of luggage. A table, maybe for employee lunches. A bulletin board full of notices.

"There's coffee," she said, and pointed. "I won't let you miss your bus. I'll come get you when it's boarding."

"Thank you," Abby and her mother both said at the same time.

Then she left them alone.

Abby sat on one side of the table and her mom sat on the other. They caught each other's eyes as they listened to the woman make a phone call.

It started in a way that seemed innocuous and uninteresting to Abby. Just the woman saying her name and where she was located.

Then it began to sound as though she was talking to someone about *them*.

"I don't know that it's an emergency," she said. "Maybe the guy won't even show up. But it seems to be a potential domestic violence situation. I just thought it might be good to have an officer here, just in case. Just to make sure they have a chance to get on the bus safely and get away. If you can spare one."

Then a long silence before the woman said, "Thank you."

Abby didn't know if she had hung up the phone. She couldn't hear that. But nothing more was being said.

She looked up and caught her mom's eyes again.

"Now I feel safe," her mom said. "For the first time in as long as I can remember I feel safe. You're such a smart girl. Sometimes I don't know what I'd do without you."

Abby waited quietly for the gripping feeling to let go of her stomach.

It never did.

—

They waved to the policeman through the bus window as they pulled out of the parking lot, and he waved in return. It made Abby's stomach buzz with a warm feeling, because he was on their side, and he had been clear about that.

Abby heard her mom sigh out a bizarre amount of breath. It just seemed to go on and on. Abby couldn't imagine how she had managed to store so much breath for so long without dying.

"We made it," her mom said.

"Well, yes and no. He'll still look for us at home."

Her mom never answered.

They rode in silence for several minutes. Through the streets of town and onto the highway, headed south. There were only a small handful of people on the bus and no one was sitting close to anyone else. It made Abby feel as though she and her mom were on their own little planet. It was comforting, in a way. But also a little disturbing.

Her mom spoke, just out of nowhere, and it startled her.

"Now *you* seem scared," she said.

"I guess."

"You never seem scared to me. I always marveled at that. Even when you were little. You were always the most courageous little girl I'd ever seen. That's not to suggest there's anything wrong with being scared. I'm just saying."

Abby didn't answer, because she didn't know what the answer should be.

"Is it all about your dad finding us?"

"I don't know," Abby said.

She didn't say more for a time, and her mother didn't push her.

"I guess it just felt different when we were going straight to Elliot's," Abby said. "I felt like I knew how it was going to be. I know we only knew Elliot for just a little bit. A few days, even though it's weird to think about that, because it feels like we knew him for a year. But he's just so . . . I don't even know how to say it. I felt like he would know what to do. Like, if Elliot says something is a good idea, it's probably a good idea. So now I feel like I don't even know where we're going or what it's going to be like."

"Are you sorry we left?"

"No," Abby said. Firmly, and without any pause for thinking.

"We might still find Elliot."

"Yeah. We might."

"We're just doing our best here, honey, and I think that's going to have to be enough for now."

"Okay," Abby said. "Yeah. Okay. That's enough for now."

———

Somewhere back over the state line into California, Abby spoke again.

"You like him. Right?"

"Who? Elliot?"

"Yeah. Elliot. You like him."

"I do. Yes. Very much."

"I knew you would. I just knew it. I don't even know how I knew it. I just did. I'm not even going to ask you any details about *how* you like him. You know. In what way."

"Probably just as well," her mom said.

They didn't talk much more after that.

# Chapter Twenty-Five

## Counting to Seven

**Elliot**

Elliot opened his eyes.

It was first light, morning twilight, and he was sleeping on the living room couch. Not because he had accidentally fallen asleep there. Because he had been bedding down there as a way of denying the massive void—the sheer loneliness—of the bed he had shared with Pat for so many good years.

He rolled onto his back and stared at the ceiling for a time.

He had expected Abby and Mary to contact him. And it had been several days. Long enough that he could feel his mood begin to crash.

He had come back to the house with the confident knowledge that they would soon join him here. That Abby's sheer optimism and the way Mary looked at him when she thought he wasn't noticing would be all the happy chaos he needed. Instead he had landed in this familiar but deserted planet.

And now it had been long enough that it was time for him to try on the possibility that they were never coming back. Not for the puppies, and not for him.

So what would he do with them? he wondered. And what would he do with himself?

Finding homes for most of them seemed to be the only solution. But how would he know for sure that it was time?

He rose, pulled yesterday's jeans on over his boxer shorts, slipped into his shoes, and turned on the coffee maker.

Then he stepped out into the laundry room, which had been layered with papers, and the puppies swarmed him enthusiastically. He opened the back door and they all spilled out into the yard together.

He had fenced off the three sides of the yard that contained flower beds, so that the puppies had one fence line and the whole grassy middle area of the yard. No point penning them in too tightly. They were bundles of raw energy, after all. A few holes had been dug here and there, but Elliot couldn't bring himself to feel that it mattered. Grass was only grass. It would grow again.

He left them to clean the laundry room floor.

Several minutes later he rejoined the puppies, who wagged as they jumped up on his legs, and felt the nagging sensation that he was not seeing quite enough of them. He counted out loud.

"One, two, three, four, five, six. Six? Hmm."

He counted again, this time to himself.

"Six. Now, wait. Now who's missing here?" He identified each individual pup. "Tippy," he said out loud. "Tippy is missing."

There was no doghouse, though he planned to add one. So there was really no place for a puppy to be hiding.

Elliot walked the fence line, looking for any breaks or breaches. There was a tiny space between boards in one spot, but Elliot couldn't imagine any living thing—even a little one like Tippy—squeezing through it.

He walked through the house and out the front door. Onto the sidewalk, where he began to call for her. It was early for that, and his neighbors might want to wring his neck for it. But he couldn't lose one of Abby's puppies. What if Abby and Mary showed up today? He had to get Tippy back.

The front door opened on the house next door, and his neighbor, Mrs. Ellison, stepped out onto her front porch holding Tippy.

"I'm guessing this is what you're looking for," she said.

Elliot stepped up onto her porch, embarrassed because he was still shirtless.

"Thank you," he said. "That's exactly what I was looking for."

"I haven't seen you since . . . ," she began. Elliot winced, knowing where she was headed with this. "I haven't had a chance to tell you how sorry I am for your loss."

"Thank you," Elliot said.

They stood considering each other for a moment. Elliot had not yet reached out to take the puppy from her.

Mrs. Ellison had been widowed about two years earlier, so Elliot figured he was in the presence of someone who knew, at least within a reasonable variation, how he felt. He wanted to ask her how she had survived the past two years, but he figured it was an unanswerable question. Probably the same way Elliot had survived the days since Pat's death—out of a lack of other, better options.

She spoke, jarring him out of his thoughts.

"She must've figured out how to get through the fence," she said. "Or under it. Because she keeps turning up in my yard."

"You mean . . . this has happened more than once?"

"Oh, yes. Three times yesterday. Every time, I put her back through the gate as carefully as I could. Before you even missed her, apparently."

"I'm so sorry," Elliot said.

"Oh, please don't be. She's adorable. And I'm flattered that she wants to be with me so badly. However she's getting out, the other puppies haven't found it. I'm wondering if she's just more motivated. I hope you won't take this the wrong way, but that's an awful lot of puppies you have over there."

"Agreed," Elliot said. "Can't really take that the wrong way. It's just a statement of fact. They're not mine, actually. I'm just taking care of them for a friend. Well. Two of them are mine, I think. I'm thinking about adopting two of them."

"Oh, so they *are* available for adoption," Mrs. Ellison said.

She was still holding Tippy against the waistband of her skirt, stroking the pup's head with her free hand. Tippy's eyes were half-closed in an expression that Elliot could only describe as blissful.

"I think they are," he said. "At least a couple of them. But I'm not sure which ones she wants to keep and which ones she'd let go of. I'd hate to make that decision without their owner."

"If you don't mind my saying so, this one is making it painfully clear that she wants to be elsewhere."

"She's not much on puppy gangs," Elliot said. "You're right about that."

"I go out on my back porch and knit, because I like the fresh air. I like to watch the sunrise and the sunset. She comes over and lies at my feet while I'm out there. That's all she wants to do. There's this feed of yarn bouncing up and down, but she never tries to bite at it or play with it. She's not all that playful. She's not all that . . . *puppyish* for a puppy. I think she must be an old soul. She just seems to want peace and quiet. And she's certainly not getting any of that across the fence with her herd."

She reluctantly handed the puppy to Elliot. Tippy squirmed to get down, as if trying to get back to Mrs. Ellison.

"Are you saying you would take her? If her owner wants to give her away?"

"You know, I really think I would. I never saw myself with a puppy. They're usually so . . . frenetic. Not really an ideal pet for an older lady like myself. I was thinking—since Alvin died—of maybe a cat. But a cat would try to play with my yarn when I knit. This puppy doesn't act much like a puppy. She just wants a quiet spot to lie down near someone."

"Well . . . ," Elliot began, ". . . as soon as I can find out, I'll let you know. I hate to make the decision on my own. But I'll let you know. Meanwhile I'll try to figure out where she's getting through the fence. There's one place with just a tiny gap between the boards, but I just can't imagine anything squeezing through it."

"Depends on how motivated they are," Mrs. Ellison said.

———

Elliot set Tippy back down in his yard and watched her brothers and sisters swarm her—and felt guilty for making her come back.

He pulled on a shirt and then searched around in the garage. Found a suitably sized board. Then he picked up the hammer, filled his pocket with nails, and stepped out again.

Tippy was halfway through the gap in the fence, wiggling. He could see the white tip of her tail swinging back and forth with her efforts.

He dropped the board and the hammer and ran to her, grabbing her just in time. He carefully wiggled her back onto his side of the fence again.

"Sorry," he said to her.

She shot him a mournful look.

Elliot retrieved the board and the hammer and patched the fence in an ugly way that offended his sense of order. But for the moment it would have to do.

He patted the head of each pup and then went back into the house to make himself a morning coffee.

By the time he carried the mug of coffee out into the backyard to sit with the puppies, Tippy was gone again. The fence patch was still in its unsightly place, but a miniature tunnel had been dug underneath the fence, marked by a pile of fresh black dirt.

Elliot counted the puppies as they swarmed his legs. Only Tippy was missing.

He sighed, and walked through the house again. Out onto the sidewalk.

He sipped his coffee as he walked next door to Mrs. Ellison's house, but he never got that far. He never needed to. Mrs. Ellison came out her front door with Tippy in her arms and met him on the sidewalk, halfway between their two houses.

For a moment they just stood, saying nothing.

"I'm not quite sure how we solve this," she said after a time.

"I think I need to make a command decision," Elliot said. "Are you sure about wanting to adopt her?"

"I would take her, yes. I'm touched by how badly she seems to want to live at my house. At the very least we can try it and see if we're all happy with the arrangement."

"I think you should take her, then," Elliot said. "Her owner isn't here to make the decision, and I am. They've been left in my care. I'm just going to assume she'd want what was best for them."

"You hear that?" Mrs. Ellison asked the pup, raising her to eye level. Tippy wagged cautiously. "You've just been given permission to be my knitting companion."

"Let me know if you need any help with anything," Elliot said, and turned for home.

"Wait," Mrs. Ellison called. "I need to know if she has a name. I heard you calling her but now I don't remember."

Elliot stopped and turned back. Walked a step or two closer.

"Her owner calls her Tippy."

"Like Tippi Hedren."

"Probably not for that reason. She's a young girl, probably too young to know that actress. I think she gave her the name because of the white tip at the end of her tail. Of course, you can name her whatever you'd like."

"I think Tippy is delightful," she said.

And she carried the puppy home.

—

Elliot took his coffee out into his backyard again and counted puppies. Just to be sure no others had made use of the tunnel. All six were
present and accounted for. The remaining six puppies seemed happy
enough to stay.

Elliot filled the hole, carefully tamping the dirt into place with his
shoe.

He walked back into his kitchen, fetched the dog kibble, and put
quite a bit out for the pups. Probably more than they would be able to
eat at a sitting.

Then he made himself breakfast and a second cup of coffee.

When he got back outside into the yard, the pups had eaten all the
food. No one had bothered to re-dig the tunnel.

Elliot sat with them for several minutes, wondering what he would
tell Abby if she showed up. How he would explain having given one of
her puppies away. Then he realized how much worse it would be if she
didn't show up. He would need to find four more homes. There was
no way he was prepared to own six dogs. And then, if he placed all but
two . . . what if she showed up belatedly, with a very good excuse for
why she couldn't have come sooner? All of her dogs would be gone, and
there would be no way to get them back again.

He might have to give her the two he had grown to think of as
his own.

It was almost hard to know which scenario Elliot dreaded most.
He knew only that the sooner she contacted him, the less stressed he
would feel.

# Chapter Twenty-Six

*Possible Descendants of Walt Whitman*

## Mary

Less than an hour after they arrived at her house, Viv brought Gerald down the stairs to the basement and introduced him.

He was a big, beefy guy. Tall. Huge, really. It made Mary feel less afraid of Stan, less afraid of her future in general, to see the man who had agreed to look out for their safety. He was wearing a tan sheriff's deputy uniform, holding the cap against his side. His hair was neatly cropped, short. A handsome guy, Mary thought.

She actually did remember Viv telling her she had gone on a first and then second date with someone. But Viv hadn't volunteered a lot of details, and Mary hadn't wanted to pry. Sometimes people like to wait and see what they think themselves before they start with the big sharing. And then Mary's problems had stolen the show.

While she was thinking this, Viv was talking. And Mary was missing a lot of her words.

"I told him what you told me. How you wanted to go back to the house," she heard Viv say when Mary had clearly offered her full attention. It sounded as though she might be repeating herself. "But I told him I thought it was too dangerous."

"It's just so important," Mary said, her voice sounding strained and desperate to her own ears. "The book with that address in it—Stan might have just thrown it right onto the living room floor and left it there for the time being. And that would solve everything. Or maybe he threw my books away in the outside garbage cans, and the trash is going to get picked up tomorrow. So I feel like I need to hurry."

Mary heard her daughter speak up from a spot in the basement behind Mary's left shoulder. "He didn't throw them away," Abby said.

Mary wanted to ask her daughter why she sounded so sure about that, but the conversation veered in a different direction.

"I think you should let me drive you over there," Gerald said. His voice was booming and deep. "And I'll wait with you while you look. It's the safest way to go."

"That would be absolutely wonderful," Mary said.

—

"The kitchen door is unlocked," Mary said. "The kitchen door is always unlocked."

They all walked through the kitchen and into the living room together. All four of them. It felt good to Mary, after having been more or less alone in this mess for so long.

"No books here," Viv said.

They stood in the living room, looking around. Nobody seemed to want to move. Mary felt overwhelmed by the chaos of the house—what had been taken and what had been left behind. The knowledge that this had been her life just a few days earlier made Mary feel almost dizzy.

Gerald was standing in the middle of the room, his legs spread wide and his arms crossed. He looked like a mountain. The pose he had struck—and the way he kept an eye on first one door and then the other—seemed a tad dramatic to Mary, yet she welcomed it. Right at the moment she needed somebody who strode through the world in such a powerful fashion.

"He might have thrown them away," Mary said. "We need to go check the outside trash."

She instinctively moved in that direction—toward the kitchen door to the backyard.

"He didn't throw them away," Abby said. Again.

Again Mary wanted to ask why her daughter felt so sure. Again the conversation moved on before she could.

"Wait for me," Gerald said. "Don't go out there on your own."

They followed him to the kitchen door. He stepped out, looked around, then motioned for them to come outside.

Mary ran to the trash cans and pulled off both lids at once. There was nothing inside except the plastic bag of kitchen trash Mary had taken out the day before they left.

"I told you he didn't throw them away," Abby said.

This time the moment held still long enough for Mary to ask.

"How did you know that, honey? Did you see him do something with the books?"

It seemed unimaginable that Abby would know something of the whereabouts of that book and yet have kept it to herself all this time. And yet part of Mary wanted to believe that her daughter really did know.

"No, I didn't *see* him. But I *know* him. Think about it. Think about how he is. He never throws anything away if it's worth any amount of money. Even if it's only a few cents. Remember that time he drove to the store to get his five cents deposit on that bottle? And you even said how dumb that was—to me, not to him—because he probably spent fifty cents in gas just going to the store and back. But he can't help himself. It's like a sickness with him, thinking something's worth money, no matter how much, and he thinks he's not getting what he deserves for it."

Mary noted that everyone was listening attentively, even Gerald.

"What do you think he did with them, then, honey?"

"Probably hauled them to the thrift store. And maybe only got, like, two dollars for the whole pile of them, but he'd still take the time to do that before he made us go."

"I'll take you over to the thrift store, then," Gerald said.

"Are you sure?" Mary asked. Even though she very much wanted him to do it. But she felt guilty taking up so much of his time. "Are you sure you don't need to get back to your job?"

"This *is* my job," he said. "Keeping the local folks safe."

They all walked around the outside of the house to the street. He held open the back door of his patrol car, and Mary and Abby climbed in. Viv sat up front with Gerald, as she had on the way over.

Gerald caught Mary's eyes in the rearview mirror as they pulled away from the curb.

"He *made* you go with him?" he asked. "Tell me more about that."

"Pretty much. Yeah. He put Abby in the car by force and then told me I had to go if I ever wanted to see her again."

"That sounds like kidnapping," Viv said, mostly to Gerald.

"It just might be," he said. "Especially if you told him straight-out that you chose not to go with him. Did you tell him that?"

"I did," Mary said. "I absolutely did. I was sitting on the porch and Abby was in the house, and he came up on the porch and got right up in my face and told me to get in the truck, and I said it. Clear as day, I said it. I said, 'I'm not going.' And then Abby came out, and he grabbed her by the shirt and put her in the truck and held her there by her arm so she couldn't get out and told me I better get in if I ever wanted to see her again."

She watched Gerald and Viv exchange a glance in the front seat.

"Think you could make a charge like that stick?" Viv asked.

"Would I have to come back and testify?" Mary interjected. "Because if I did, and they didn't convict him . . ."

"I don't know," Gerald said. "I don't know." His voice sounded strong, almost dismissive. Like he was trying to fight away all the verbal interference so he could think. But he didn't sound critical of the ideas he was hearing. More like he needed a moment to get his thoughts together. "I don't know if I could make it stick. I don't know if Mary would have to press charges or if the DA would take it up on a 'versus the people' sort of a basis. There's always a lot of gray areas in situations like this. I really couldn't say in advance how I think it would go. But I can tell you one thing for a fact. I can arrest him and charge him with kidnapping and I can hold him two days before he's legally entitled to an arraignment. And that's a fair amount of time for these two to get somewhere safe."

A silence fell. Mary knew what she was thinking, and she wondered if the other three were thinking it as well. If they could find Elliot's address, it was more than enough time. It was perfect.

But they hadn't found Elliot's address yet.

No one said out loud what they were thinking.

———

They spilled into the thrift store together, all four of them, still moving as a team.

The store was owned by an older married couple, and the husband, Irv, was manning the cash register.

"Well, hello, Mary and Abby," he said. "Hello, Viv." He seemed not to acknowledge Gerald, but maybe only because Gerald was new in town, and almost no one knew him by name. "I must say I'm glad to see you, Mary. When Stan came in here with all those books and household items, we didn't know what to think about your situation. Ethel and I talked about it a lot—spent a good amount of time hoping everything was okay in your world. Stan being a little . . . well, you know . . . hot headed and all."

"Yes," Mary said. "I know all right. So he *did* bring the books here. Can you show me where in the store you put them?"

Irv ambled out from behind the counter, his pace maddeningly slow, and led Mary to the back of the store. Just the two of them. Everybody else waited up front.

"Oh!" Mary said as they neared a corner area of the bookcases. She was following the sweep of Irv's hand with her gaze. "I do see some of my books here!"

She moved up close to the shelf and began touching each spine with her fingers. From one row to another. Stan had sold a lot of her books. But she didn't see the Emily Dickinson book. In fact, she didn't see any of her poetry books at all.

"Were they shelved all together?" she asked Irv.

"Should've been. But, you know how it is . . . customers come in and mix things up. I can't say for a fact they still are."

"Abby!" Mary called out. "Viv! Come help me look."

Gerald showed up and helped look as well. They touched the spine of every used book Irv and Ethel had in their shop for sale, speaking the name of the author out loud as they did. Just to be sure nothing was overlooked.

"It's not here," Mary said.

She could hear the defeat in her own voice.

"Don't get upset now, honey," Viv crooned, "Gerald can still look up the records on that property."

"But not till Monday," Gerald's booming bass voice added.

"Oh, it's the weekend? I've totally lost track of all that. Irv, any chance you remember who came in and bought my poetry books?"

Irv looked up and to the left, as though it helped him think to do so. "I haven't sold any books this week. Not that I can recall. Must've been when Ethel was manning the shop. I could ask her. But she's doing some errands now. I could call later, when she might be home. I could let you know."

Of course Ethel would not have a cell phone, Mary thought. They were old school, Ethel and Irv, and besides, why pay for a phone that will never get reception anyway?

She wrote down the number at Viv's, and Irv dutifully folded it and tucked it in his shirt pocket.

Then they piled back into Gerald's patrol car and headed back to Viv's house.

No one said a word on the drive. Mary could tell that her sense of defeat had infected everyone. As if defeat were a contagious disease, they had all succumbed to Mary's despair.

———

It was nearly three hours later when Viv carried the phone down into the basement and handed it to Mary.

Mary's heart leapt disturbingly, not so much because she thought she would hear what she needed to know, but because she was fairly sure her hope was about to be stomped to death again.

"Hello?" she said into the phone.

"Mary? Darling, it's Ethel. Irv told me you were in looking for some of your books that Stan sold. I had a bad feeling he was doing that without your permission, Stan being who he is and all. I didn't want to buy them, for just that reason, but he seemed perturbed and Irv didn't want to stand up to him in that moment. I don't honestly remember selling them, because I'm not as good at that as Irv is. He remembers things like that. Like who bought what. I nearly never do."

Mary felt her heart drop again. Just as expected.

"But I do know who likes to come in and buy poetry," Ethel continued. "It's Mrs. Whitman. You know her? The widow?"

"I don't think I do. Mrs. Whitman, you say? No. Doesn't ring a bell."

Abby, who was standing close and listening, began to jump up and down on the concrete basement floor.

"I know her! I know her, Mom! She's the one who drove me to the county shelter with the puppies that very first day."

Meanwhile Ethel was still speaking into Mary's left ear.

"She has a soft spot for poetry because of her last name. Whitman. She thinks her late husband might have been related to the poet Walt Whitman but she could never get him interested enough in genealogy and she couldn't quite figure it out on her own. But she still thinks so, which I guess is why she fancies herself something of a connoisseur of poetry."

"I could ask her," Mary said. "Would you happen to know where she lives?"

"Can't say as I do, darling, but she's probably listed. Look under her husband's name. Gregory, I'm pretty sure. Single ladies who live alone don't like to list in the phone book under their own names—in case you don't know that, having been married for so long. I wish I could be more helpful to you, darling. I hope you're okay. Irv and I have spent a lot of time hoping you and your daughter are okay."

Mary hoped she and her daughter were okay, too, but she didn't say that out loud.

"No, you were very helpful, Ethel. Thank you."

Then she put her hand over the phone and asked Viv to run upstairs and see if she could find a local phone book listing for a Gregory Whitman.

Meanwhile Ethel, who Mary had forgotten was quite a talker, was still talking.

In fact, Ethel was still talking when Viv came back to the top of the stairs to give Mary a hugely welcome thumbs-up.

—

They arrived at Mrs. Whitman's house in a four-person group, but Mary asked to go to the door by herself. She didn't want to scare the poor woman by bringing a small army, including a uniformed officer, to her door. And Stan would never expect her to be here anyway.

Gerald parked his patrol car a couple of doors down, and Mary walked up the carefully tended path alone.

The house was ancient and seemed to be crumbling, but the garden was meticulously tended, with bright flowers everywhere.

Mary knocked on the door.

It opened just a few seconds later, and Mary looked into the face of the tiny older woman who was about to either solve all her problems or plunge her back into hopelessness. It was a lot to put on a stranger who wasn't even expecting her. But here she was.

"You don't know me—" she began.

"I know you," Mrs. Whitman said.

It surprised Mary into silence.

Mrs. Whitman looked more like her garden and less like her house. Her white hair was gathered up carefully at the nape of her neck, her apron freshly cleaned—even starched, from the look of it. She wore it over a loose pair of jeans and a checked yellow shirt. The short sleeves of her shirt had been rolled up high, which Mary noted as seeming remarkable to her. Mary was already covering her upper arms because she thought they looked too old and saggy. Mrs. Whitman obviously had no such insecurities.

Mary had seen this woman a few times around town, but nothing more as far as she could recall.

"Well, I don't *know you* know you," the older woman added. "I know your daughter. I drove her to the county animal shelter that day not too long ago when she rescued those half-drowned puppies. And I know her a little bit just from around town. I've really only seen you, but I suppose I felt as though I knew you. I took an interest, though I realize your life is really none of my concern. I'm about to be very forward, and I hope you'll forgive me, but you and your daughter always struck me as seeming unhappy, and I guess I wished there was something I could do to help."

"There just may be," Mary said.

"Come in, dear. Come in."

Mary cast a glance over her shoulder at the three people waiting for her in the patrol car, but it was hard to see much at the distance.

She stepped inside.

Mrs. Whitman's home was cluttered with knickknacks, paintings, and crocheted items, but dust-free and well organized. Mary sat on the couch when she was invited to.

"I think you might have bought a book of poetry that belonged to me at the thrift store. My husband sold it without my permission."

Mrs. Whitman looked disappointed.

"Oh," she said. "I see. I thought you meant I could help you with something that went closer to the root of your unhappiness. Looking back, I have no idea why I thought so."

"But you can!" Mary said, agitated now. "It really would make me happy. You see, I left my husband because I thought I had a place to go. A new friend with a guest room invited Abby and me to stay with him. He even said he might be able to get me a job. But I was hiding the card he gave me in one of those books, and when my husband took it out of the packing boxes and left it behind, he cut me off from my solution. You have no idea how much happier I would be if I had it back."

"Oh. I see. That is rather critical, isn't it? Which book?"

"The Emily Dickinson."

Mrs. Whitman rose and walked to her bookshelves. As she did, it struck Mary that if she were reading a book from the thrift store and came across a bookmark from an old owner, she would simply flip it into the trash. In fact, Mary had. On more than one occasion.

Mary's heart seemed to try to jump out through her throat as she saw the woman take a small, thin book down from the shelf. As she walked back to the couch with it, Mary attempted to swallow her heart—or what felt like her heart—back down into place.

Mrs. Whitman stood over her and let the book fall open in her hands. She seemed to be reading, which made Mary's head spin. Waiting for her answer felt unbearable, though it was only a couple of seconds.

"'A Prison gets to be a friend,'" Mrs. Whitman read out loud. "My. That really is strangely apropos, isn't it?" Before Mary could ask, she added, "Is this what you were looking for?"

And she held up Elliot's business card.

Mary opened her mouth to say it was, and unexpectedly burst into tears. Somehow the sight of that card smashed the dam she had erected to hold back all of her doubt and fear.

She took it into her hand when it was offered, and looked at it. Colvin. Elliot's last name was Colvin. She would not forget that again.

She sat there on the couch and cried for a while longer, because there seemed to be nothing else she was capable of doing.

Mrs. Whitman sat next to her and placed a hand on her shoulder. In most cases Mary didn't like being touched by strangers, but this touch felt comfortable enough.

"Not to beat the prison analogy to death, but you came in here with a look on your face like a person just released from prison. Or what I imagine that look to be, in any case. That kind of wide-eyed overwhelm. The world is scary just by its nature of being so huge, and filled with so many options, and that's a hard thing when everything is changing. I suppose that's why a lot of people released from prison find themselves right back in. I hope you won't. Please don't. I've felt for a while that your daughter deserves better, and now I feel the same way about you."

—

"So, do you want to call him first?" Viv asked. "You can use my phone if you want to call him and tell him you're coming."

"No!" Mary shouted. She hadn't meant to shout it. And the fact that she did, combined with the way she did, revealed just how panicky she felt. Revealed it to her and to everyone else, all at the same time.

They were sitting upstairs in Viv's kitchen, drinking homemade lemonade. Viv had a lemon tree in the backyard that was so laden with fruit she could barely use it up fast enough.

All eyes turned to Mary, but her throat felt as though it were welded shut, and she said nothing.

"You sound really scared," Viv said, her voice soft.

Mary pulled a deep breath and forced her voice to function. "I am. I am really scared. I'm walking into something I know nothing about. I barely know this man. What if I call him and he says he changed his mind? If Abby and I just show up on his doorstep, it'll be harder to turn us away."

"He's not going to turn us away," Abby said.

"You don't know that, honey."

"I *do* know that. I know it because I know him."

Mary looked up at Gerald, who had added nothing to the conversation. He was staring at his sweaty drinking glass, running his finger in patterns through the moisture on its sides.

"Can't I take my car?" she asked him. "It's just sitting there in front of the house, doing no good for anyone."

That seemed to wake him out of his partial sleep.

"I wouldn't," he said. "Even if it's in your name only, he'll have paperwork around the house with the license number. If it's in his name only, or his name too, he can report it stolen. If you really want to get effectively lost, you should let us put you two on a bus."

"I just feel like . . . ," Mary began. "I mean, I had a little money. It wasn't much but it took forever to save it, and I spent most of it to get us back here from Oregon. I don't even know if I have bus fare for both of us to the city and even if I do, I'll be dropping on poor Elliot's doorstep with no car and without a penny in my pocket. Who wants *that* in a guest?"

"I can float you a little loan," Viv said.

"I hate to ask it of you."

"You didn't ask. I offered. It's no big deal, honey. Pay it back to me later when you have a job. Just go down to the basement and pack your things and put them in my car and we'll get you out of here safely."

———

Mary would marvel later at how secure she had suddenly allowed herself to become. All day Gerald had stayed at her side or gone ahead to be sure all was safe, and now, in that final hour, it had seemed to Mary as though they were out of the woods and nothing could possibly harm them.

Maybe Gerald hadn't intended for Mary to go outside alone to take the duffel bags to Viv's car. But, without thinking too much about it, Mary did just that.

She really never thought to question the move until two strong hands grabbed her upper arm, and by then it was too late.

"Just walk," the deeply, disturbingly familiar voice hissed into her ear.

"I'm not going with you," Mary said, her voice breathy with panic.

He wrenched her arm around more tightly behind her back, and Mary cried out. In fact, she cried out far more loudly than the pain required, because she needed someone in the house to hear her.

"Quiet!" Stan barked.

Mary looked up to see his truck standing, idling, in the traffic lane of Viv's street, its driver's side door yawning open.

"What about your daughter?" Mary asked desperately. "You're just going to put me in the truck and leave without her?"

Mary wanted Stan to go into Viv's house to get Abby, because Gerald was in Viv's house.

"She knows where her aunt and uncle live. If she wants a roof over her head, she'll get herself back there."

"She's thirteen! She's a child! She can't go all that way on her own!"

"Hell, you know what all I did when I was thirteen? Worked a real job, like a man."

They were only a few steps from the truck now. Mary felt that the moment he pushed her inside, all would be lost. Abby would likely not follow. She would stay with Viv, hoping her mother could get away again. Mary would have to get away again. Or maybe Gerald would send the Oregon police to rescue her. Abby would know where she was.

Mary thought about screaming again, to try to summon help.

Before she did, she glanced over her shoulder. The door to Viv's house was standing wide open, and Abby was racing in her direction.

Mary heard a familiar "oof" sound. A rush of air mostly, but in it she recognized her daughter's voice. Abby had slammed into Stan's back and was riding him, feet off the ground, her arms wrapped around his throat. Stan let go of Mary and violently threw his daughter off his back. Mary watched helplessly as Abby landed hard in the street. She could hear the rushing sound of her daughter's wind being knocked out of her.

Without any conscious thought about doing so, she ran to Abby, who was still sprawled on the tarmac.

"Honey! Did he hurt you? Are you okay?"

"I'm fine," Abby said in a breathless whisper. "I'm fine."

But she sounded shaken up.

Mary helped her daughter to her feet, and they both turned back toward Stan, expecting him to be on top of them again. Instead they saw him facedown in the street with Gerald's knee in his back.

Mary held her daughter close to her side, feeling her heart begin to settle, and they watched Gerald handcuff her estranged husband's hands behind his back.

"You're under arrest for kidnapping and assault," Gerald barked, pulling Stan to his feet and pushing him toward the patrol car. "You have the right to remain silent. Anything you say can and will be used against you in a court of law. You have the right to an attorney. If you cannot afford an attorney, one will be provided for you. Do you understand these rights?"

Stan never said whether he understood them or not.

"You can't arrest me for that!" he bellowed. "She's my wife!"

"Sure. And I'm your arresting officer. But that doesn't mean you own me."

Gerald shoved Stan into the back of the patrol car and slammed the door. Then he walked back to where Abby and Mary stood in the street, still in a mild state of shock.

"You okay?" he asked Abby.

"Fine," she said. "I'm fine."

"Good. You've got forty-eight hours. Disappear."

# Chapter Twenty-Seven

## Six out of Seven Ain't Bad

*Abby*

"You still seem scared," Abby said.

They were on the bus, on a winding section of the little two-lane highway, heading down out of the foothills and toward the city. Her mom had been silent, and Abby had mostly satisfied herself by looking out the window. But so much fear had been radiating over from her mother's seat that, in time, Abby couldn't help but address it.

"Just shaken up," her mom said.

"But you seem *more* scared the farther we get from home. The closer we get to there."

"Oh," her mom said.

Then nothing was said for a time, and Abby didn't want to push.

"It *is* kind of scary," her mom said after a while. All on her own and with no urging. "Just showing up on his doorstep like that."

"He said we could, though."

"I know."

Abby looked out the window again. But what she really wanted was to say something helpful. Something in support of her mom.

She watched that big nice new gas station flash by—the one where she and her mom had talked in privacy on the way up to Oregon. It felt satisfying that someone whose job it was to enforce the law agreed to call it a kidnapping, whether the charge stuck or not.

She took a deep breath and did her best with the supportive talk.

"I get why you would be scared," Abby said. "I'm scared, too."

It was a remarkable thing for Abby to hear herself say, because she hadn't known. She had felt the ragged, jangling feeling in her belly, but had thought, right up until she heard herself say it, that she was picking it up from her mom.

"Because it's all so new?"

"Maybe. But I think mostly because I don't know if he still has my dogs, and if I still get them back or not. And I know, I know. Don't even say it. It was a dumb kid thing to take them all and I was always taking the chance of getting my heart broken. You don't even have to tell me again."

"I wasn't going to say a word," Abby's mom said.

———

They stepped into the bus station, Abby carrying one of the big duffel bags on each of her shoulders. At first they strode with great purpose, as if in a hurry. Then, about halfway across the highly waxed station linoleum, they slowed. Then stopped. Then turned to look at each other.

Abby had to drop one of the bags to see her mom's face, which looked surprisingly troubled, even considering their situation.

"What now?" Abby asked.

But there was no answer. Her mother just stood, transfixed.

"Do we call him to come pick us up?" Abby asked.

That broke her mother out of her stupor.

"No!" she cried, too loudly. The four people sitting on wooden benches turned to stare, so she lowered her voice. "No. We need to just figure out how to get there. Walk, or take the bus. I don't want to do that to him. It's too much bother. Who wants that in a guest? 'Hi, we're here. Drop everything and come be our chauffeur.' No, we'll get there on our own."

Abby waited for her mom to say more. While she was waiting she set down the second heavy bag.

When her mom did not say more, Abby asked, "How?"

"Oh. Um. I guess I have to start by figuring out where to find this address. You wait here. I'll see if anybody who works here has a map."

"A *map*?" Abby asked. Incredulous. As if her mom had just said she would ask around to see who might have a unicorn or a dragon.

"Yes, a map. You're unfamiliar with the concept?"

"Like, a printed map? Nobody has those anymore. They have navigation in their cars and they find their way with maps on the internet, or on their phones."

Abby watched her mom's face redden, and she wished she had spoken more gently. Yes, the world had left them behind while they lived with her dad in that tiny house with no cell phone reception, and Abby should have been nicer about pointing it out.

"Fine," her mom said. "Then I'll go see who has a virtual map."

They must still have been talking a little too loudly, because three of the passengers waiting on benches jumped up and opened the map apps on their phones.

—

Elliot's house was a place that might well have appeared in Abby's dreams, waking or sleeping, if she had imagined the house where she would have chosen to grow up. Not fancy, but two-story and clean and nice, with shutters on the windows and flowers growing in beds on both sides of the door. And carefully trimmed hedges marking the property lines on either side.

She walked up his path, then turned to look at her mom, but there was no one beside her. She spun all the way around, turning the bags on her shoulders as she did. Her mom was still frozen on the sidewalk.

"Mom," she called. "Seriously. Come on. I know this is scary, but we didn't come all this way to get scared and then not do it."

No reply.

"He's not going to turn us away."

Still no reply. But Abby saw her mom's eyes go wide. She was staring at a spot over Abby's right shoulder, looking as though she'd seen a ghost. So Abby turned to look.

Elliot had opened the front door and was standing in the open doorway, watching them.

Without realizing she was about to do so, Abby dropped the bags and ran to him, throwing her arms around his waist. He seemed too surprised to hug her in return.

She stepped back quickly, thinking maybe she shouldn't have. But he wasn't even looking at her. He was looking past her at what Abby could only assume was her mom. He had that look on his face that grown-ups get when they forget to be anything other than exactly what they are. When they forget to pretend the world is easy, and nothing in it much affects them, and that they're not feeling the slightest bit vulnerable.

She looked back and forth between them for a moment, wondering if anyone was ever planning to speak.

"Um . . . ," she began, and that seemed to wake Elliot and unstick him.

"You made it," he said. "Thank goodness you made it. Come on in and I'll show you where you'll be staying."

"Where are my puppies?" Abby blurted out. "You still have them, right? We got here as fast as we could. Please tell me you still have them."

A small dark cloud seemed to pass through him. Abby looked into his eyes and watched it move. It scared her for just a moment. But then he opened his mouth and spoke as though all was well.

"Okay, fair enough," he said. "We'll start our tour in the backyard."

Abby left the bags in the hallway, just inside the front door, and followed him through the house. It seemed a bit dark to Abby—if it had been up to her, she would have walked around and opened all the drapes and shutters—but it also had a comfortable feel. It had beautiful woven rugs and an old, valuable-looking grandfather clock, and furniture that might have been antique. As though somebody lived here who hadn't been dead broke their whole life. Abby wasn't used to that. But she figured she could *get* used to it.

Those thoughts were promptly dislodged from her head as they stepped out into the yard. Elliot had fenced off an area—maybe three-quarters of the yard—for the puppies to run, as though he'd figured they'd be staying a while.

And when they saw her, they ran.

They leapt into the air, higher than Abby knew they could jump, trying to get closer to her face. She fell into a cross-legged sit on the grass and they swarmed her, yipping and crying in their excitement and nipping at her fingers and chin. Trying to wag their tails but overdoing it and wagging the full lengths of their soft little bodies.

"They got bigger! Is that even possible? It's only been a few days."

She heard Elliot say, "They grow fast at this age."

Abby felt a few tears come. She tried desperately to keep them from getting out, but was only partly successful. She looked up at Elliot, who was standing over her, watching.

"You kept my puppies," she said. "Thank you. Really, thank you. You have no idea how much I love you for keeping my puppies."

Then she closed her mouth quickly and firmly, and regretted what she had just said. She wasn't supposed to love Elliot. He wasn't her father. He was just a guy they'd known for a few days who was nice to her and the dogs, and had done them some favors.

That uneasy look passed across his face again.

Abby looked back down at the wildly excited dogs.

"Wait," she said. And she quickly counted. "One, two, three, four, five, six. Six? Who's missing? Oh, I know. Tippy. Where's Tippy?"

She looked up again at Elliot, whose expression had turned down-right queasy.

"I had to make a decision while you were gone. I hope—"

"Oh no! Something happened to her? What happened?"

"No. Nothing happened to her. She's fine. She's right on the other side of that fence."

And he pointed.

Abby brushed puppies away and climbed to her feet. She walked to the fence, vaguely aware that Elliot was walking right behind her. She had lost track of where her mother was, but somewhere in the yard watching all this, she figured.

The board fence was six feet tall, so Abby had to grab the top of it and walk her feet up a few steps. Then she was able to hang there and look over. Elliot was tall, and he stood beside her, slightly up on his toes. They looked into the neighbor's yard together.

An old woman was sitting out on the back patio, knitting. She was looking up at the trees and the sky, not down at her work, which she seemed to be able to do by feel. Tippy was sleeping at her feet.

"Tippy!" Abby called.

The pup's head shot up, and she raced to the fence to greet Abby.

"Tippy, Tippy, Tippy. I missed you! What're you doing over *there*?"

She walked the soles of her sneakers up a few more steps and hooked her armpits over the top of the fence. But when she reached down in Tippy's general direction, the pup turned and ran back to the old woman's porch again. Tippy glanced quickly over her shoulder at

Abby, as if in apology. But she kept retreating. Then she settled again at the old woman's feet.

"She kept squeezing through the fence," Elliot said. "Or digging under it. She wanted to be over there so badly. Finally I started to feel guilty for making her come back."

The old woman waved at them. Elliot and Abby waved back.

"So that's why you looked kind of queasy when I asked if you still had the puppies," Abby said.

"Pretty much, yeah. I had to decide. Have you noticed how Tippy's the one who never seems to want to stay with the litter? It's too much commotion for her. She likes things quieter."

"I *have* noticed that, yeah."

"So . . . did I do the right thing?"

Abby took a deep breath and cast a wistful look back to the little black pup. Tippy still felt like Abby's dog. It hurt as she sighed the breath out again—hurt to let go of something she loved.

"Yeah," she said. "You did the right thing. I'd've decided the same thing if I'd been here."

# Chapter Twenty-Eight

## The Pros and Cons of Hauntings

*Elliot*

Elliot stuck his head into the guest room, hesitantly, to see if they needed anything, and how they were settling in. It felt like an invasion of their privacy. But, on the other hand, he figured they wouldn't have left the door wide open if they were changing, or exchanging confidences.

Abby was looking out the window into the backyard. Watching her puppies, he assumed. Mary was hanging up their clothes in the guest room closet.

"Need anything?" he asked.

Mary jumped the proverbial mile, then put one hand to her chest.

"Sorry," he said.

"No, it's not you, Elliot. It's me. I've been edgy the last few days."

"I can imagine."

"I don't think we need another thing right now. Thank you for asking. I'm just so grateful. We're both just so darned grateful. It's a lovely room. And with this nice private bathroom and the huge closet and a comfortable bed for each of us. I'm just so relieved to have this nice place for us to land."

"You must be hungry," he said.

"Starving!" Abby yelled over her shoulder.

"Abby!" Mary said. "That was very rude."

"Sorry," Abby said. "Sorry, Elliot. But I *am* hungry."

"I could take us out to dinner," Elliot said.

"Absolutely not," Mary said. "I won't hear of it."

Abby craned her neck around to look at Elliot, who was still standing respectfully in the doorway. She looked positively crestfallen. He leaned his shoulder on the doorjamb, settling in for a longer conversation.

"Everybody needs to eat," he said.

"Restaurants are too expensive, though. It's enough that you're letting us stay. I won't have you spending all that money on us. I want to *save* you money, not *cost* you money. I'm a good cook. I can make us all something."

"She *is* a good cook," Abby added from her perch at the window.

"Maybe tomorrow," Elliot said. "In fact, tomorrow it would be great to have home cooking again. But today I'd have to go out and shop first. There's really nothing in the house."

"Oh, I doubt that," Mary said.

To his surprise, she brushed past him and marched off in the direction of his kitchen, talking all the way. He followed her down the stairs, saying nothing. Just listening.

"Everybody always says they have nothing to eat in the house, but most of the time they're just speaking figuratively. There's usually plenty, but it just doesn't happen to be what they feel like having, or they don't really cook so they don't really know how to put it all together into something they can make. Now, of course there's a chance your kitchen is about to make a fool out of me and there's really actually nothing, in which case I'll apologize for jumping to conclusions."

He followed her into the kitchen and watched her open his refrigerator door, then briefly pull out the vegetable crisper drawers. Then she closed the fridge and opened his pantry, which she examined carefully.

"Just as I thought," she said. "I don't owe anybody any apologies. Dinner will be ready in about half an hour. I'll go tell Abby to set the table."

———

When Elliot walked into the dining room, following the call to dinner, he felt a lump in his throat that threatened to close off his airway. He paused a moment in the dining room archway, looking at the scene he had been invited to join, and attempting to swallow.

The table had been set with a linen cloth, and with his cloth napkins. Mary had lit taper candles in the center of the table. There was a salad presented in the wooden salad bowl he hadn't used or even seen for years. Two steaming serving bowls sat on trivets by his place, which seemed to be at the head of the table. One contained what looked like some kind of vegetable curry, the other was nearly overflowing with cooked noodles that he assumed would go underneath.

And, best of all, there were people there to eat with him. Abby and Mary sat in their places on either side of the table, waiting for him to join them.

"Did I do something wrong?" Mary asked. Her voice sounded hurt.

Elliot swallowed hard and forced himself to speak. "No, I like it," he said. "I like it very much."

"You look so . . . devastated. I mean . . . more than I'm used to. Oh, I'm sorry. I'm making a mess of things."

"Not at all," he said, and moved to his seat. Sat down at the head of the table. "I just got to feeling a little emotional for a second there."

All three plates had been placed in a stack where Elliot sat, so he dished up noodles and ladled curry on top and handed the meal to Mary. Then he turned his head slightly toward Abby and spoke to her as he began to dish up her serving.

"Say when," he said, and placed an enormous mound of noodles on her plate.

"Keep going," Abby said.

"Abby!" her mom barked.

"But I'm hungry."

"She's a growing girl," Elliot said in her defense.

"At least say it politely. 'A little more, please, Elliot.'"

"Okay. Sorry."

He served up an impossible amount of food and handed it to the girl, then made up a plate for himself.

Nobody started eating. Not even the starving girl. They waited for him.

"It's just . . . ," he began. Then he stalled for a few beats, wondering if he really wanted to go there. "When I saw all this, it just took me back. Pat used to cook, and she would set a lovely table like this. But then she got sick. And I'm not much of a cook, so I'd just get takeout or whatever. So it's just been a long time, and it hit me kind of hard when I saw it."

"No explanation necessary," Mary said quietly. "We haven't forgotten what a hard time this is for you. Which makes it extra wonderful that you're willing to offer us your hospitality at a time like this."

"Eat," he said. "Don't let it get cold."

"Don't you get it, Mom?" Abby said. "He's trying to say it's nice not to be alone."

"Abby," Mary said, quiet and a little stern.

"No, she's right. It's exactly what she just said."

He took a big bite of the curry. It was coconut milk based, mild but nicely spiced.

"This is wonderful," he said.

"I'm glad you like it."

"I still can't believe I had all this in the house."

"Oh, everybody has bits and pieces of stuff around the house. They just don't know how to get it to add up to something good. When you've been cooking for years, you start to understand how to do that kind of math."

—

Elliot's first day back at work came four days later.

When he arrived downstairs in the kitchen, Mary had coffee made, and all the fixings for an omelet cut up and measured out on the counter beside the stove, ready to cook.

There had been shopping in the intervening days. Much shopping.

"Would you like me to pack you a nice lunch?" she asked, pouring the beaten eggs into a skillet.

"Oh. Well. Let me think. I hate for you to go to all that trouble. I was figuring I'd just go out for lunch. Or maybe get something in the company cafeteria."

"It's no trouble. If you really *want* to go out to eat, that's fine. You should do what you like best, especially on your first day back. But I don't mind making you a lunch, and that's a lot more economical. And probably healthier."

"If you really don't mind," he said.

"Don't be silly. With all you're doing for us? It's the least I can do."

Abby wandered in, fully dressed but looking mostly asleep.

"Oooh, omelets," she said.

"This one is for Elliot, hon. You have to wait and have the next one, because Elliot has to go to work. You're on summer vacation, so you've got all day."

"That's fine," Abby said, and sat down. Rubbed her eyes. "Besides, I have to let the puppies out of the laundry room and into the yard. And clean up if there's anything to clean, and feed them." But for the moment, she just sat. "I have a question," she said, addressing Elliot. "I understand if the answer is no. Totally understand. But do you think they might ever be able to come into the house?"

"Oh, honey . . . ," Mary began. But then she waited. Gave Elliot a chance to weigh in.

"If you could housebreak them and teach them not to chew things that aren't theirs. But that's an awful lot of training."

"I'll train them. I don't mind."

"We'll have to roll up the rugs."

"But they'll be housebroken."

Mary and Elliot both laughed.

Abby looked hurt.

"What's so funny?" she asked. "I told you I'd train them."

"Dog training involves a lot of trial and error," Elliot said.

"Oh."

"Maybe let's not trouble Elliot with this on his first day back at work," Mary said.

"I don't mind talking about it. It would actually be nice to be able to have them inside with us."

"All six of them?" Mary asked. Then, to Abby, "Honey, you really might want to think about finding good homes for a few more of them. Six dogs is still an awful lot."

"Nooooo," Abby whined, drawing the word out into multiple syllables. "They're *mine*. I would *miss* them."

Elliot found himself right on the verge of letting out that same long, whiny "no."

"What do you think, Elliot? Do I have to give some away?"

"I would miss them, too," he said. He glanced over at Mary to gauge her reaction, but she didn't look up from the cooking of his omelet. "I mean . . . they're just so cute. You get attached to them much faster than you think you will."

"See, Mom? Elliot's on my side. Besides, two of them are his. Right, Elliot? So that's only four for me. I mean, four is still *sort of* a lot of dogs, but it's not ridiculous. Right? Which two do you want, Elliot? Did you decide for sure?"

"Not really. I'm not sure how much it matters. We're all here together."

"We should decide, though. You know. For later. When we go. Get our own place and all."

But Elliot didn't want to talk about them moving on. Didn't even want to think about it.

That must have shown on his face, because Abby added, "I'm sorry. Did I say something wrong?"

Mary set a plate in front of him with his omelet and some cut fruit. Elliot was grateful for the distraction.

"This looks wonderful," he said. Then, to Abby, "I guess we can cross that bridge when we come to it."

———

Roger stuck his head into Elliot's office at ten minutes to noon.

"I'm going to the coffee place for lunch. Want to join me?"

"What can you have for lunch at the coffee place?"

"Coffee," Roger said.

"But . . . food-wise. All they have is pastry. You're going to have pastry for lunch?"

"Just the opposite. I'm on a diet. I'm having coffee for lunch. The caffeine helps me control my appetite."

"That doesn't sound like a very good way to . . ." But then Elliot stopped himself. Let the sentence trail off. Changed direction. "Sorry," he said. "I guess that's none of my business. I'll just stay in my own lane."

"So, you coming?"

"Mary made me a lunch," he said. He opened his big bottom desk drawer and pulled it out, in its brown paper sack, as if Roger would need to see proof. "And it looked good when she was packing it."

"So bring it along," Roger said. "Get a coffee and eat it there."

"I guess I could do that."

If he was honest with himself, he had been hoping that he and Roger would get a chance to talk.

———

"I'm obviously missing something," Roger said.

He was staring at Elliot's sandwich like a starving man. In his defense, it was an amazing sandwich. Mary had made it with three kinds of cheese, and mustard, on thick slabs of sourdough bread that she had baked and sliced herself.

"What are you missing?"

They were sitting at one of the outdoor tables, where Elliot hoped no one would take offense to his having brought his own food. The day was nicely warm, and the sun felt good on his back. He took another huge bite.

"I guess," Roger said, "the part of this whole situation that's anything but good. She cooks for you, and keeps the place tidy, and does the shopping. And you say she's nice to be around. So . . . what's the problem?"

Elliot finished chewing, and swallowed. He felt a wave of something like heartburn as the food went down. But it might have been entirely unrelated.

"I didn't say it was a problem."

"You didn't have to. Something is obviously bothering you about it." He stared longingly at Elliot's sandwich again. "Oh, wait," he said. "Got it. Sorry, old boy. Sorry for being so thick. It's like having a wife again. And it's nice. And you feel guilty because you like it."

Elliot set the sandwich down on the paper Mary had used to wrap it.

"Something like that. Yeah."

"Do you have anything to feel guilty about?"

"No. Why would I? I just wanted to help them out."

"So you don't have feelings for her? At all?"

Elliot looked down at the remaining half of his sandwich and realized he had lost his appetite for it. For anything.

"I don't know," he said.

"Got it," Roger said, and sipped at his coffee.

"What do you get? How can you get it? *I* don't even get it."

"Anything short of a flat-out no is pretty telling, old boy. If you don't know if you have feelings for her or not, then you're saying you at least *could.* Somewhere down the line. And that's why you feel guilty."

Elliot opened his mouth to argue. Then he closed it again. Because there was no argument to be made.

"I think I'm mostly confused," he said in time. "I just lost Pat, and my mind and my emotions are all . . . discombobulated."

"Interesting word," Roger said, "'discombobulated.' Ever notice how nobody ever says they're feeling combobulated? I just always thought that was—" Then he stole a glance at Elliot's face and ended the sentence abruptly. "Sorry. Too soon. Wrong room. Wrong audience. Go on with what you were saying."

"I just feel like . . . in the middle of all this grief, I don't even know how to know what I feel. Maybe I just like having her around these past few days because being alone was so awful."

"Still not hearing the problem," Roger said.

"Then you're a terrible listener, Roger. I just stated the problem. The problem is not knowing."

"Not knowing is not a problem."

"It sure feels like one."

"You're talking about something that'll come clear over time. We should all have such problems. There are no problems here, old boy, except the ones you're making in your own head."

Elliot didn't answer. He was trying on what his friend had just said. Considering the idea that Roger might be right.

"I mean . . . ," Roger began, ". . . what would Pat say?"

"Oh, there's no *would* about it. She *did* say. She spoke loud and clear on the subject. About a year after she'd been diagnosed. When she was sick, but not so sick that she couldn't speak loudly and clearly. I remember almost word for word. She said, 'Elliot, you're a handsome, vital man, and your life's not nearly spent, and I won't have you putting yourself on a shelf for the rest of your time on this earth. When this is over, you're to get out there and live. Or else.'"

"That sounds like Pat. Did she ever say what the 'or else' was?"

"Oh, yes. Like a fool, I asked. She said, 'Or I'll come back and haunt you.'"

They both just sat a minute, smiling at their memories of her.

"Well, you wouldn't want that," Roger said, still staring at Elliot's half-eaten sandwich.

"Oh, I don't know," Elliot said. "It would be nice to see her again."

Then, much to his own surprise, he picked up the sandwich because he felt like eating it now. The slightly queasy sensation had passed.

# Chapter Twenty-Nine

## Time

### Mary

It was nearly four months since they had gone to stay with Elliot, and Mary was settling at a small table in the Meade Industries cafeteria with her sack lunch.

She reached into her purse and took out the pad of paper she had brought. Dug around for a pen. For the moment she let her sandwich sit uneaten. She was given a full hour for lunch before she had to be back at reception.

She wrote the date on the top of the first sheet of paper and began a letter to Viv.

> *Dear Viv,*
> *Every single day I've been wishing I could pick up the phone and call you. I mean, since that first quick call just to let you know we got in safely. There's so much to catch up on. But the problem is, it's always somebody else's phone. I don't want to stick Elliot with any more long-distance charges, and of course the phones here at*

*work are not for personal calls, which is probably true no matter where you work. So I finally decided to break down and do this the old-fashioned way.*

*I've been on the job for three weeks, and I've already gotten my second paycheck, so when I get home I can write you a check for half of what I owe you, and I'll put it in the envelope with this letter. Be sure to look.*

*The people here are really nice. They know I'm (sort of) with Elliot, and they all really like him and feel bad about Pat, and they want him to be happy again. I think they're being extra nice to me because of that. But . . . I know this may sound strange but I'll go ahead and say it . . . that just puts more pressure on my situation. I'm sure you know I have feelings for him and I think he probably knows it, too. He's not stupid. And I'm pretty sure he doesn't feel the same. So that's one reason I think Abby and I will need to go soon. Because that's just too hard for me, the way it is.*

*Interestingly, though, Elliot got me this job, and he's the one who recommended part time. Just so I could have some money for my own stuff, and to pay you back, and clothing and such. And of course I'll need a lawyer to handle the divorce. Abby says his suggesting a part-time job means he wants us to stay. She always seems to be able to read him. Better than I can, anyway. So at first I got my hopes up over that, but now I think he just really likes having someone to cook and clean. Which is okay. After all he's doing I can at least do that much in return, but if Abby and I are ever going to get our own place, I'll have to ask the Meade folks to take me on full time. I can't even afford my own car at the rate I'm going, but Elliot has a car and a truck and he's nice about letting me borrow one or the other. Still, I can't do that forever.*

*I don't mean to make it sound like he decided for me that I should only work part time. He's not like Stan that way. He's not like Stan in any way. He just sort of suggested that part time would be a good option. And, oh, I hate to even write this to you, Viv, but at least a lot of the time I'm still the same person I always was. I couldn't bring myself to ask what that meant. If he was saying he wanted us to stay, or what the message was in that. I guess it takes a long time to change who you are. More than a handful of months, anyway.*

*Still, even if he did want us to stay, there's still the problem of my having these feelings that I don't honestly think he returns. I mean, of course, his wife just died. I understand how he's not ready. I just have this hunch that this is a problem that isn't going away, even when he is ready. Not really sure why I say that, but it's the impression I get.*

Mary reached the bottom of the page. She tore the sheet off, flipped it over, then decided not to write on both sides of the paper. The ink had bled through, and it would be too hard for Viv to read.

She sat a moment in front of the clean new sheet of paper and wondered what more, if anything, she had to say to her friend. Probably she should tell her about her talk with Abby that morning before she left for school, and how bad Mary felt about making her daughter cry.

A voice startled her out of her thoughts.

"Done with what you were writing?"

She looked up to see Elliot standing over her table. He was carrying the lunch she had packed for him.

"Oh. Well, for now. Yes."

"Want some company?"

"Sure."

He sat across from her and they exchanged small, awkward smiles. Everything involving Elliot seemed to grow more awkward by the day, which felt like another reason to find a way to move their lives along.

"I saw Abby before she left for school this morning," he said. "She was crying."

"I know. I'm sorry."

"She said you told her she has to give up at least two of the dogs."

"I didn't mean to make her cry."

"So you did tell her that."

"I did, yes."

"But *why*, Mary? Why did you say that to her?"

His voice sounded so plaintive that she braved a quick glance at his face in the glaring fluorescent lights of the cafeteria. Then she looked quickly down at the stainless steel tabletop. He looked hurt. It briefly flickered through her mind that he could only look so utterly hurt if he cared, but she immediately decided that it likely had nothing to do with her. He liked Abby, and clearly enjoyed her company, and he adored the pups as if they were his own.

"I know it's harsh," she said. "But you must know why. Do you have any idea how hard it'll be to find a place of our own with even *two* dogs? With four I might as well give up before I bother to start."

She braved another quick glance at his face, then immediately wished she hadn't.

"Are you not happy at my house?"

"Oh, no! How could you think that? Of course we're happy there. It's wonderful at your house. Abby and I both love it."

"Then why go?"

"Well, we have to sooner or later, don't we? We can't just rely on your hospitality forever."

"I don't see why you can't. It's a big house. And we get along well."

Mary felt a cold tightening in her stomach. Because she knew it was time to do something brave. She had just confided on paper to her friend Viv that she had been a coward where Elliot was concerned. And now life had handed her a chance to do better.

Her stomach a sickening riot of butterflies, she pushed the letter to Viv across the table to him. He picked it up and began to read quietly to himself.

Mary died a thousand times in the waiting.

She looked out the window because she couldn't bring herself to watch his eyes. It was a windy day. There was a line of tall trees outside, marking the edge of the Meade campus. She watched their branches sway in the wind. She could hear a chorus of birds through the glass, but she couldn't see them. Then, all at once, they lifted up from two of the trees and flew away, hundreds of them at once, a black polka-dot cloud.

"You probably already knew," Mary said, carefully avoiding looking at his face.

A couple of seconds later he set the letter down. She wanted to look at his expression for clues, but couldn't bring herself to do it.

"You didn't give me time," he said. He sounded almost absurdly wounded.

"Time for what?"

"You aren't giving me time to *see* if I feel the same."

Mary shifted her gaze from outside the window to the tabletop. Her stomach had begun to soften and buzz, as though the ice of it were being melted with warm water.

While she was nursing that sensation, he said more.

"You said yourself I'm not ready. Which is true. But why would you just assume that even after that . . . even after I've had a chance to adjust to this loss. I mean . . . *why* did you have a hunch that it would still be a problem?"

"I don't know," Mary said. Then she felt herself fall deeply into some pit of honesty, and knew that the next words out of her mouth would not be disconnected or defensive. Or utterly altered by fear.

"Complete lack of self-esteem? Or maybe I'm just not used to things going my way."

She waited, in case he had anything more to say. When he didn't, she stole a glance at his face. He looked lost in thought, and sad. Or just plain lost.

"So what if I give you time and it still doesn't work out that way?" she asked. Bravely, she thought.

"Well . . . so what if it doesn't? People share a house together when they're just friends. It happens all the time. It's so much nicer with you and Abby there. It's like the house is alive again. She's so happy and friendly, and I love the way you cook and take care of the place. And the puppies! I love those puppies. Even if you do move, please don't make her give any puppies away. I would miss them as much as she would. I'll keep them if you can't take them along, and she can come see them. She can even come back and get them later if she has a place for them. But that's if you *have to* go."

"But you don't want us to."

"No."

Mary sucked in a huge breath of air. She heard it enter her. She heard it blow out in a sigh. She knew he heard it, too. She had no idea how much stress it had caused her, thinking she and her daughter were about to have to move. She hadn't fully perceived the weight of it on her shoulders until she felt it lifted away.

"Then we'll stay," she said. "And I'll give you lots and lots of time. However much you need."

"Good," he said. "I feel much better getting that off my chest. I'm guessing there's not much pain in this world that lots of time and six puppies can't at least help heal."

They ate their lunch together in a comfortable silence. The way friends do—friends who don't always need to fill the air with noise. It felt like enough to Mary. Or, at least, enough for the time being.

When she got home, she could tear up the letter to Viv and write an entirely new one to go with the check. Since everything she had just written was old news now.

"Hey," she said out of nowhere, and it seemed to startle him. "Do you have your cell phone on you?"

"Sure. You need to make a call?" He slid it out of his shirt pocket and extended it in her direction.

"It's local."

"No worries. Go ahead."

She took the phone from him. She had the number of Abby's new school in her wallet. Just in case of emergency. The school would not categorize this as an emergency. But knowing how Abby must have been feeling that day, after their talk, Mary did.

An officious-sounding woman picked up immediately, and said, simply, "Office."

"I need to speak to Abigail Hubble, please. I'm her mother."

"Hold, please."

As soon as she heard the click on the line, Mary regretted not asking the woman to please tell her daughter, right up front, that it was not bad news.

"This will take a minute," she said to Elliot, and he nodded.

While they were waiting, their eyes met, and they smiled at each other. And it wasn't awkward. Not even a little bit. They even held each other's gaze for a beat or two, and in that moment Mary saw the admiration and newly minted affection he held for her that she had foolishly missed.

It must have been a longer moment than she realized, because suddenly Abby's voice was there on the line.

"What? Mom? What is it? What's wrong? Did something happen?"

"No! Everything's good. I'm so sorry to scare you, honey. It's good news. Really good. So good that I couldn't make you wait all day to hear it."

—

Abby came blasting through the front door at a little after six. She had begun staying late at her new school, practicing hard in their pool to make the swim team.

Mary was in the kitchen having a snack of homemade cookies with Elliot, but she could hear the enormous sounds of her daughter's arrival. It was followed by the slam of the front door behind her, then the thump of her book bag landing in the corner of the hall—under the hat rack, Mary assumed, because that was where it lived.

Abby sprinted through the kitchen, barely glancing at her mother and Elliot. Not bothering to address them at all. She was chanting an excited litany of the two words "My puppies, my puppies, my puppies." Over and over and over.

Then she was out the back door into the yard. Gone.

"That was rude," Mary said. "I'm going to go have a talk with her."

"Not on my account," Elliot said. "Please. She's excited. This morning she thought most of them *weren't* her puppies anymore. Of course she'll want to go see them first thing."

"She might've taken a moment to acknowledge that the reason they're still her puppies is because of you. She might've said a simple thank you to you. Even 'hello' would've been a step in the right direction."

"Maybe she'll get to that," he said. "You know. On teenager time."

Just as he finished the last word of the sentence, the kitchen door burst open again, and Abby came running in. She swung the door toward closed behind her, but it failed to latch, and three puppies came bounding in.

She ran to where Elliot sat at the kitchen table and threw her arms around him.

"I love you I love you I love you," she said, the words tumbling over each other. "I'll never forget you for this. I'll never stop saying thank you."

Mary looked past them and saw the other three puppies stick their heads through the open doorway, cautiously. Then, seeing their siblings inside, they bounded in and began tearing around the house.

"Oops," Abby said. "Better go catch my puppies."

She stopped briefly at Mary's chair on her way by and gave her mom a vigorous kiss on the top of the head. "Love you, too, Mom. Thanks for everything."

Then she ran into the living room to round up the interloping pups.

Mary looked up at Elliot and smiled, a little shyly, and he smiled in return.

"That wasn't half bad," he said. "For teenager time."

# SEVEN PERFECT THINGS
# BOOK CLUB QUESTIONS

1. The novel opens with Elliot facing a tremendous loss in his life. What are some of the coping mechanisms he utilizes to help him through this difficult time? How do they contrast with how Mary copes with the challenges of her situation?

2. When Abby witnesses a wriggling sack being thrown into a river, she reacts by impulsively jumping into the freezing water to save whatever is inside. What does this say about her character, and how do her traits help her survive what she must face ahead?

3. How have the puppies acted as both a catalyst and a healing element throughout the story?

4. Mary is in an abusive marriage, constantly living under the threat of a vicious and controlling husband. When Mary has self-doubts due to the circumstances she has lived through, Elliot explains that Stan gaslighted her, sowing seeds of doubt in Mary, making her question her own perceptions. Why do you think victims of this manipulative technique find it so difficult to recognize this is happening to them?

5. Occasionally Abby shares her frustrations about her father with Elliot. What qualities does she see in Elliot that enable her to open up to him in this way?

6. Elliot is very perceptive about human nature. At one point he tells Mary that when we demand that people live the way we think they should, it's never helpful. Do you agree with this statement?

7. Before Stan kidnaps Abby and her mother, Mary hides Elliot's contact info in a book of poetry. How does this clever choice work in her favor and also add other complications?

8. Eventually Elliot is able to help Mary and Abby by opening up his home where they can be safe. He discusses this with his friend Roger, and accidentally reveals his own feelings of guilt. Do you think Elliot made the heathiest choice for both himself and his guests? Why or why not?

9. Mary confides in her friend Viv that she has been a coward with her feelings where Elliot was concerned. What is it from her past that makes her fearful that she doesn't deserve love or a second chance?

# ABOUT THE AUTHOR

Catherine Ryan Hyde is the *New York Times* and #1 Amazon Charts bestselling author of forty books (and counting). An avid traveler, equestrian, and amateur photographer, she shares her astrophotography with readers on her website.

Her novel *Pay It Forward* was adapted into a major motion picture, chosen by the American Library Association (ALA) for its Best Books for Young Adults list, and translated into more than twenty-three languages in over thirty countries. Both *Becoming Chloe* and *Jumpstart the World* were included on the ALA's Rainbow list, and *Jumpstart the World* was a finalist for two Lambda Literary Awards. *Where We Belong* won two Rainbow Awards in 2013, and *The Language of Hoofbeats* won a Rainbow Award in 2015.

More than fifty of her short stories have been published in the *Antioch Review, Michigan Quarterly Review, Virginia Quarterly Review, Ploughshares, Glimmer Train,* and many other journals; in the anthologies *Santa Barbara Stories* and *California Shorts*; and in the bestselling anthology *Dog Is My Copilot*. Her stories have been honored by the Raymond Carver Short Story Contest and the Tobias Wolff Award and have been nominated for Best American Short Stories, the O. Henry

Award, and the Pushcart Prize. Three have been cited in the annual *Best American Short Stories* anthology.

She is founder and former president (2000–2009) of the Pay It Forward Foundation and still serves on its board of directors. As a professional public speaker, she has addressed the National Conference on Education, twice spoken at Cornell University, met with AmeriCorps members at the White House, and shared a dais with Bill Clinton.

For more information, please visit the author at www.catherineryan-hyde.com.